PJ

THE WORLD IS DEAD

"A stunning collection of stories, each of which grabs the traditional zombie story by its scrawny throat, rips out its innards and rearranges them into something completely original. If you thought the only thing left to do with a zombie was shoot it in the head, prepare to think again. [This] is a collection of eighteen incredibly original, extremely well-written stories."

—David Moody, author of *Hater* and *Autumn*

"This book is essential. I've read a lot of short story collections, and this one just blew me away. Kim Paffenroth and his crew have given us a terrifying glimpse of our future, and in the process they've shown us more than your standard zombie fare of violence and guts. They have taken us through the entire emotional register from profound love and loss to heartbreaking confusion and longing. This collection shows what we all knew the zombie story was capable of becoming."

—Joe McKinney, author of *Dead City* and *Quarantined*

"*The World is Dead* is not what a person would expect from a zombie-themed anthology. Sure, there are grotesque things that shamble along, but in all, those aren't what makes this collection remarkable. The stories themselves harness more than revulsion and fear. At once horrifying and humanizing, this collection represents the best of zombie literature."

—Scott A. Johnson, author of *Deadlands*

OTHER BOOKS FROM KIM PAFFENROTH:

Dying to Live
(from Permuted Press)

Dying to Live: Life Sentence
(from Permuted Press)

Valley of the Dead
(coming 2010 from Permuted Press)

History Is Dead
(from Permuted Press)

Gospel of the Living Dead
(from Baylor University Press)

Orpheus and the Pearl
(from Magus Press)

THE WORLD IS DEAD

A ZOMBIE ANTHOLOGY EDITED BY
KIM PAFFENROTH

Permuted Press
The formula has been changed...
Shifted... Altered... *Twisted.*
www.permutedpress.com

A PERMUTED PRESS book
published by arrangement with the authors

ISBN-10: 1-934861-25-1
ISBN-13: 978-1-934861-25-7

Cover art by Christian Dovel
Interior by Ryan C. Thomas

10 9 8 7 6 5 4 3 2 1

Table Of Contents

WORK

Dead Men Can't Complain
by Peter Clines

"**Mr**. Secord?" said the voice. "Mr. Secord, can you hear me?"

He felt his eyes moving, but a red veil hid everything. "I . . . Yeah. Yeah, I can."

"Okay, that's good. Hang on, let me open your eyes."

Something pressed against his face and the world exploded into existence, carried on waves of white light. "Oh, geez. Geez that's bright."

"Sorry, we need it for the vision test. Can you see okay?"

The brilliance dimmed and an Asian man loomed over him, inches from his face. He leaned back and revealed a loose tie and white coat. Behind the doctor was a spectacled blonde in hospital scrubs. Her curly hair was pulled back into a high ponytail, almost a top knot.

"Yeah, fine. Where am . . . " His lungs ran low and he coughed.

"Deep breath. Just think about doing it. There you go. What color's my tie?"

"Red."

"How many fingers?"

"Two."

"And now?"

"Four," he wheezed.

"Don't forget to breathe. And now?"

"Two again."

"Excellent. Can you make a fist? Good. Other hand? Good. Hold onto this pen as tight as you can. Very good."

"Where am I? Am I in the hospital?"

"Just a few more quick tests, Mr. Secord. Can you feel this? How about this?"

"Yeah, that."

"Incredible. Do you know the year?"

"It's 2109, unless I've been out for a really long time. May 17th."

"It's the 18th, actually. You've been gone for a day. What's your name?"

"Lawrence. Homer Lawrence Secord."

"Birthday?"

"Last month. April 28th. I'm forty-four."

"Who's the President?"

"Wesley Lohan. Vice President is Jeffrey McGuire."

"Very good. You a political man?"

"Die-hard Whig."

"Ahhh."

Lawrence raised an eyebrow. "Why ahhh?"

"This'll probably be rough on you. What's the last thing you remember?"

"I . . . " He mulled over the gray images in his head until he found a colorful one. "I was at work."

"Where's that?"

"Dynotech. I'm a portfolio specialist."

"And then?"

"I headed home. I'm supposed to go to some cocktail party with my wife." He grinned. "Guess I got out of that."

The doctor smirked. "Yes, you did. Do you remember what happened next?"

"I drove home. I always do."

"You drive a classic, right?"

"Yeah, a Tesla. I'm going to miss that car."

"Right," nodded the doctor. "And . . . ?"

"Oh. Oh, hell! Somebody hit me! Some jerk in a truck."

"It was a bus, actually. You tried to cross the busway and got hit by the Green Line."

"Oh, son of a . . . Am I . . . Wait. You did all those tests. I made it out. I'm okay."

"You're lucky, that's for sure," nodded the doctor. "These days, only one person in a thousand still carries the ex-virus. And only one out of a thousand of those has strain seventeen."

"What?"

"You almost didn't make it. The windshield practically decapitated you. If one of the residents hadn't run a blood test we would've just shipped your body off to the incinerator."

The blonde smiled and gave a little wave.

"What are you saying? You did the tests. I'm okay, right?" He wiggled his fingers and toes to find the unspoken problem.

The Asian man nodded. "You're fine. You made the transition with no apparent loss of mental ability."

"The transition? What are you talking about?"

The doctor held his hand back and the blonde placed a mirror in it. "This may be a bit of a shock, but it's best just to get it over with."

The H. Lawrence Secord in the mirror looked a bit pale, and his hair was messy. There were a few small cuts on his forehead, but none of them were bleeding. His eyes looked black, and he realized the pupils were wide open. Then he turned his chin and saw his throat.

Stitches ran around his neck, coarse black threads coated with gummy blood. He could still see the raw, ragged gash that ran across his Adam's apple and out of sight behind him. The edges were pushed together and caked with dried gore. The skin above the wound was a shade paler than the flesh below it.

"You're dead, Mr. Secord," said the doctor. "But you had the ex-virus, so you came back. You're a zombie now."

"Life-challenged," murmured the resident.

"Right," nodded the doctor, "whatever."

Lawrence flipped through his billfold. "Someone took all my cash," he growled. "What kind of place is this?"

"Hospital policy," the resident explained. "It's how they cover costs for any repairs and orientation."

"Are you insane? Give me my money back and send me a bill."

She shook her head. "Sorry. They have to do it this way."

"Why?"

"You'll understand soon enough." She guided him down a delivery hallway, away from the other patients. The staff members they passed stared at him.

"What's that supposed to mean?"

"Look, let me give you a couple of tips, okay? Off the record." She looked around and patted his thigh. "Probably about this time tomorrow your legs are going to feel stiff and swollen. Your feet are going to hurt. That's lividity setting in."

"What?"

"Without your heart pumping, all your blood and bodily fluids are going to drain down. You're still moving around, so that'll force some capillary action, but not much." She pushed a bright blue scalpel into his hand. It was sealed in a sterile wrapper. "You'll want to slit your ankles on either side of the Achilles tendon and let everything drain out. Cut up and down, go as deep as you can, but make it clean. Remember, you don't heal anymore, so if you cut the Achilles you'll cripple yourself. Shake your legs a lot. You probably want to do it in the shower or outdoors. It's going to be messy."

"I . . . Okay."

"Second thing is to keep clean. You don't want to rot. Rub yourself down with alcohol whenever you can. Don't forget to do your eyes, ears, nostrils, and your rectum. Drink some of it, too, but not too much."

"Oh, geez."

"You'll want to buy some Lysol or some kind of antiseptic spray. It'll help keep bacteria away and hide your smell. Oh, and some eyedrops. Your eyes are going to be the biggest challenge. You might want to consider contacts to use as protective covers."

"This is some kind of joke, right? This is all a sick . . . " He ran out of air again and had to will himself to inhale.

"Third, don't try to eat anything that isn't raw meat. Chicken, fish, shellfish, doesn't matter what. But if you try to eat anything cooked or processed you're just going to throw it back up again."

"I can't eat raw meat."

The double doors clanged open and they were outside on the loading dock. The sun was heading down. The resident's owlish glasses flared and her hair looked like gold in the afternoon light. "You don't have a choice," she told him. "If you don't you're going to last a year at best, and half of that'll be pretty miserable. Be thankful you've got enough brains left to control your appetite."

"I don't . . . " He closed his eyes. "What else?"

"Last thing. San Diego's not a good place for your kind."

"What do you mean," he growled, "my kind?"

"For ex-humans," she said. "It's not a good climate, temperature-wise. The heat breeds bacteria. Think about moving somewhere with real winters. But not so cold you'll freeze." She glanced around and held out a fifty. "Take this. It should get you home. Hillcrest, right?"

"Yeah. I . . . I'm still trying to process all this."

"Your family, they Whigs, too?"

"Of course."

"Ahhh. Well, maybe things will go well for you."

"What do you mean? I've been married fourteen years. My family loves me."

"Your family loved Lawrence Secord," she said with a sigh. "He died yesterday in a car crash. You're just an ex."

"**Oh**, thank God you're dead, Lawrence," said Kimberly. "If you'd lasted much longer I probably would've poisoned your whiskey."

"What? What's that supposed to mean?"

"It means I'm happy for the first time in years." His wife walked back into the dining room. She wore the red dress with the inappropriately-low neckline and the just-as-inappropriately-high slit up the side. From the looks of it, she wasn't wearing underwear, either. She took a deep sip of champagne from the oversized goblet she'd answered the door with. "Well, I've been pretty happy when I'm with Danny, I guess."

"Danny?" He was still dwelling on the dress and champagne in a goblet and it took a few moments to process. "The pool boy?!"

"Pool man, for your information." Her grin was wicked. "A little after-the-fact advice, Lawrence — stamina. Our wedded life would've been a lot more satisfying if you could've lasted longer than three minutes."

"What are you…"

"Timed you. More than once." She gestured at herself with her free hand. "Do you know what it's like being the most lusted-after woman at every social event and having to come home to three-minute Larry? Our first time Danny went for sixteen minutes without even trying. After eleven years with you it was like paradise. "

"Eleven? You've been sleeping with the pool boy for the past three years?"

She laughed and took another sip of champagne. "At least now we've got free run of the place. The pool house was getting kind of old."

"You told me you were making an art studio out there."

"Oh, he's an artist, believe me."

Lawrence clenched his fists. "I want you out."

"What?"

"Out!" His bellow shook the glasses hanging above the bar. "Get out of my home!"

Her smile was wide and beautiful. "You don't even realize, do you? Oh, this is delicious. All your political rants at every party and you don't even know where you're standing, do you?"

"What are you talking about?"

"You're dead, Lawrence. You don't have a home. You don't have anything. I inherited it all when you died yesterday."

"What?"

"You know how it goes. You 'damned exes' don't get a thing. It's my house, my money, my . . . everything. I signed all the paperwork this morning." Kimberly downed the last of the champagne and glee-fully threw the goblet to smash across the room. "Tell you what, out of the goodness of my heart, you can go up to the bedroom and pack a suitcase. Make sure you grab all of your cologne. You're already starting to stink."

"Screw you."

"Had your chance, darling. There aren't many limits to my vices, but necrophilia's one." She pointed down the hall towards his study. "If you want to hang outside the window and watch, Danny's coming by in about an hour. I was going to ask him to bend me over your desk. When he takes me from behind, it's when he can go the longest."

He thought of a lot of things to say, but bit his tongue.

"Oh, and in case you're having any naughty zombie thoughts, I might call the police and say I heard a prowler. They'd probably be here in ten minutes or so." She wandered back to the bar. "Just leave your keys on the hall table when you go."

In the back of his closet was an old gym duffle with a shoulder strap. Bigger than most of his luggage and easier to carry. Four of his better suits. Some shirts. Jeans. Lots of socks and boxers. One of the scarves he wore to the opera went into the bag and the other he threw around his neck.

He searched the bedroom and found a couple hundred split between two of Kimberly's purses. A bunch of fifties he kept hidden in an old book. Some twenties and change from his nightstand. Almost a thousand dollars in cash. He saw her wedding ring sitting on the bathroom sink and scooped it up. Then he stopped, reconsidered for a moment, and dumped her jewelry box into the duffle.

Lawrence was two doors down the road when the police car passed him. He adjusted the scarf around his surgical scars and glanced over his shoulder as they pulled up to the house. Kimberly smiled and waved to them with another drink.

He walked to the corner and stumbled once. His left foot was sluggish.

The dead man held up his arm and a taxi buzzed up. The teen at the wheel glanced back as the trunk popped open. "Where you headed, sir?"

He dropped the bag in the trunk. "I've been thrown out, my friend," he said. "Take me somewhere nice for the night."

The driver took in his breath to ask something as Lawrence settled in behind the rear-view mirror, then decided against it.

The Horton Grand dominated downtown, a block-sized building two centuries old. The driver had been silent through the whole trip, but Lawrence gave him a large tip and tried not to notice as the teen flinched from his fingertips. He shouldered the strap of his bag and marched up the steps to the lobby. His toes caught once at the top, but he grabbed a railing and told himself he just looked like a drunk.

The dark carpet and soft music soothed him in a few steps. The thought of a single-malt scotch crossed his mind and he tried to ignore the rumble from his stomach.

Somehow, he'd never noticed the valet exes on previous visits, even through there were a dozen in the lobby. Each one had a black plastic muzzle winched over its head, half-hidden by the strap for a little red cap. Their wrists were handcuffed to their luggage racks.

The well-dressed clerk at the desk, a slim man about Lawrence's age, saw him approach in the wide mirror and swung around like a dancer. "Good evening, sir."

"Good evening. I was wondering if I could get a room for the night. Possibly a few nights. I'm afraid I don't have a reservation."

The other man made a show of opening an old-fashioned reservations book and running his finger down the page. "I believe we have some available, sir. Card?"

He handed over the plastic and the clerk waved it across the scanner. His brow wrinkled just for a moment. "I'm sorry, sir, it's been declined."

"Ahhh," said Lawrence. "My fault. Please, try this one."

The card crossed the scanner panel and the clerk shook his head again. "I am very sorry, sir."

"What if I just pay cash?"

"I'm afraid we would still require a card for the room deposit."

"I could pay the deposit in cash as well."

There was a long silence as the other man studied Lawrence's face. He wondered if the scarf had slipped and berated himself for not checking it after the taxi drive. "Sir," said the well-dressed man, "please forgive my bluntness, but are you . . . dead?"

He straightened up and squared his shoulders. "I am," he said. "What of it?"

The clerk closed the reservations book. "I'm afraid the Horton Grand has a very strict policy regarding ex-humans. I'm going to have to ask you to leave. Sir."

A pair of large men in suits appeared at either end of the desk.

Just outside the hotel lobby was an ATM. Lawrence paused at the kiosk and glared at the two security men. It took his card and he tapped in his six-digit code. The machine hummed and flashed a message.

I'm sorry. That account has been closed.
Can I help you with something else?

He muttered, switched to the savings account, and tried for another thousand.

I'm sorry. That account has been closed.
Can I help you with something else?

He banged his finger on the red button and held his hand out.

This card is being held.
Please contact the number on your statement about a replacement.
Thank you for your business.

He slammed his palm against the machine but it had nothing else to say to him.

Half the taxi drivers on the street glared at him. The others ignored him. When he shouted at them to give him a ride, a police officer jabbed him with a stun baton and he found himself on the ground. One of the drivers tried to peel off his watch and he yanked it away from the man.

"Shame to see a nice watch like that on a dead guy," said the driver to his friend.

"Real shame," nodded the other man. They followed him to the end of the block before they got bored and wandered back to their vehicles.

It took an hour to cross the city, trying every hotel along the way. The icy woman at the Hyatt threatened to call the police before a group of drunken conventioneers dragged him out to the street. The doormen at the Marriot wouldn't let him in. Security at the Sands grabbed him halfway across the lobby. The old motel on 11th offered him a supply closet until morning for two hundred dollars, but the kid behind the counter wanted to lock him in.

Another half hour and he found himself on the outskirts of the park. When he realized how far he'd gone, he congratulated himself on being in great shape at forty-four. Then he remembered the real reason he wasn't out of breath.

A monument loomed there, four bronze figures on a marble base. It had been old when he was still young. The statues were the heroes of the outbreak a hundred years ago, the Zombocalypse as it was called. He couldn't remember all their names, but the tall man was named George, which he always remembered as a child because it was an awkward first name to grow up with, like Homer. The woman had been some kind of celebrity. He knew the huge robot looming behind them was named after a dog.

The base of the pedestal had four thick buttresses which made a set of nooks sheltered from the wind. He tossed his duffle into one of the spaces and wished he'd packed a blanket.

Something slipped in the grass behind the monument. An ex stumbled into sight, a dead woman with patches of oily hair. Its body was gaunt and wasted, its skin the color of old newspaper. One eye was an empty, withered socket. Each bare foot dragged behind it as it walked, a swollen sock of meat and bones it didn't know enough to lift.

Lawrence flinched back from the dead thing. It had a muzzle, but even from here he could see the plastic was white and brittle. There was a splash of yellow across the ex's side, a paint ball marking it for a pick up. Its lopsided path was curving it around to his duffle, and he was struck with the thought of it tripping and falling on him while he slept.

The dead woman shuffled alongside the statues and her one-eyed gaze passed over him without interest. He took a cautious step forward and tried to remember all the ex-safety classes from school. There was a rhyme about fright and sight they drilled into kids until sixth grade, one most of them forgot by eighth.

Another careful step put him next to it. The ex still didn't react. He put his hands on the woman, tried not to think about the greasy way her clothes slid on her arms, and turned her away from the monument and away from him.

The dead thing paused for a moment, as if confused by the shift in view. Then it stumbled forward, still dragging each foot as it staggered away. The off-kilter movement would carry the dead thing out onto Park Blvd in a while, and into traffic.

Lawrence took a moment of pleasure in the thought of the ex getting splattered by a car, and then noticed his own papery hand. He sighed and looked up at the statues. "You'd all kill me on sight, wouldn't you?" He hunkered down out of the wind and tried to get comfortable.

In the morning, everything would be better. He'd go into the office, throw himself into the Hammond account, and have his secretary rent him a little place somewhere. Everything was going to be fine.

He was stretched out with his head on the duffle bag for an hour before he realized he didn't sleep anymore.

"**Mr.** Secord?" the woman at the front desk yelped.

"Good morning, Judy."

"But you're . . . they said . . . "

He tilted his head at her. "Is there a problem?"

"No," she yelped. "Just let me get Mr. Parson." She pressed a few buttons and whispered into her headset.

As he waited, he saw his reflection in the big glass doors that led to the inner office. He glanced at his hand and saw his skin was the soft gray of thick clouds. The fingernails looked pale in contrast. His calves were sore.

Three minutes later the doors hissed open and Ray Parson strolled out, six feet of color-treated hair and pearly veneers. "Lawrence." He held out a hand, then changed his mind. "Sweet sexy Jesus, so the stories are true."

He tried to smile. "I guess. What stories are they telling you, Ray?"

"Just that you had a car crash and turned into a man-eating monster."

"That's about half right."

"Hah," barked Ray. "Well, what can I do for you? You here for your stuff?"

"My . . . ?" He blinked and felt his lids drag on his eyes. "I'm here to work. We're really close on the Hammond account."

His boss's grin flickered for a moment. "To work?"

"Yeah. I'm pretty sure we can close it this week. You can't afford to lose me."

"Well, no, Lawrence, no I sure can't," he said. "Thing is, you don't work here anymore. He's not the best, but I had to put Greg on the Hammond account."

"What?!" He counted to three, and lowered his voice. "You're firing me?"

"Well, not exactly," said Ray. "I mean . . . you died."

"Not really. Okay, sort of."

"Oh, come on," his former employer said. "How many times did you and I talk about just this sort of thing over drinks? The dead taking jobs from the living? Trying to destroy our way of life?"

"That's ridiculous. You know me."

"Used to. I have to be honest, your . . . " He chose some words. "Your new legal status has a lot of people here worried, Lawrence.

There are trust issues. And we have to think of our clients. Are they going to do business with a company that employs . . . "

"Portfolio specialists?"

"Zombies," he said. "Let's just call a spade a spade. You're one of the walking dead and no one's going to feel comfortable around you. Heck, my skin's crawling a bit just looking at you."

"I'm the same guy! Jesus, Ray, I was going to be Anna's godfather."

"Good thing that didn't happen, eh? Can you imagine trying to explain that to her now? She'd want to keep you as a pet or something." He shook his head. "Was good working with you, Lawrence. Your stuff's in the break room. We got it all into two boxes, but I think Greg may have stolen your stapler."

"Marty?"

On the screen, his friend peered at the camera. "Lawrence? Is that you?"

"Yeah, it's me."

"This isn't your extension. Why can't I see you?"

"I'm using the break room phone and the . . . the video's broken I think." He pressed his thumb against the lens a little harder. "Look, have you talked to Kimberly recently?"

On the other end of the link, Marty shifted in his seat. "No," he said. "You two having a fight?"

"Yeah, sort of. Are you free for lunch?"

"I've got to be in court at three, but I think I could swing it. How's Rey Muerto sound?"

"Sounds great."

"Good. I'll see you at one."

"See you at one." Lawrence tapped the button to break the link.

The patio of Rey Muerto got enough sunlight to be bright, not enough to be blinding. From across the street Lawrence watched his friend take their usual table and lean back with the menu.

He slid in through the fire gate and dropped into the chair across from him. Marty leaped up. "Son of a whore!"

"Calm down," said Lawrence.

His friend looked around at the other patio diners and took in a deep breath.

"Marty calm down, for Pete's sake. It's me." He reached up and slid the glasses away from his eyes.

He froze. "Lawrence?"

"Yeah."

"Oh, sweet Allah," said Marty. "What the hell?"

"Will you sit down?"

"Are you . . . I mean, you're not going to bite me or anything, are you?"

"Sit down."

He sat down. "What happened?"

"Car crash. I tried to beat the Green Line and lost."

"Shit."

"Yeah, tell me about it."

"And now you're . . . dead?"

"Yep."

"Shit."

The waitress approached and he pushed the sunglasses back up. "What can I get you two gentlemen?"

"I'd like the cold roast beef sandwich," said Lawrence. "No lettuce. No tomato. Heavy on the beef, as rare as you can cut it."

She gave him a look but shifted her attention to Marty. "And you?"

"Vodka martini," he whispered. "Make it a double. Two doubles, in fact."

"And to eat?"

"Another martini."

She walked away with a last glance at Lawrence.

Marty drummed his fingers on the tabletop and looked anywhere but at his friend. "Why did you call me?"

"I need some help."

"No, seriously." He glanced around. "Why did you call me? Do you know what it could do to me if I'm seen with you?"

"Marty, I am screwed right now, okay? I've got no home, no job, nothing."

"Of course you don't. You're an ex."

"I'm an ex but I'm not like them," he said. "Look. We're just talking. No biting. No ripping."

The other man shuffled back.

"Will you stop acting like I'm a leper?"

"You're worse than a leper! Lepers are still alive."

"That's just stupid."

"You used to say that all the time."

"Yeah, but I didn't . . . I didn't mean it for people like me." He leaned back and twisted his foot back and forth. His ankles ached.

The waitress set two martinis down on the table. Marty grabbed one and downed it. "What the hell were you thinking, coming back like this?"

"You think this was a choice?"

"Well, no, but . . . Can't you just kill yourself? Or re-kill yourself or something?"

"Jesus, Marty. I could use a little more support right now."

"What do you want from me?"

"I want you to calm down, for starters."

"Calm down? You're an ex, you idiot. If the partners found out I was talking to you they'd throw me out."

"They can't throw you out for talking to me."

"You're an ex! For all they know I'm collaborating with you."

"Collaborating?" He tried to laugh but there wasn't enough air in his lungs.

"Look, just tell me what you want."

"What do you think? I want Kimberly out of my house and me back in. I want my job back."

"You lost your job?"

"Of course I did!" he snapped. "Look at me. Why would they keep me on staff?"

"See?" Marty stabbed his finger down and the bread plate clattered. "You know it yourself. That's why I can't be talking to you."

"So you're just going to bail on me?"

"Just like you would on me, yeah." He thumbed through his wallet. "Look, there's this guy in North Park named Wells. He's some sort of zombie-rights nut, does a lot of pro bono work." A card flew down and clicked on the table.

"Marty . . . "

"I have a family. Did you think of them? Do you know what would happen to them if the authorities thought we carried the ex-virus? That we've been hanging out with one every weekend for Allah knows how long."

"Just explain it to them. They'll understand."

"How much brain did you lose? You know what'll happen. Hell, you campaigned for half those laws. No job, no outside contact, nobody would hear from us for years at best. Probably never again." He stood up, dug through his wallet a bit more, and threw a wad of bills down on the table. "That's around six hundred," he said. "It's the most I can do, and you didn't get it from me. Don't call me again."

"I won't."

His friend marched into the restaurant, reappeared on the sidewalk, and vanished down the road. Lawrence watched for a moment, reached down to rub his calves, and a roast beef sandwich inched into view. The waitress was holding the plate at arm's length. A large busboy stood behind her. Half the patio diners had vanished inside.

"Oh, just give me the damned sandwich," he sighed.

Lawrence marched away from Rey Muerto with a small moral victory, no friends, and a fluttering hunger. The sandwich had smelled okay, but his stomach was churning. The roast beef had not been rare enough.

And his legs were in agony.

He sat on the concrete wall next to his shoes and socks and watched sheets of water cascade down. The big fountain dominated the plaza between the two museums. At night the lights filled it with color, but right now it was just curtains of silver reflecting the blue sky. He could almost feel the cool liquid on his feet. They looked white underwater.

The sterile-wrapped scalpel was still in his coat pocket. He pulled it out and tapped it against his knees, then his knuckles. Two little tabs made it easy to tear the paper away.

Clenching the scalpel between his teeth, he dragged his ankle up onto the opposite knee. The veins were thick and black against his pale skin. He poked at his Achilles tendon. It was getting stiff and hard.

He balanced the blade in his fingers. It felt warm against the flesh of his ankle. He gritted his teeth and pushed down. There was no pain, and the resistant meat reminded him of carving a Christmas ham. He worked the scalpel deeper, until the plastic handle touched his skin, then dragged it up his calf.

Dark blood welled up and he swung his leg into the fountain. He watched the water cloud as he lifted his other ankle and sliced through the flesh. His cuffs were getting bloody, so he pulled them up and bunched them above his knees.

The dull pain flowed out of him and he relaxed.

"Whatcha doin?"

He turned and saw the girl. She was five at the most, wearing a bright red Mighty Dragon shirt. She leaned over the edge of the fountain and looked at the clouds of dark blood.

"You made the water dirty."

"I did," he smiled. "I'm sorry."

"Why?"

"I was trying to fix my legs."

"Why?"

"So they wouldn't hurt."

"Why?"

He thought for a moment and fell back on the oldest of infections. "I've got cooties," he explained, "and it makes my legs hurt."

"Ewwwww," grinned the girl. "Cooties."

He nodded.

"Misha says cooties are forever."

"They are."

"No," she said with a sage shake of her head. "Daddy says Misha's wrong. They can cure cooties now."

He laughed. The air scraped his windpipe and it came out like a bark. The girl jumped and squealed.

"Lettie," called a woman across the plaza. She took a few strides towards the fountain. "Stop bothering that man."

"S'okay," she yelled back. "He has cooties but his legs don't hurt no more."

His laugh grated the air again. "You are so cute," he said with a grin. "I could just eat you . . . up . . . "

The mother looked at him in horror. His heart sank.

He put his hands up. "It's just a figure of-"

"Ex! Ex in the park!" She yanked the little girl into her arms and the child began to cry. "Somebody help!"

"Lady, it's okay," he said, standing up. "Honest, I just meant she's a really adora—"

"Get away from my baby, you monster!"

A few other people wandered closer. Fingers pointed. People gasped.

"Did it bite that kid?"

"Jesus, look at all the blood."

"Somebody call the cops."

"People, please," he shouted. "This is all jussss . . . " His air ran out and the words faded into a throaty moan. He stumbled over the fountain's edge, back onto the cobblestones.

"It's attacking!"

"The head! We have to smash its head."

"Is the little girl okay?"

"Oh, God, there's so much blood."

A police car buzzed up over the stairs and skidded to a halt. Two officers, a man with a thick mustache and a burly woman, leaped out with stun batons ready. "Mother of God," said the man. "I knew one'd get loose some day."

Lawrence tried to talk, coughed, and remembered to suck in another lungful of air.

"Everyone stand back," shouted the female officer.

"It tried to eat my little girl," screamed the mother.

"She's been bit," yelled someone else. "She's bleeding bad."

"It's my blood," he shouted. "There'sssss . . . " Yelling used up his air faster than he thought. He took another breath and they hit him with the batons. The cobblestones rushed up to smack his shoulder.

The policeman kneeled on his back. "Get the muzzle around its head!"

"I'm not an it!"

"Hold it still," she yelled.

The plastic straps cinched down across his nose and cheeks, and a steel rod the width of a finger slipped between his teeth. Another set of bands pulled tight under his jaw and across the top of his head.

"Whaa tha fugg ith ronn wit yuu peepa?!" he bellowed around the bit.

Nicholas Wells looked like every other lawyer Lawrence knew. Dark suit, perfect hair, and a trustworthy, pasted-on smile. His bland features could've been anywhere between thirty and fifty. There were a dozen photos of him around the office with a dozen different public figures. He looked the same in every one.

Wells leaned back in the chair. "The police say you had my card in your pocket."

Lawrence nodded.

"And you're a seventeen. You can talk."

He drummed his fingers on the chair arm and pointed at the bit in his mouth.

"Oh, sorry. Just too used to seeing those on." Wells reached into a drawer and slid a pair of scissors across the desk to the dead man. Lawrence forced the plastic strap between the blades and levered them shut. The muzzle came apart with a bang and he spit the steel rod out.

"Thanks," he said.

"Again, sorry about that. You want a drink or anything?"

"I don't think I can anymore, but thanks."

"Actually, the high-proof rums are great for you," said the lawyer. "Sterilize your insides."

"Really?"

"Really."

"I'll have a double, then, thank you."

"There's also some hamburger in the mini-fridge, if you want it. Vat meat, but it does the job."

Lawrence's eyes flicked to the white box but he stayed in his seat.

"You're not my first dead client, Mr. Secord." Wells handed him a glass. "I'm guessing the past two days haven't been that great for you."

"Not really, no."

The lawyer sat down on the edge of his desk. "Have some meat. You'll feel better and it'll be easier for you to focus while we talk."

He got up and made it to the fridge without stumbling. His tongue trembled as he unwrapped the ground chuck. It tasted like heaven. He couldn't remember any meal ever tasting so delicious.

"Good?"

"God, yes," he said between bites. "Thank you."

"No problem." He gestured at the chair with his own glass and

Lawrence sat back down. "So, what can I do for you?"

"I just . . . I want my life back."

Wells smiled. "I think you need to be in a church to make that request."

"No, I know that. I'm dead. I understand. It's just . . . a few days ago I had a home. I had a job. And now it's all been taken away and people are looking at me, people I thought I knew, and they're . . ." He settled back in the chair. "They treat me like a monster."

"I know," said the lawyer. "People look at you and they just see an ex. They don't care that you can control your appetite. They don't care that you want to be left alone. They just see a flesh-eating monster that wants to swallow their children."

"Exactly," nodded Lawrence. "But that's not who I am."

"But it's what you look like."

"Yeah but that's . . . that's profiling, isn't it?"

"It is, but what are they supposed to do? Assume that little old lady might try to gnaw someone's face off and slap a muzzle on her? That's counter-productive and you know it. It's not fair, but that's how it goes." He shrugged. "I could help you get a job doing construction, if you want. Maybe janitorial work. There are a couple pro-ex companies here in the city."

"I've been in finance for twenty years. I'm a portfolio specialist for investors."

"Who got fired this morning, yes? People get nervous seeing someone like you behind a desk. Or working in the food industry. They want to see you doing harmless work in a muzzle."

"You have to be joking."

Wells shook his head. "You'd only have to wear it during work hours. There are models with buckles. You could take it off back at the shelter."

"I don't want to go to a shelter, I want to go home!"

"You don't have a home!"

"I do. It's a mile and a half that way. We could go look in the window and watch the pool boy bang my wife."

Wells sighed and set his glass down. "Mr. Secord . . . Lawrence. You have to accept this. You don't have a home. You don't have a wife. You're lucky they're not deporting you."

"How can they deport me? I'm an American. Are they sending me back to Connecticut?"

"You aren't an American anymore. That's what you need to understand. The moment you died, your citizenship was declared null and void under the Ex-Patriot Act of 2057. You can't own property or hold currency. You have no legal rights under the law as it currently stands. Technically I'm not even supposed to talk to you."

He shook his head. "This is just . . . it has to be illegal. I'm an American. A taxpayer. People can't just walk in and take everything I own."

"You were an American. You were a taxpayer. And you lost ownership of everything the moment that bus hit your Tesla."

"There has to be something I can do."

Wells sighed and stood up. "I'm sorry, but at this point in time there isn't."

Lawrence glared up at the bronze heroes glimmering in the moonlight and wished he was dead. For real. If they'd done their jobs right, he would be.

He had a job again. In three days he started hauling pressboard at a lot near Old Town. They were willing to pay him three bucks an hour. Wells had arranged a bunk at an ex-shelter where he could get vat meat and a place to lay down.

A rustle echoed across the night time park. The same ex he'd seen there before. The dead woman. It tilted its head and stared past him with the empty eye socket. Then it shuffled away. The ex's legs were swollen and fat with rotted blood. It was no wonder she shuffled.

He took a few steps and pulled the scalpel from his pocket. One hand went against her knee, the blade sank into the bloated flesh, and he dragged it down to her heel. Blood oozed out like pudding to splatter on the grass. He cut the other ankle and more black clumps ran from the ex's skin.

Its expression never changed, but he was sure it moved a little easier and lifted its feet a little higher as it stumbled away. Closer to a walk than a stagger.

"That was nice of you," someone said.

He leaped to his feet, arms up.

It was a pretty blonde, her hair tied up almost in a topknot. She smiled at him over her owlish glasses. "I'm not going to hurt you," she said.

"I remember you," he said. "You were at the hospital."

She nodded. "I saved you from the incinerator."

"Ahhh," he said. "You'll forgive me if I don't jump up and down thanking you for that."

Her lips twisted. "Not going well, I guess?"

Another dry laugh echoed around the monument. "No," he said with a wry smile. "Not going well."

"How bad is it?"

"Why do you care?"

"You're dead, but you're still a person," she said. "That's how I see it, anyway."

"For all the good it does me," he said. "Sorry. I know you were trying to do me a favor."

The intern took off her glasses and held them out to him. "Can you hold these for a second? I'd like to show you something."

Homer took the spectacles and she glanced around. With one quick motion she tugged her shirt up around her neck, revealing a powder-blue bra against flawless, milky skin. She tugged on the bottom of the cup to reveal a soft, pale curve of flesh and something dark. He took a breath without even thinking about it.

Just below her right breast was a deep, ragged gash. It had been cleaned, but showed no signs of healing. The flesh around it was bruised and wrinkled. She let the bra settle back in to place and pulled her shirt down. He looked up at her face and she blinked out a blue contact, revealing the cloudy gray eye underneath.

"I've been passing for two years," she said. "It's not too hard in a hospital. Harsh lights, lots of topical antibiotics, eye drops, and no one questions it if you smell like chemicals. Just have to be a bit careful no one sees too much of me in the locker room."

"Why . . . why didn't you say anything?"

"People need a couple days to work through stuff, get their minds around what's happened." She shrugged. "If I'd told you then you just would've outed me to the hospital staff."

"I would've." He nodded. "What happened to you?"

Her smile was the nicest thing he'd seen in days. "It sounds stupid but . . . jogging accident."

He barked out another laugh. "A what?"

"Here in the park, actually," she said, and pointed off past the bridge. "I was running on one of the back trails. I slipped on some loose dirt and fell on a broken branch."

"You're joking."

She shook her head and tapped her chest. "Right through the lung. It collapsed and it took me about twenty minutes to smother to death."

"Sounds horrible."

"It was, but I was lucky. It was a Tuesday night. If it had happened on a weekend, someone would've found me immediately and that would've been that." She shrugged. "As it was I woke up dead the next morning and only missed one shift at the hospital. My supervisor docked me two days pay to teach me a lesson."

"And now you help any exes that come through?"

"No." She smiled again. "I've been waiting for you."

"Careful. I'm a married man."

"Yeah. How'd that work out?"

"Apparently the past three years have been great for the pool boy."

"Ouch."

"I'm starting to realize it's not that big a loss. So why were you waiting for me?"

She leaned back and looked up at the sky. "We've had four seventeens come through our hospital since I made the transition," she said. "Two put themselves down almost as soon as we released them. One went crazy and attacked a few people. And the last one got a lawyer and tried to get his house back from his bitch of a wife."

He chuckled and followed her gaze up to the stars.

"I want to leave San Diego," she said. "I want to head north and find somewhere better. A place where people like us can have a regular life. I just . . . " She looked over at him. "I didn't want to go alone."

"So you've been waiting for me so we can go on a road trip together and find zombie paradise?"

She laughed. "Well, when you put it like that…"

"I think that'd be nice."

"Good."

He held out his arm. "What's your name, anyway? I'm Lawrence."

She hooked hers through his. "Promise not to laugh?"

"I promise to try."

"I'm Eve."

"Eve." He smiled. "Of course you are."

They walked off together into the night, heading north.

The Office Party

by Walter Jarvis

"It's not like you're actually going to be partying with dead people," his girlfriend told Gerald as she tried to talk him into going to his
office Christmas party. "Who cares if they're locked away someplace
down the hall? You know that's not the real reason you don't want to
go. "

"You're right. Actually, I'd rather socialize with the arbies than
some of my co-workers," he said.

"Look, Gerald, I know you don't like your job—"

"Hate it with a passion."

"—but you still get a decent paycheck from the place, and you and
I both know that jobs are hard to get nowadays. So if you want to get
ahead in your career, you better show up and mingle. You can always
come home early."

He was silent for a moment, then said, "They've told me I'm going
to be replaced by the first of the year."

"What? When did you find that out?"

"Yesterday. You want to know what's worse? My replacement's
an arbie."

"That's impossible, Gerald! They can't do the things you can do."

"Apparently Esperionex thinks they can."

"All the more reason for you to go, then. It'll give you a chance to network and see what else is out there."

"Replaced by a corpse," Gerald said, shaking his head. "What does that say about my marketability?"

The arbies weren't dead in the strictest definition of the term, for they did possess mobility, some memory and a prodigious capacity to do work. The authorities called them Resuscitated Reprogrammed Bodies, or R.R.Bs. The public had shortened that acronym to "arbie," although the more politically incorrect designation of "zombie" was still widely used. They had become a common sight in America's workplace, despite establishment squeamishness and blue and white collar resentment and fear. The reason was simple: they worked cheap.

There were four of them assigned to Gerald's office. God only knew how many were utilized by the Esperionex Corporation world-wide. They filled in when people were out either on vacation or on sick leave. Most of Gerald's fellow employees had acclimated themselves to the arbies at this point. If you overlooked the small flashing diodes embedded in their jaws, you might think they were rather taciturn temps who needed to get out in the sun more.

"What they are," Mr. Nichols, Gerald's office manager and supervisor, declaimed at one point, " are terrific labor saving devices. They don't take any breaks, never call in sick. And you can forget about overtime."

"But Mr. Nichols," Gerald had said, "they're still *dead*."

"Only in a manner of speaking. I prefer to think of them as being recycled. After all, we do it with glass and plastic, so why not with people?"

Occasionally one of them would be moved into Gerald's work

sector when someone was out—usually as a replacement for Johansen who was a chronic absentee. Gerald found them a distraction; he could not help but steal glances at them out of the corner of his eye. Often it was a male arbie who wore the tag MXA-123 on his gray uniform whom Gerald found planted in Johansen's cubicle.

When the clock on the wall signaled five o'clock, Gerald and his fellow workers would, almost in unison, clear their desks, log off their computers, and leave. MXA-123, on the other hand, would keep on working. Gerald didn't know at what time he was led back to the storage closet and parked for the night, but apparently it was long after the living had left. Perhaps he was shepherded away by the cleaning crew, who might have been arbies themselves, for all Gerald knew.

When Gerald arrived, the office party was well underway. A pleasant hum of conversation rose over the piped-in Christmas music—the band had not yet arrived—broken occasionally by the sounds of slightly inebriated laughter. The Christmas tree glittered in one corner and there was a good crowd around the open bar. A buffet had been laid out against the opposite wall and people were lined up to help themselves to steaming trays of hot hors d'oeuvres.

Gerald got a drink and joined Jake Carruthers, his best friend at work, whom he had spotted putting the make on a new girl who had just been hired for the office secretarial pool. She was blonde, pert and had an innocence in her eyes that had not been corrupted yet from toiling at Esperionex.

"Carrie here is worried about one of the zombies taking her job," Jake said, "but I tell her it's not going to happen. Nichols isn't going to have some dead person answering the phone."

"But they're becoming better and better at what they can do," the girl said anxiously. "Who ever thought they could learn to type? And I've heard they can be taught to speak. What I say when I answer the phone is almost totally scripted, anyway."

"But you still have clients coming into the office," Jake pointed out. "Do you think management is going to have some gray-faced, dead-eyed thing greeting the people who ultimately pay the bills?"

Gerald listened silently. The conversation left him with a sick feeling in the pit of his stomach. He wasn't going to say anything, but, of course, Carrie could be replaced. If they were going to replace him, whose job demanded a much higher skill level, with an arbie, then she was expendable, too. He didn't want to dampen her spirits by saying anything, though. Certainly not at the Christmas party. Besides, he hadn't told anyone yet he was losing his job after the first of the year; he was too ashamed about how it was going to be filled.

"You've got nothing to worry about," Jake said again. "If you ever want to practice your spiel, I'll be glad to give you some constructive criticism. Maybe at my place, after work."

Nichols, the division manager, had taken the microphone and was smiling at the crowd. As far as Gerald was concerned, he represented everything that was bad about Esperionex. He was arrogant, uncaring, and driven to pare costs to the bare-bone minimum. It was because of him that Gerald was going to receive a pink slip.

"Ladies and gentlemen, welcome to the annual Esperionex West's Christmas party," he said. "This is our small way to say thank you for your dedicated service. I realize that we have asked many sacrifices from you this year to keep the company competitive in the global economy, and I'm proud to let you know that your efforts have not been in vain: our corporation has shown a two percent increase in profits for the fourth quarter. We should all be proud of the contribution we've made to Esperionex's long-term viability."

Gerald felt his old anger return. If there had been some kind of year-end profit, he was sure that Nichols had gotten a fat bonus. If he could replace Gerald with one of the arbies in the months to come, his reward would be even greater next year. Gerald wished he could figure out a way to wipe that self-satisfied smile off his supervisor's face.

"And now it is my great pleasure to introduce Benjamin Middleton," Nichols went on, "chairman and CEO of Esperionex, who has taken time from his busy schedule to fly from New York City to be with us tonight."

A polite round of applause. Middleton was a tall, vulpine-looking man with hair so carefully styled that it looked like he were wearing a bad wig when it was really his own. His dark blue suit, cut from some expensive Italian fabric, shone with a faint iridescence when the spotlights over the podium caught it.

"Old Benjamin's the most boring humanoid on earth," Jake whispered. "I've heard him speak before. Nothing but corporate bullshit. I'd rather listen to one of the arbies."

"Speaking of which," Carrie said, "I wonder if they can hear the sounds of the party from the storage room? That would be too cruel."

"Doesn't matter," Gerald said. "It's not like they feel anything. You have to be alive to have emotions."

A respectful silence settled over the room as Middleton began to speak. Jake was right: he was incredibly boring. He was talking about how Esperionex looked on its employees as "family," when nothing could be further than the truth. The only relationships that the corporation cared about were measured in dollars and euros. If Middleton could replace all of them with zombies tomorrow and put the savings against the bottom line, he would do it.

"I've got an idea how to liven this party up," Gerald whispered to Jake. "Let's let the zombies out of storage."

"What? Are you crazy?" Jake hissed.

"Nobody will know it was us. Half the time they forget to lock that door. Don't you want to see the look on Nichols face when he turns around and finds an arbie at the punch bowl? These guys think that they've got everything under control, from our paychecks to when we're supposed to applaud. Well, let's show them we're not completely programmed yet!"

Everyone was listening to Middleton drone on and on, so it was an easy matter to slip away from the crowd. When Carrie glanced at him, Gerald smiled back and mouthed "bathroom." Jake had slipped out the opposite direction; it wouldn't be good for them to be seen leaving together.

They met at the entrance to the storage room. Down the hall they could hear the muffled, monotonous words of Middleton's speech. As Gerald suspected, the room had been left unlocked, and he opened the door. The interior was dimly lit only from the spillover illumination from the hallway. Squinting into the darkness, he could barely make out the outlines of the arbies, lined up against the back wall as rigid as soldiers standing at attention. The sight was so disconcerting that Gerald suddenly had cold feet. He was about to close the door, when one of the arbies haltingly stepped forward. It was followed by another and another.

The light must stimulate them, he thought.

"They'll be attracted by the noise," Jake whispered. "They'll head straight to the party. We better get out of here."

Middleton was just wrapping up his speech when they rejoined Carrie, trying to look as unobtrusive as possible. He found his heart was beating wildly.

A murmur ran through the crowd and Gerald thought he heard a woman shriek faintly. Middleton looked in that direction, and the smile faded from his face. People moved aside, revealing the four arbies standing motionlessly in the entrance to the hall.

They were wearing their standard dull gray jackets and black trousers, their usual work uniform, and they appeared to be waiting for someone to step forward and give them an assignment. Gerald guessed this was the position they took every morning before the office opened

"This is not funny," Nichols said in an angry voice, looking around the room. "Someone in our midst has done this. Well, if this is your idea of a joke, you're going to be very sorry. Lacey, Wilson," he ordered two men standing near the arbies, "please escort these things back to the storage area."

When the two men hesitated, Nichols grew angrier still. "That's an order, gentlemen."

"Just one moment, please," Middleton said, a serene smile on his face. "This is, after all, the Christmas season. Perhaps we should extend the hand of fellowship to our R.R.B's here, who toil ceaselessly throughout the rest of the year with no recognition from the rest of us."

"Well, if you really think that's a good idea," Nichols said, his expression making clear that he didn't.

"I want Esperionex to be known as a progressive, open-minded company. Let's share some of our blessings and our companionship with our R.R.B. co-workers."

Middleton went over and extended his hand to the nearest arbie, which happened to be MXA-123. "Welcome to the Esperionex Christmas party," Middleton said. "You are among friends tonight."

Expressionlessly the creature stared at him and then, as if it were a delayed reaction, clumsily shook his hand.

A sigh went up from some of the partygoers, and there was even a scattering of applause. Taking a cue from Middleton, several of his sycophants gathered around the other arbies, wishing them Merry Christmas and trying ineffectually to strike up a conversation. Gerald noticed that Nichols was first in line.

"I've got to give him credit," Jake said in a low tone. "Old Middleton's quick on his feet."

Nichols, trying to win additional points with his boss, and casting his squeamishness aside, had led one of the arbies—was it MXA-123? Gerald was having trouble in telling them apart—over to the buffet, and with a great show of solicitude was serving him a plate.

"How stupid can you get?" Gerald asked. "Everybody

34

knows that arbies don't eat."

Much to his surprise, though, the arbie, following Nichols' example, took one of the eggrolls and put it in his mouth. Was it Gerald's imagination, or did the faintest trace of a smile touch the other's bloodless lips as its jaws crunched down on the golden crust? Perhaps the pastry had awakened some long dormant taste buds that were supposed to be as dead as the rest of its body.

The arbie began to clear the plate, stuffing its mouth with food. Disconcerted, Nichols took a step back. "Wilson," he called out, "would you make sure this R.R.B. gets enough to eat? I'm going to rejoin Mr. Middleton."

Another arbie was at the far end of the table, dipping its hand into a silver hot tray and taking fistfuls of food, which it was swallowing whole.

"I think I'll pass on the mash potatoes," Jake said, eyeing the thing with disgust.

Perhaps to distract the other partygoers from the sight of their food being consumed so rapaciously, Nichols ordered the band, which had just set up, to begin playing. They started out half-heartedly enough, their spirits tempered by the sight of the arbies, but Nichols said something to the director, and the tempo picked up immediately. Soon a handful of couples were on the dance floor, moving to the slow beat of "Unchained Melody." Gerald saw Middleton cross the floor to the single female arbie who was standing alone and motionless at the edge of the crowd. *He's not going to do what I think he's going to do,* Gerald told himself.

Middleton gently whispered something in the arbie's ear and then, taking her by the hand, led her out to join the other dancers.

Clumsily the arbie tried to follow his steps as they circled the dance floor. Middleton wore the self-satisfied smile of a man who wanted to say, "Look, if I'm this empathetic with a creature who isn't even alive, how much more so will I be with Esperionex's living workers, who need time off and sick leave and all those other inconvenient necessities of employment?"

"Get a picture of that," Nichols ordered Ms. Sarapour, who handled

PR, "for the company newsletter."

Dutifully the woman began taking pictures, the flash going off in rapid succession. Others got out their cell phones and digital cameras and began photographing the two dancers as well. Out of the corner of his eye, Gerald saw the arbies at the buffet freeze suddenly, their eyes drawn toward the bursts of light. Their diodes were flashing rapidly and had turned a bright crimson.

Without warning, and giving a raptor-like screech, the female arbie suddenly wrapped her fingers around Middleton's neck and began to choke him. One of the arbies standing by the table grabbed a carving knife and with an inhuman cackle plunged it into the chest of the nearest man in line. Another grabbed a serving fork and rushed a woman in front of him, stabbing her again and again.

The party-goers panicked. People were yelling and screaming and trying to crowd through the narrow doors that led to the elevators. Gerald looked over his shoulder and saw that Carrie was safely exiting down the stairwell. The next thing he knew he was sent crashing to the floor As he struggled to his feet, he saw a big burly man careen into Jake and knock him down as well. His friend disappeared beneath a surge of stampeding bodies. Gerald tried to reach him but was swept toward the door. He glimpsed the female arbie chewing on a severed arm, its mouth dripping with blood, and wondered dumbly if it might be Middleton's. Trying to work his way back to Jake, he was sent hurtling into the wall and struck his head. The hallway went black, and he did not have to witness the rest of the carnage.

Gerald arrived to work 20 minutes' late, but he knew he didn't have to worry about having his pay docked. The new management cut the old employees—those who had survived the Christmas party— quite a bit of slack. Until the doctors removed his leg brace—someone had stepped on his knee while he lay unconscious in the hallway, crushing it—he had an excuse to be late.

Stepping into the office every morning was like entering a winter's clearing in which all noise was deadened by surrounding banks of snow. People had gotten into the habit of speaking in low voices, or even whispers; the telephone rings had deliberately been muted. The bloodstained carpet had been removed, the shattered window through which someone had been hurled had been replaced. Middleton's smiling picture that had hung near Nichols' old office, still empty, had been replaced by that of the new CEO. Carrie had quit the day after the Christmas party and was now working for a company that had an iron-clad policy of not using arbies.

There were no longer any arbies in the office except one. The four that had gone on the rampage had been captured, tested extensively to see what had gone wrong, and subsequently destroyed. There had been talk at the highest levels of management about doing without the arbies altogether, but there were certain profit goals that could not be met without them, so it was decided to keep a few at least.

The newest and only arbie at Esperionex West had been extensively vetted and declared to be perfectly free from all aggressive tendencies. Because it was already familiar with office procedures, and had to shoulder the workload of its missing brethren, it was being used 24 hours a day. Of course, the thing never protested about being overworked.

It had been placed in the cubicle next to Gerald's. He tried not to look at it, but sometimes he had to. Gerald always regretted when he did, because that reawakened the old guilt. If only we hadn't opened the storage room door, he told himself over and over. Once or twice he had to fight back tears.

The first day he was back, when he was sure that nobody was around, Gerald had been tempted to speak to the thing. He leaned over and whispered, "I'm sorry, Jake. You don't know how sorry I am." It kept on working, as if it had not heard Gerald, its gray face expressionless, the dead eyes focused on the key board, and that made his pain all the worse.

Gather Round, Gather Round

by Dave Macpherson

A time back, I made a living traveling compound to compound selling Captain Riley's Death Elixir. We weren't the only ones selling the stuff. It was like a franchise. We bought into the grift. For the money, we got the sales pitch and the special labels. There was probably a half dozen Captain Rileys roaming about the Compound Land back then. Our Captain Riley was a fellow named Smith.

We'd roll into town, wait out quarantine and sell the shit. It didn't matter what the elixir was; we made it from whatever liquids we had about, and iodine. There way always iodine; it had to have that medicine taste to make it all work. If it didn't taste like shitty medicine, no one would believe you. Smith would be wearing this stained old lab coat and strut out into the common and start his spiel. He said he was part of a Los Alamos research team that was like seconds away from cracking the ultimate puzzle when the walkers broke in and ate everyone—except the great and glorious army doctor, Captain Riley. Only he escaped. With him were scraps of the formula. He spent years recreating it and finally he had it for sale today

The Death Elixir. Drink it and when you die, you die. No resurrection, no walking. Just oblivion. The turn of the con was when Smith showed charts with crazy chemical symbols. He'd talk amino acids, neural transmitters, retro-viral disintegration. Nonsense, but it sold the deal. Science. It was bullshit and fancy footwork.

It was a sweet pitch, because we could sell out our supply and be 3 compounds down the road before our little experiment would be tested.

This worked for months until we ran out of iodine. Smith told me to mix up a new batch of the joy juice, but we needed something to make it medicine. I went into an old factory and in a cabinet found a jar with its label browned and unreadable. I swear, it smelled like iodine. Okay. I suppose it wasn't. Don't know what it was.

That night, we sold twenty-seven bottles. By morning, all twenty-seven of our clientele were dead and hungry. They ate us out of our potential customer base. This little old lady, who the day before I pegged for the easiest mark, just up and bit Smith on the leg. We were packing up the truck when she chomped down on him and he looked at me all confused. All I could do? Pushed my ice pick through his eye, cracked the old biddy's skull with Smith's trench shovel, finished tying down the gear, and popped the clutch. And that's how I left the employ of Captain Riley and his Death Elixir concern.

I suppose you are asking why I tell this tale of woe and liars. Because I have reformed and speak only truth. I ask you to look at my arm. Observe the scar. Two years back a walker gave me this love peck. So the question is—how am I here today? I was cured. The infection was nullified.

And not only that, this item I have has other amazing abilities. A way to bring death after life. Friends, in my possession is a remnant, a fragment of cloth from the first walker. He came way before the scourge, but he was the first and if you touch anything of this long ago walker, the powers of nature will reverse. There will be no more returning.

Friends, survivors, have any of you heard of the Shroud of Turin? No? Well, settle yourselves and let me tell you a tale of its origins and how I came to hold it here before you. Don't worry, no need to push to the front. No grabbing at it. It will be worth your wait. Trust me.

Working Man's Burden
by David C. Pinnt

Harold knew things were about to go cock-eyed when Betty 248 stuffed the chicken guts in her mouth.

He sat up on his stool and flicked off the Mossberg's safety. The rest of the Z- crew—Betties and Barneys they called them in the break room—continued to work the eviscerating carousel, shoulders slumped and jumpsuits sagging, hands moving slowly but efficiently as the chicken carcasses rotated on the hooks. Grabbing the breast with the left hand, right plunging into the gut slit and a quick pull and tug, dropping the offal to the stainless steel mesh. Heart, gizzard and liver onto the conveyor and the rest down the trough to the waste bins. The regulators implanted in the backs of their skulls, leads burrowing into their shriveling limbic systems, winked green, a slow happy cadence to a shift boss like Harold.

But Betty 248, he'd been watching her close anyway. So new she hardly looked dead, flesh sagging just a bit on her face, deep circles under her eyes. She'd been in the line three, four days? Soon enough her skin would take on a gray, waxy sheen and eventually, despite the hosing down with chlorine each night, it would break open. Dark, dry tissue, the blood long clotted. The sores opened at the knuckles first, then the elbows. Harold knew the repetitive motion—hour after hour gutting the chickens—was just too much for the dead flesh to bear.

Harold swung off the stool and edged around the carousel to see her face. The other crew kept at their jobs, jaws slack, weight tilting from side to side, their various numbers stenciled large across their backs and small over the left breast. The chickens, gleaming white skin still oozing droplets of blood from the defeatherer, swayed on the carousel. Emaciated fingers in rubber gloves grabbed, twisted, pulled, and separated.

On the far side of the carousel Harold stooped, a ratcheting pop sounding off in his left knee. Sure as shit, Betty 248 had a crimson smear across her cheek where she'd crammed the guts into her mouth. The other Z-crew stared straight at the carcasses or worked with eyes closed, but 248's sunken orbs rolled left and right and Harold fancied he could hear a high keening rising from her smeared lips.

He jacked a shell into the Mossberg and thumbed open his radio. "This is Harold in EVR 4—I've got a situation. Send a crew down." Maybe his voice tipped her over, or maybe it was the chewed entrails hitting the desiccated, empty stomach, but Betty 248's regulator failed for certain. She yanked a carcass off its hook, ripped out a mouthful of pearlescent flesh, and turned on the Barney next to her, yellowed teeth gnawing the side of his face, latex-tipped fingers raking his cheap cotton jumpsuit.

"Holy shit," Harold flicked the radio open again. "Right now. I need a crew right now."

The Barney, 109 on his chest, shuffled sideways his regulator working fine, still trying to gut the chicken before him, as Betty 248— shrieks rising in her throat—slavered and chewed at his neck. Harold crab-walked under the carousel, keeping one eye on the Z-crew, not knowing if the fracas would overload their regulators too. His boots squelched on the wet floor, stray clumps of feathers and gobbets of meat in the treads.

Betty 248 ripped off Barney 109's ear, shriveled gray flesh on a zombie so old. The wound lay purple black under the harsh fluorescents.

With one economical step Harold slipped behind the pair, socketed the Mossberg's barrel at the base of the Betty's skull, just below her regulator—now amber—and pulled the trigger. The top of Betty 248's skull vaporized—bone, hair and brain splattering across the carousel, the Z-crew and the chickens. Her body dropped to the floor, head gone from the nose up, jumpsuit collar smoldering. Barney 109 turned back to the carousel, left hand twitching for the next chicken.

Levi and two rustlers banged into the evisceration room. The rustlers held lollysticks, steel tubes six feet long, a wire loop at the far end and a shank handle at the other to pull the loop tight. Pistol-gripped Mossbergs hung over their shoulders, barrel down.

Levi took in the scene—Barney 109's gaping head, Betty 248's still lump on the floor, and hooked his thumbs through his belt loops. One of the rustlers slapped the red kill switch by the door, shutting down the assembly line, chickens jerked and swayed on their hooks and the Z-crew stopped, limp.

"Goddamnit Harold, you shot her? Protocol is to wait on the rustlers. We just got her last week. Five thousand dollars! She had a good six months in her. Jesus Christ!"

Harold bit back his first reply. Still cradling the Mossberg he tipped its barrel toward Barney 109's ragged head. "Her regulator failed all the way, Levi. Look at that one. She'd taken him down, the whole bunch might've tripped over." He cocked his head toward the rest of the Z-crew, now complacently shifting from foot to foot, staring at the denuded chickens. "They could have all tripped over, you know? Every one. You want that happening?" Harold felt a thick muscle swell in his neck, veins bulging out along his temples. Christ, he'd been working the evisceration room for a dozen years before this ass-wipe was hired and now here he stood riding him on protocol. "They trip over and you got two dozen rampaging around the plant, who knows what happens. I'd be dead, the rustlers you send down dead. Who else? A hell of lot more than five thousand dollars I can tell you that—a hell of a lot more."

Levi opened his mouth, red flush creeping into his ears, and then seemed to think better of it. He pulled the radio from his belt. "I need status check on the regulator for F-248. Variances for the last twenty-four hours."

While Levi waited for answers, the rustlers moved in closer to Harold. One held his lollystick in a two handed grip.

"Any contact?" the second asked peering at Harold's bare arms, his neck.

"Contact? Christ, no. Only contact was with the Barney there." They continued examining him, made him open his hands, show them his knuckles. Harold felt the post-adrenal surge working from his body. He needed to sit down. Even one scratch, Harold knew and the loop would be over his head, dragging him into a quarantine room, waiting for the infection to surface.

Levi's radio crackled and he held it to his ear, nodded as if the speaker could see him. "A bad regulator, dipped 15 minutes ago and went off-line."

Harold had been in the control room before. A technician monitoring all five hundred Z-crew in the plant, watching the output from the regulators, making sure the urge, the overriding urge that moved them, stayed dampened, the creatures docile.

Harold spit between his feet, prodded at Betty 248 's flaccid corpse. "Tell you what, Levi. This'll happen again, the company going on the cheap like this. An approved regulator won't drop completely in 15 minutes with no stimuli. Half this crew's up from Nogales, ain't it? Undocumented. What's the cost now to slip in under the CDC?"

Levi's tongue probed at his back teeth, lips parted. His ears stayed red. "You want to watch what you're asking there, Harold. Two, three years to pick up your pension? Wouldn't be right for man your age to be turned out this late in the game."

When Harold didn't reply Levi allowed himself a small, self-satisfied smirk and clipped the radio to his belt. He beckoned the rustlers. "Move this crew out and get the room sanitized. Get this mess cleaned up." He prodded Betty 248's corpse. "And the chickens—shit, those four are gone. Run the rest back through the baths." Barking orders now, the flush left his face. A rich pall of cordite and the yeasty smell of the Betty's brains hung in the air, fighting through the ever-present chlorine, through the chicken offal's briny scent.

"Harold, head up to H.R. Fill out your incident report and clock out. Take the afternoon off."

Traffic on the drive home was light so early in the afternoon, giving Harold time to ponder. At Federal and 12th panhandlers stood four abreast. Some made eye contact, others kept their heads lowered, shuffling alongside the cars trapped at the stop-light. WILL WORK FOR FOOD—HARDWORKING DISABLED VETERAN—ANYTHING HELPS—and the last—ZOMBIES TOOK MY JOB.

Harold did his best to ignore them and fight the guilt at the same time. There but for the grace of God and such. He caught the left turn signal at 17th as it flipped to amber. These blocks had taken it hard during the Epidemic, lot after vacant lot, the burned foundations poking through the weeds. There'd been talk of rebuilding, townhouses or something, but there were too many empty houses now. Why build more?

Though fifteen years had passed since the Epidemic began, since the first corpses clawed their way from their black rubberized body bags in Houston, Harold still marveled at the way society slipped back into normalcy.

The first dark days were right there if he closed his eyes—the world in chaos, round-the clock coverage on all channels, the cities burning with soldiers rattling through the streets in their Humvees. He and Val had worked hard and furious when the reports first started, screwing plywood over the windows, double nailing closet doors horizontally over the front and back entrances, listening to the relentless *thump, thump* against the wood.

The tanks and APC's at last roaring into the city to restore some semblance of order, of safety.

And then Stephen had come home.

Harold rubbed at his dry eyes, willing the memory away. He knew the Z's must have some vestigial intelligence down there under their all-consuming hunger. Maybe that's what had brought Stephen north from Colorado Springs, to their doorstep.

All the blood and terror of those first days boiled down to mere seconds on his front porch.

"And look now," he muttered as he made the wide arc around Custer Park. A Z-crew shambled about the grounds, running push mowers back and forth, their overalls spattered green to the knees. Two city foremen and three Rustlers watched them. Another bent over his transponder board, eyeing the regulators' discharge.

One foreman turned his head as Harold's truck rattled by, a shotgun propped on his hip and the sunlight winking from mirrored sunglasses. The city crew looked in bad shape, skin sloughing and lips pulled back in rictus grins. At the plant, after the second shift, all the zombies were herded downstairs and into the safe room, where the day's offal bins were rolled. They were locked up and the control boards shut down, letting them come alive, plunge into the viscera, gobbling it down. Harold had watched a time or two on the security monitors. The technicians waited until the offal was gone, until the first Barney tried to take a bite from his neighbor, and then flipped the regulators back on, leaving them all shuffling aimlessly, stupid, staring at the cement walls.

Such quick and loose use of the regulators was prohibited if a company was using Z-workers. The CDC would shut them down in a blink if they caught wind of it, but Levi and the management thought it worth the risk. The workers lasted longer if they could feed. Still, maybe flipping the regulators on and off weakened them, the way taking too many pain pills eventually stopped helping with the arthritic grinding in his knee.

"**Y**ou're early today."

Harold twisted the bolts on both locks and dropped the counter-weighted bar, snugging it against the steel sheathed front door. Val sprawled on the couch, one hand working the remote and other rubbing her bare foot. In the back room the swamp cooler thrummed, pushing damp air through their little rambler. She had unzipped the front of her polyester cleaning blouse, and a few strands of hair hung loose at her temples. Sweat beaded on her neck and the bags under her eyes were so dark they seemed purple.

"Had one the Betties flip over today." He rummaged a beer from the refrigerator. Recounting the afternoon's events between swallows, he tried to sound casual, not mentioning how the flesh crept along his scalp as he slid under the carousel, or how his guts sloshed as he thought the others were going to flip over.

"Levi threatened your job? Really said that to you?"

"I tell you Val, they're cutting costs across the board. Bring in those Z-crews on the cheap. I know they couldn't have been certified. They're setting themselves up for one big mess."

Val thumbed the mute button, sighed, and rubbed the inside of her wrist across her forehead. "Well, it's a hell of a day for us, I'll tell you that." She looked off in the distance as she always had when bringing up bad news. "I lost the Chavez Building account today. They came at me with a bid so damn low I would've had to clean the whole place myself to make any money. It was my biggest account. I had to let Esmeralda go. She's got kids, too, you know. It was hard. Said I'd bring her back if business picked up, but there's not much out there."

"Cheap," Harold ran his finger around the bottle top, moisture rippling up in a tiny wave. "Were they—"

"Yep, some outfit out of Greely. I guess they can make 'em push a mop, empty trash cans. Can't think they'll do a decent job." She was silent for a moment and when she spoke again her voice quavered.

"Those . . . things. Those goddamned fucking things." She tossed the remote on the coffee table. "You know it seemed the world went to hell overnight and then we pulled it back up, but it's just sinking again, in a different way."

Harold glanced at the mantle, at the picture of Stephen in his cadet uniform, so bright and earnest, the world at his feet. He wished, not for the first time, Val had been the one to look through the peephole that night. Would she have only seen her son? Would she have turned a mother's blind eye to the twigs in his hair, the dirt rimmed lips and nostrils, the dried bloody tendrils snaking from his scalp and ears. Maybe it would have been better than all this, better if she had opened the door wide and let him lurch into the house, better to have had it all end then.

On the television two talking heads shared a screen, below them crawled the words—*A Shifting Economy?*. Harold turned up the volume. "This has the potential to skyrocket the GDP, vault us over Asia and Europe—"

The blow-dried head's adversary cut him off. "But isn't it just slavery under another name? Aunt Mildred kicks the bucket and her family gets a quick thousand to ship her off for processing, regulator implanted in her skull and the next day she's making widgets. Free labor."

"Well certainly there will be some birth pains—they are all but taking over the unskilled job market. Ultimately it will bring us all a higher standard of living. People are going to have to become better educated, more skilled workers." He leaned back and chuckled. "I know no zombie could do my job, though I'm not so sure about Chet here."

Harold clicked the television off before Chet could reply.

He sat the empty bottle on the table. "You know it wouldn't be so bad if the controls were followed. They're supposed to be burning ninety percent of the bodies, strict protocol for the regulators, but—"

"But they're greedy," Val finished his sentence.

Harold nodded. It was an old topic for them. "Trucking them up from the border. Who knows how cheap their circuits are. Business, it's greedy, and the government's turning a blind eye to it. I guess you can't blame them down south for selling the bodies off. Even if they get five hundred dollars each, it's more than most of those folks see in a year."

Val let her hair loose, rubbing her neck.

Harold felt a small hitch in his chest when he realized her brown eyes were shiny with tears.

"I can blame them. Look what we've become." Her mouth softened. "We're sinking into hell and all anyone cares about is 'Can I make another dollar on this?'" She slumped. "There was a time when you would just work. You could go to work and care for your family. If you were willing to work hard, it was enough. You could raise your family and have a decent life."

"Well, we did that. We had a decent life before . . . " He lost steam, fumbling over the right words. "I'm sorry," Harold said. He hoped she knew what he meant.

"I just don't know." Her voice hiccupped. "I just don't know how it can keep moving. The world. I don't know how we can keep moving."

"I don't see we have a choice. I know Stephen—"

Her voice rose, cutting him off. "Don't."

Later, in bed, he splayed a hand across the swell of her hip, her nightgown cool beneath his fingers. Her breath caught and he knew she wasn't asleep, but she kept her eyes closed and turned her back to him, burrowing her head into the pillow. Harold's hand dropped.

He knew better than to say their son's name in front of her. She would spiral down for days, breakfasts and dinners with a palpable wall of silence separating them. Her eyes glossy and staring past him—mouth, cheeks and forehead creased with hard shadows.

He was already gone, Harold thought. He knew it. The dried blood, the dirt and twigs. Yet still that part of his mind which took such masochistic delight in waking him deep in the night, asked the question again and again. Was he? Was he really? How fast did you bring the shotgun up Harold? Didn't you see a glint, just a flash of awareness in his eyes?

He'd buried Stephen in the soft ground of the garden along the back fence. Zipped his near headless corpse into a day-glow orange mummy bag and shoveled dirt over him, blocking out Val's wailing from the house, letting her anguish blend with the braying sirens, the clattering Strykers and staccato bark of AR-15s filling those first days of the Epidemic.

No man should have to bury his son with his own hands.

Harold turned over. Outside a low warbling siren grew closer. Revolving red and blue light seeped through the cracks of the heavy plantation shutters bolted to their windows.

He rose and levered the shutters open, filling the room with muted moonlight and the oscillating flash of an emergency vehicle. A sheriff's SUV, blue and white, stopped at an angle across his street. The virus, the infection—whatever had caused the dead to walk—was still in the air, weaker, but enough to keep the crematoriums busy.

About every third corpse now became infected and sometimes people died alone in their homes, no one to strap them down or phone their death into the CDC.

A Barney shambled along the street—an old man, eighty-five or ninety, sloped shoulders and sunken chest curled with wisps of white hair. His flaccid belly jiggled with his stiff-legged walk, toothless mouth gaping and his pee-soaked pajamas falling off his scrawny backside.

A second sheriff pulled up in front of the Barney. The competing headlights threw perpendicular shadows on the ground. The first SUV's door opened and an officer stepped out, shotgun at port arms. He circled around the Barney, who had stopped as the second set of lights washed over him, circled until the other officer was free from his line of fire. In what could have been a replay of Harold's movement earlier in the day the Sheriff took two quick steps, nestled the shotgun in the back of the old man's head, and pulled the trigger.

Before the echoes rolled off down the street and the Barney's frail body hit the pavement, Harold snapped the shutters down, not sure if he should get back in bed, knowing there'd be no more sleep tonight.

The next morning Harold slipped into his usual parking space at the plant. Val hadn't woken when he'd told her goodbye. Or if so, she'd done a good job of hiding it, keeping her breathing slow and regular. He'd snipped a rose from one of the bushes out front and left it in a tumbler of water on the kitchen table with a scrawled "I love you," on the back of an envelope.

Harold tucked his thermos under one arm, lunch box swinging from the same hand, when he saw Bert, one of the QC's, striding across the parking lot. Bert's fingers tapped an erratic rhythm against his pant leg and the muscles in his jaw bunched like he was swallowing a pair of marbles.

"Knocking off already?" Harold smiled and squinted into the rising sun.

Bert unlocked the door to his Chrysler, his eyes feverish, burning in their sockets. "Knocking off for the rest of the week, Harold. Shit, I guess knocking off for good."

"You're quitting?" Bert's time was as short as Harold's.

"Not quitting." Bert's gaze skittered around the parking lot filling up for the morning shift. He nodded his head at the pebbled cement walls of the processing plant. "Listen, I got to get out of here before I do something stupid. Go talk yourself to that sonofabitch, you want the story. Tell Levi he better hope I don't see him on the street. Kick his fucking teeth down his throat if I do." His hands shook as he opened his car door. "Tell him that if you see him."

"It can do the job, Harold. Don't see why you're so worked up." Harold had button-holed Levi near the end of the wrapping line, packages of 8-piece fryers slipping along. A Barney stood at the line's end, head jerking left to right as the packs rolled before him. "It's not like I didn't offer Bert another job—he's just too proud to take it"

"Back on the gut crew? Swilling out eviscerators at the end of the night, half as much money? What'd you think he would do?"

"It can do the job. Watch." Levi grabbed one of the shrink-wrapped packages off the rollers. He tore loose an edge of the cellophane, pulled a drumstick half out, and set it back on the conveyor. As the fryer crossed in front of the Barney his head jerked down and he snatched the damaged pack off the rollers, dropping it in a bin at his feet, his sunken, milky eyes unblinking as more clicked by. "Now why would we pay someone eighteen bucks an hour, when we've got him?" He slapped the creature's shoulder. "They're just tools Harold. A business is going to make money. You can't be afraid of tools."

"Christ, Levi, don't you remember? It hasn't been so long. Don't you remember being boarded up in your own house, watching your friends, your family torn apart? Don't you think about what they are— what they were?"

"It's progress Harold. It's the new order of business. People like you had their way we'd still be living in caves, shitting ourselves during a thunderstorm."

He made a point of glancing at his wristwatch. "You been on the clock now for about half an hour? Maybe you ought to be worrying we aren't training one of these guys to watch for green lights to go blinking off."

Through the rest of his shift Harold fought to stay focused, watching the Z-crew as they gutted the chickens, but his mind hiked out on its own tangents. Had they really forgotten what brought these things forth? He raised the Mossberg and sighted along the backs of their heads. The regulators winked green at him over and over. What if they hadn't found a way to control them in the first place? Would it have been better if they all burned?

Levi's words echoed in his head. Maybe he ought to be worrying about his own job, never mind Bert's. He was a secondary warning system, nothing but another set of eyes, where the technician in the control room leaning over the transponder board had the ability to turn the regulators on and off at will.

Harold straightened his leg from the stool, wincing at his knee. The Mossberg held five shells and he carried another twenty in his utility belt. He could shoot them all right now, walking along, firing and reloading. They wouldn't blink. Each would keep pulling at its chicken guts until he put the barrel against its skull, squeezed the trigger. What would they do? Fire him, maybe charge him with destruction of property?

They've forgotten what they are, he thought.

The clean-ups come so easy in the middle of the night now. Sanitary. Two cops in front of his house. The old Barney falling limp like a string-cut puppet. It's like the entire world had forgotten.

He avoided Levi the rest of the day.

Val's Honda was still in the driveway when Harold came home.

He threw back the deadbolts and stopped, one foot on the rug. The swamp cooler wasn't running. The television wasn't on. His breathing echoed through the still rooms, the heavy air.

"Val?" In the kitchen the water glass stood empty, a flower stem on the table and a small pile of petals on the floor. Beneath his scribbled note Val's spiky handwriting filled the bottom of the envelope.

I'm so tired, Harold. Tired and sorry. I know I haven't shown it but I never blamed you for Stephen. I just couldn't say it to you. You did the right thing and you've carried that awful burden alone. I pray you'll do the right thing again if you have to. With all my heart.

Harold read the note a second time, tracing fingertips across the words. "No, Val, you couldn't have," he whispered. "You wouldn't do that to me."

He couldn't leave the kitchen. The rose petals were soft, wilted, curling in on themselves in the heat. The only dishes in the sink were his from this morning, a coffee cup—brown stained porcelain as he'd forgotten to rinse it—and a bowl and spoon with flecks of shredded wheat gluing them together. He filled a glass with lukewarm tap water and drank it down. Rinsing the coffee cup and bowl, he gazed out the window at the vegetable garden.

Stephen was down there, bones wrapped in down-filled nylon.

The second tumbler of water was cooler and he passed its cold curve across his forehead, hearing the faint pops and creaks of the old house as it expanded and eased in the evening warmth.

After what seemed hours, as cool blue shadows crept across the back yard, Harold opened the hall closet and grabbed the Remington pump, the one they'd left loaded by the front door through all these years after the Epidemic.

He walked heavily to the bedroom door, twisted the knob and cracked it open. With shades drawn tight the room was cave-dark, cooler than the rest of the house.

"You didn't do this to me," he whispered again, but the air in the room carried a sour undercurrent, vomit and urine. He took in Val's still form, the comforter pulled to her armpits, the empty brown Valium bottle on the nightstand. She lay turned on her side, back to the door and one hand splayed on her thigh.

Harold eased himself onto the bed, shifting quietly as if he might wake her. He held the Remington awkwardly in his left hand and thumbed the safety off. With his right hand he grasped Val's cold, slack fingers, interlaced them with his own.

He knew the accepted thing was to block the door and call the CDC, the police. They'd be out in minutes, zipping her up and whisking her away to the crematorium, but he also knew the virus had waned over the years. There was a better-than-even chance Val was dead, dead and gone. At some kind of peace now. He couldn't bear the thought of some group of haz-matted strangers clomping through their house, tumbling her body into a rubber-lined bag.

"In the morning, Val. I'll call them in the morning." He closed his eyes and tried to conjure memories of their first days together, her quick step and the bright sparkle in her eyes.

The bedside clock read 11:45 when her fingers clenched hard on his. Her back arched and her heels drummed into his thigh.

"It's all right," he whispered, and canted the Remington across his chest, barrel pressing into her skull. He pulled the trigger before a sound could escape from her writhing lips.

Harold spent the night lying in the dark, ears ringing.

"Harold, didn't you call in sick?" Sally at the front desk smiled at him as he stumbled by. "Jonas's been on your shift three hours."

"A bug, but I'm better now," Harold mumbled. He stepped quick down the corridor to the locker rooms. How long before Sally phoned Levi and the little prick came snooping around for him?

In the echoing tile-floored locker room he tugged on his vest and pulled the Mossberg from its brackets, thumbing the red cartridges into the magazine. In his locker door's seam he had tucked a photo of Val and Stephen, taken some twenty years before at Lake Powell. They both wore goofy, sunburned grins, squinting into the camera lens, framed by placid blue water and smooth sandstone cliffs.

"It'll be okay." He slipped the photo into his shirt pocket.

Would this make any real difference? Deep down he had the answer. One man can't shift the world's balance. But people needed to know, to remember what happened. He couldn't be the only one who thought like that.

He pressed the Mossberg along his leg as he left the locker room, turning right toward the control center rather then left to the hydraulic push doors into the plant itself.

Harold didn't know the technician inside the control room, which was just as well. The man slouched in a rolling desk chair, a slight cowlick sticking up as he sipped from an insulated coffee mug. Video monitors stretched across the far wall, tiny black and white images of the plant jerking back and forth. To the left a flat screen monitor displayed a rapid cycling of numbers and digits, each culminating with a tiny green dot—F237, M24, M458, F17.

The technician turned his head, catching Harold's reflection in the screens as he stood with door propped open by one foot. "Hey you know the rules, buddy. Nobody but management or control crews in here."

"Yeah, I know the protocol," Harold stepped into the room, keeping the door open with the barrel of the Mossberg. "This door's supposed to be locked down too, isn't it?"

"Hey." The technician's eyes darted to the shotgun, and he leaned to put his coffee cup on the desk. Harold stretched his free hand forward, clamping down on the bird-thin bones of the technician's shoulder, his thumb pressed against the seat back. He jerked and the man rolled backward, past Harold and through the open doorway. The chair bounced hard over the threshold and the technician spilled into the corridor. Harold kicked the chair out after him and slammed the door. On the inside was a thick bolt. The control room was designed as a refuge of last resort. He threw the bolt and turned his back on the technician's pounding and indignant squawking, narrowing the sounds from his consciousness.

The control board was clearly labeled and no great challenge to decipher. Harold thumbed off the override controlling the plant's electronic doors. Every door would swing free and easy until he turned it back on. A flurry of activity in one of the monitors caught his eye —Levi barking into his radio, rustlers running haphazardly before the camera. Maybe they'd all leave the work rooms, come thundering into the corridor.

Harold removed the photo of Val and Stephen and propped it beside the screens. All he had held dear in one faded scrap of paper.

"I guess this'll about do it." His voice was a cracked whisper. This might shock them back into reality, make them remember what everyone had so easily forgotten.

Something heavy hit the control room door and it shook in its frame but he paid it little mind. The technician's radio squalled over and over. Harold cycled up the regulator controls and began shutting them down, one hundred to a screen. Five screens filled with urgently winking amber pinpoints when he was done.

On the video monitors the Z-crews stopped their methodical movements, heads twisted back and forth, hands jerked, clawing at the air as they looked for something, anything to quell their hunger

Harold shut the monitors off one after another. This wasn't something he wanted to see. Thin screams seeped through the walls, between static bursts of the radio. On the last monitor Levi and a half dozen rustlers were in the corridor outside. They stopped pounding at the control room as, from the far end of the hall, a pack of Barneys and Betties surged through the swinging doors, coveralls stained dark, gloved hands and mouths smeared and clotted.

They'd soon be out of the plant, lumbering into the city.

Harold laid the shotgun up across his knees. When the noise died down he'd throw the bolt open and go out.

He'd go out and see if he couldn't get his family together again.

FAMILY

Bridge Over the Cunene
by Gustavo Bondoni

Botoso was singing some innocent rhyme about the horrors of the great change at the top of his lungs. It was a new phase, and Lara was fervently hoping that it would pass as quickly as the rest had.

It seemed only last week that the little five-year-old had contented himself with running around inside the stockade, happy to let his universe be defined by the log walls. But, suddenly, he'd become obsessed with the world outside. First, he'd gone through a period of curiosity about the Pale Ones, never going to bed unless he'd first been told a story about them, and the things that had happened during the change. He'd cover his head and pretend to be terrified, but never had nightmares, and always came back for more.

Then, seemingly simultaneously, every little one in the village had begun to sing the songs that their parents had sung. Songs about the Pale Ones, songs about the change. It was incredible how these songs, that had been buried for years, reemerged all at once. Nonsense songs, but their verses contained references to the horror of the times.

Lara noted that her son was looking at her quizzically. But he was silent at last, which was a relief. She could get back to mending the shirt.

"Mama," his thin voice piped up. "Do you think I could be the headman, some day?"

"Of course, dear," she replied absently.

"Just like Simao Zaboba?"

"Yes, dear."

He wandered off, and she breathed a small sigh of relief. There were clothes to mend, thatching to do. And he could be a demanding child sometimes.

He'd done this for all of his adult life. His predecessors had done the same. It was as natural as life on the veldt, and had been part of the cycle of life even before the great change, and would be part of it after the Pale Ones were a faded memory.

Simao Zaboba was at peace with himself, with the bright noon sun and the fresh June breeze whispering through the trees. He knew enough to be thankful for his role in the natural cycle. Twice a month, the offering was made, and twice a month, it was accepted. A pig on the full moon—valued for its brains, a goat on the new moon—desired for its blood, and safety, even a measure of protection, for the village all month long. It had always been thus, although in the times of his grandfather, the offering of a chicken or a cow were made on a less regular basis, to other, less tangible, spirits. But even those sporadic devotions must have had some effect, since the village had survived nearly unscathed, while others . . . well, others had been absorbed into the nests.

Today, he was leading a well-fed goat on a leash of metallic rope, enjoying the three-hour walk to the neutral zone across the river. It was a clear day, and he could see forever, but knew that he would never see one of the Pale Ones while the sun was up. Like all spirits that had once been day-walking humans, they were nocturnal creatures.

The bridge was a rickety affair, long poles lashed together with vines. His father had told him that the Cunene had once been bridged by dozens of concrete structures designed to last for generations. But these had been torn down in a desperate, failed attempt to stop the plague from spreading north to Angola. The village had avoided the change only because it was so far off the beaten path. By the time they'd been rediscovered, the Pale Ones had evolved, and had even reached the point where they could be reasoned with. Spirits were like that.

As they approached the neutral zone, the goat began to show signs of nervousness. It seemed to sense, somehow, that hundreds of its brothers and sisters had perished very nearby. Close enough that the smell of death was still present.

Or maybe it sensed something else. Something hungry.

Simao was unconcerned. He dragged the now openly resisting, panicked animal towards the clearing the way he'd done hundreds of times before. The stained ground and scattered bones seemed to give the animal added strength, and it left four furrows in the dust as its feet slid along.

He reached the tree and looped the end of the metal cable around the trunk. As always, he double-checked the clasp; the consequences of the goat escaping were too ugly to contemplate.

Leaving the grunting goat straining against the unbreakable bonds, Simao walked, as he'd done countless times before, back towards the village.

He wasn't expecting to see little Botoso crouching behind one of the bushes, because he'd never been there before. And that was probably why he didn't.

Botoso knew he was in trouble. He had no idea how in the world he was ever going to get back to the village. He had no idea where the village was. This was the first time he'd ever been outside the stockade without his mother or one of the other village adults to take care of him, and the sun was setting.

But he wasn't frightened. He told himself that a future headman would never be frightened just because night was about to fall. He would laugh the night off, and keep walking until he found the river. He knew the river was near his village.

He also knew that he would make a great headman someday. He was smart and compassionate. After Simao Zabobo had left the clearing far behind, Botoso had emerged from hiding and immediately noticed that the headman had forgotten the goat. The boy knew how important goats were to the village—he was old enough to know that the village's very survival depended on the supply of goats.

So he worked at the clasp tying the goat to the tree and began his walk back the way he'd come. At some points, it was difficult to decide which way he had to go, since one patch of low grass or clump of trees looked just like the next, but he wasn't worried. A headman would never get lost.

But he had. And now the sun was all the way down, and it was hard to see where he was going. The goat, sniffing the air, had been getting more and more restless, and, suddenly, it gave a mighty jerk and broke free of Botoso's five-year-old grasp, dragging the leash off into the darkness.

Botoso gave chase, following the tinkling of the metallic cord until an unseen hole in the ground sent him tumbling onto a patch of thorns. He lay there silently, listening to the tinkling which grew fainter and then died out, and to the night, which was suddenly alive with scurrying and wildlife sounds. He knew that some of those sounds weren't alive.

He told himself that he wasn't afraid, but the tears that streamed down his face seemed unaware of it.

Lara was frantic. She'd been waiting for Simao Zaboba outside the village ever since she'd realized Botoso was missing. Now, off in the distance, she could make out a dark, tiny speck coming towards the village from the south. She knew, she had to believe, that the speck, as it grew nearer, would resolve itself into two figures, a large, thin one, and a slightly rotund smaller speck less than half the height of the first.

As the speck grew into a smudge, her hope waned, but then she rallied. The headman probably made Botoso walk behind him, as a punishment. That's why she could only make out one figure approaching in the afternoon glow.

But even that hope soon faded. She ran out to Zaboba, stood before him, clutching his arm, getting her breath back and finally panted, "Did you see Botoso?"

The headman looked her over, perfectly still, his impassive gaze showing no emotion. "There was no one on the path. How long has he been gone?"

She hung her head. "I'm not really certain. I looked for him, to eat the midday meal, and he was nowhere to be found. We looked all over the village." Lara was holding back tears now, desperate, her nails digging into his motionless forearm.

Zaboba looked at her knowingly. She felt that he could see through her, that he knew her deepest secrets, that he knew she was holding back. Finally, she could hold back no longer. "I think he followed you," she sobbed, and broke down completely.

"This is grave news," Simao said. "Go gather the elders." He pushed her gently towards the village, and walked slowly after her as she ran, stumbling, to do his bidding.

Other than Simao Zaboba, there were four village elders, and they all looked gravely on as she explained her plight. Finally, Satumbo, a toothless old man, by far the oldest man in the village, broke the silence. "A boy lost in the night is a job for the father," he said.

"My husband is dead."

"The uncle, then."

"He had no brothers."

"Then the boy is lost. The village cannot risk the men we have. No wife will let her man go. There is no way we can defend ourselves from the Pale Ones outside our walls in the night. The night belongs to them, and if we violate that agreement, we forfeit our lives."

Simao Zaboba spoke unexpectedly. "I will go," he said. "I know where the boy is. The mother must come as well—she will have a choice to make."

Lara swallowed. Nothing was more important to her than her son, but what Satumbo said was true: the night belonged to the Pale Ones. She suddenly imagined herself being torn to shreds, her bones cracked for their marrow, her blood drained from her body, her brain sucked from her skull through a hole in the top of her head. But then the image in her mind changed, and she saw Botoso there in her place.

"I'll go," she said.

"You will go alone," Satumbo replied. "Simao Zaboba is much too valuable to the village."

"No, I am not. I am just a silly old man whose only value to the rest is that he leads an animal to a dangerous place once a fortnight. And besides, I will certainly return tonight. I speak the language of the Pale Ones."

"The Pale Ones will kill you when they see you."

"It may be so, but I don't think so. They have changed since your childhood. And even since mine. I will be all right." He turned to the still-open gates of the village, retracing the steps he'd taken to return to the village that afternoon. He didn't look back to see whether Lara was behind him.

And he didn't seem at all surprised when she appeared beside him. Only Lara knew that she almost hadn't come. Only she seemed to have noticed that no matter how confident the headman had been of his own return, he'd said nothing about hers.

It was a typical night. The veldt was cool and the sounds seemed somehow louder than they did from inside the village compound. That was ridiculous, of course; the open-topped wall of logs wouldn't have done much to filter the sounds of the nocturnal animals— the hoot of an owl, or the scurrying of rodents, or the buzz of insects. But it still seemed that the sounds were louder out here without the wall.

They'd been walking for two and a half hours, their way illuminated only by the starlight and the knowledge of Simao's feet which had tread this same path for thirty years. At first, she constantly called out for Botoso, but, as they neared the bridge, Simao Zaboba told her to be quiet. Sound carried a long way on these grassy plains, and soon, the sound would carry all the way to the nest.

He didn't know where the nest was located, exactly, but he suspected that it was just a little beyond the clearing in the neutral zone— a clearing that was less than half an hour away on foot.

The night sounds seemed to get louder and louder the farther they got from the village, as if the animals, far from the noise and smell of human habitation, grew bolder. But Simao knew it had less to do with the actual noise than the fact that he was listening harder, trying to distinguish the sounds that didn't belong to the night. The sounds that meant that there was a something out there walking noisily on its two hind legs—something that hadn't been designed to prowl in the darkness, despite having originated near the very same plains millions of years before.

Something that, despite not being human, would have the arrogance and fearlessness that had, until the great change, allowed humans to walk the night knowing that no matter how much noise they made, no matter what they stirred up, it could be dealt with.

But now, with the few surviving humans huddling behind thick walls or in underground bunkers as soon as the sun went down, only the Pale Ones walked the night that way. They could be easily heard by someone who knew what to listen for. And it wasn't long before

Simao Zaboba distinguished the telltale sounds. His heart sank when he realized that the noise of multiple Pale Ones milling around was coming from the clearing where he'd left the goat that afternoon. It came from their destination.

He looked over at Lara, but she seemed lost in her own thoughts and not to have heard anything out of the ordinary. Her features were set, and she was grimly putting one foot in front of the other. She thought that he would know where to look.

She was right. He knew exactly where the little boy would be, but he dreaded what they'd find once they got there. He began to hope that they would be intercepted before they arrived, dreading each step. Soon, his fear had grown to the point where he was only reluctantly putting one foot in front of the other. By the time they were a hundred paces from the clearing, Lara was dragging him along.

Even in the dark, he could tell the clearing was crowded. Darker shapes could be made out in the darkness, and Simao Zaboba felt as though someone was running cold hands up his spine.

"Welcome," a voice said out of the darkness in front of him.

Lara jumped, but Simao had known it was coming. The word had been spoken in their harsh guttural language, the language that the villagers feared and reviled. They called it Palespeak. The Pale Ones themselves called it English—it had been the tongue of the southern land before the change. Only the headman and a few others could speak it.

The voice went on, "We suspected you come soon." It was a ragged, sighing voice—as if it had been unused for so long that it had to be dug up from deep within the Pale One's thorax. And yet, the speech was clearer than what he'd heard when, as an apprentice, he'd accompanied the old headman to make the agreement that exchanged an occasional goat and pig for their lives. During that meeting, the Pale Ones had spoken in grunts and single, almost incomprehensible words—and it had been impossible for them to understand any but the most rudimentary concepts.

Simao knew that how he responded could make the difference

between life and death, but he also needed to understand the situation a little better. "I make fire to see," he said, glad he'd practiced his Palespeak all these years, despite never having had to use it.

His pronouncement was met with hissing and an unseen step forward from his right. Zaboba tensed, but the original voice replied before any action was taken against him. "Small fire," it said.

"Small fire," he agreed. One of his precious, irreplaceable matches was used to light a torch.

The clearing was bathed in flickering yellow light. The Pale Ones looked much worse for the wear. Nothing with skin as tattered and decomposed as the inhabitants of this clearing had any business being animate. Their once-mahogany skin, already pallid from the change, had become even more gray with the years. They looked like dolls made of stained rags.

Zaboba looked around desperately, searching for a smaller figure. His gaze was attracted by a commotion behind the nearest Pale One.

"Mama!" a high-pitched voice screamed, and suddenly a small brown bullet shot from the shadows and buried itself in Lara's stomach. She cried and bent over to hug him, protecting him with her arms. "Thank you, thank you," she was saying, to no one in particular, without thinking about it, just repeating the mantra—happiness and disbelief mixed.

"Thank you," Zaboba told the Pale One in front of him.

The other acknowledged, inclining his head. "We no eat little ones. Little ones grow, turn big ones. Bring us food. Other nests eat little ones, eat big ones too. Other nests die out. No food."

Zaboba was shocked at this. He couldn't believe what he was hearing, couldn't believe the sophistication of the Pale One's thought processes. But he had no time to dwell on it then. "We leave now," he said, bowing.

"No."

Zaboba realized that the semicircle of Pale Ones in front of them had expanded, and was now a complete circle, ahead and behind. They could not leave unless they were allowed to. There was no way they could break through that line unscathed—and even a scratch meant the end of human life, and the beginning of a twilight existence as a Pale One. He turned calmly back to the spokesman.

"We no have food," the Pale One said.

And suddenly, Zaboba lost his calm. He understood that what had been his worst fear, in the back of his mind, had actually come to pass. He knelt beside little Botoso and, trying to keep the fear and urgency from his voice, said, "Where's the goat?"

And Botoso, sensing the fear, began to cry. "It ran away. I tried to catch it, but I fell." And, finally, accusingly, "You forgot the goat."

Zabobo turned back to the Pale one.

"We no have food," it repeated. "Give food."

Lara turned to him, eyes wide, understanding. She seemed on the verge of panic, so he calmed her down. "Do not worry," he said. "I will stay. I am an old man, almost fifty summers. The village does not lose much."

Gratitude flashed on her face, but was almost immediately replaced by doubt and then fear. "But how will I find my way? It is still a long time until dawn. What happens if we get lost?"

"You must not become lost."

"What happens?"

"If you get lost, you will both die." He cursed the moonless sky. Even the small illumination from the barest crescent might have made the return trip possible. "Once you leave the neutral area, you are fair game unless you are on a clearly defined path towards the village. If you are anywhere else, other members of the nest will take you, since they have no way of knowing you are from our village."

And Lara knew it. She cried softly, silently, as she accepted what she must do. Botoso, who had lifted his head to see what was troubling his mother, suddenly cried again as he found himself transferred to Simao's care.

Simao took a tight grip of Botoso's hand. He knew the boy would have to be kept in check.

"Will you take care of him?" Lara said.

Simao nodded.

"What will become of him, an orphan? His options will be few."

"His options," he replied, "will be one. He has seen the Pale Ones, and it seems he will survive the encounter. He will be headman. I will take him on as an apprentice."

Pride flickered across her face, but lasted only a fleeting instant. She had remembered that she would not be there to see it. "Tell them," Lara said.

"One will remain," he told the leader of the Pale Ones, who nodded in reply.

A rustling sound behind caused Simao to turn. The Pale Ones behind had disappeared.

"Ones who go, go now."

Simao Zaboba took a tight grip on Botoso's hand and began to walk towards the village. At first, Botoso came readily, but then realized what was happening.

"Mama!" he said.

But it was too late by then. The circle had reformed, with them on the outside. The headman dragged the resisting boy towards the village. He was even thankful for the boy's calls for his mother, as they somewhat drowned out the screaming. At first, a single cry of protest, then a series of long, drawn out screams of agony which grew hoarser and hoarser. The final scream was a ragged cry, mercifully cut off in the middle.

The boy seemed to understand; his struggles stopped.

But the sick feeling in Simao Zaboba's stomach wasn't caused by the sounds of a pretty young mother being torn to edible chunks behind them. It was caused by the knowledge that the Pale Ones had, in their way, discovered farming—or at least a way to get small but sufficient quantities of live food without having to hunt for it. At present, they needed the village to supply their meat, but how long would it take them to figure it out for themselves? After that, the village would serve no purpose other than as a breeding ground for their favorite dish—or, worse, the site of one spectacular nighttime binge.

His reverie was broken by a slurping and panting noise from the feeding ground behind. He shuddered and hoped it would fade soon. But sound carries a long way over the veldt.

Glorietta

by Gary A. Braunbeck

Pining to live, I was constrained to die,
Here, then, am I . . .

Poor soul; he suffered. But, at end, no child
Ever more gently fell asleep.

He smiled.
As if all contraries were reconciled.

—Walter de le Mare, "Epilogue"

The first questions are always the same, as are the responses:
Mom? Dad? Sis? Do you recognize me this year?

. . .

Do you like the Christmas tree? Remember when I made this decoration in kindergarten? You liked it so much, Dad. Remember? See,

I even strung popcorn.

. . .

Yet another Christmas spent both above-ground and alive. You can't understand why you still bother, why it is you hang on to a pitiful, even pathetic, shred of hope. Some nights, watching the lights as they blink on the tree and the Christmas music fills the empty rooms of the family home, you can almost— *almost*— pretend that everything is fine, you're still ten years old and that this year you *will* stay awake long enough to catch Santa slipping down the chimney, even if there is a banked fire blazing.

. . .

You'll listen, as always, and hope for something; a sound, a whisper, a spark of recognition in the eyes. Listen and hope, but all the while know what you'll get.

. . .

Still, even their silence is a sort-of gift, isn't it? Because at least they remember enough about their previous lives to come home for Christmas. They remember the house. They remember in which rooms they spent the most time during the holidays. They remember where everyone sits around the tree and how to turn off the lights so only the glow of the tree and tinsel and the fire provide illumination. They remember all of this, all three of them.

. . .

They just don't remember you.

At age forty-eight you have learned a new, albeit nearly useless, lesson: something about your disease repels the living dead. The first time you realized this, in the days and weeks following the awakenings, was when you had no choice but to leave the house and go in search of food and medicine. There was still power then, and the unlooted grocery stores and pharmacies still had plenty of supplies, much to your astonishment. You were in the pharmacy, gathering up the boxes of hypodermics, the vials of Dilauded, and the steroids you'd need to keep yourself alive and pain-free. You were almost finished when you decided, what the hell, grab some Percocet and Demerol, as well, because sometimes the Dilauded made you far too weak and woozy. Six large shopping bags you had, filled with enough prescription medicine to keep you going for a couple of years, even if you took more than the prescribed dosage. You were on your way out when you walked right into a group of five of the living dead, gathered around your car in the parking lot. You thought, *This is it*, as they began stumbling toward you, but as soon as the first one was close enough to touch you, something like a shadow crossed its decomposed features and it pulled away its hand, and then simply stood there *staring* at you. The rest did the same. After what seemed an hour but was in fact only a minute or two, the five of them turned away from you and shambled on.

You used to keep a gun, but that's long been thrown out. They want nothing to do with you. You spent months afterward in search of others who were sick—cancer, AIDS, leukemia—something, *anything* that marked them as *persona non grata* to the living dead. You did find a few people, but they were so far gone that there was no community made with them; you even helped a few to end their suffering, and then used their guns to pulp their brains so they wouldn't come back. The eleven-year-old boy with leukemia thanked you as you sank the plunger, sighing into sleep, dressed in his Spider-Man pajamas. You hated shooting him, but you'd promised, and he'd kissed your cheek before falling asleep for the very last time. You sat there, holding his hand until you were certain he was gone. Then did what had to be done.

You no longer search out the marked ones. Though you know what you do—what you *did*—was the right thing, it still hurt too much, caused too many sleepless nights, gave you too many bad dreams and sick-making memories. It's better this way. You keep telling yourself that. Maybe one of these days you'll even start to believe it in your heart of hearts.

And then came that first Christmas after Mom, Dad, and Jenny died in the automobile accident when Dad had swerved to avoid hitting a cat that had frozen in fear. You handled all the arrangements, set up viewing hours, sent notices to the paper. The day before the funeral all of the dead opened their eyes, stood up, and began walking around. You did not see the mangled remains of your family until Christmas Eve, when you awoke from a nap to find all three of them sitting in the living room, staring at the spot where the Christmas tree was usually displayed. So you did what a good son and older brother would do under the circumstances; you went to the basement and dug out the tree and all of the decorations and began setting up everything. A few minutes into your project, your family began removing decorations from the boxes and hung everything exactly, precisely where the traditional decorations always went. Your little sister even arranged the Nativity set on the fireplace mantle.

But not a one of them looked at you with anything like recognition.

Still, it was better than being alone. It is always better than being alone—another thing you tell yourself constantly in the hopes that you will one day believe it.

Merry Christmas, everyone, you say to them every year.

. . .

Merry Christmas.

. . .

This year will be no different. Oh, some of the accoutrements will change—you taught yourself how to make turducken, and your recipe is pretty good, if you do say so yourself, and you'll set four places at the dinner table, knowing that you'll be the only one eating. The menthol cream you rub under your nose kills most of your family's stench, so you at least can keep an appetite, providing you don't look at them for too long, or too often.

$\mathcal{I}n$ the years since the awakenings, you have become a good carpenter, a decent-enough electrician, an excellent plumber, an all-around first-rate handyman. The gas-powered generators keep the electricity flowing into the house, though you're careful not to waste power. You use only the downstairs, having boarded up and sealed the entrance to the upper floors after removing everything you might need or want.

You stand in the kitchen watching them decorate the tree, arrange the Nativity set, string the popcorn. *It's a Wonderful Life* is playing on DVD in high-definition Blu-Ray, Jimmy Stewart's face filling the 65-inch flat-screen plasma television you took from an electronics store last year. A digital home theater system guarantees exquisite sound. You couldn't give less of a damn about any of it right now— although you find that you've come to appreciate the middle of the movie much more, the part where it's all dark and hopeless. You recognize that look of terror and grief and helplessness that is a permanent fixture on Stewart's face in these sequences. You see something like it every time you glance at your reflection in a mirror. You laugh at the heavy-handed melodrama of that thought. It's an odd sound, hearing your own laughter at Christmas time. It's almost like the old days, the good days, the happy-enough days.

They've rotted away so much, you wonder how it is they manage to move around at all, but somehow they manage. They drip, they leak, sometimes sections of flesh or a digit falls off, a tooth drops to the floor, yet they keep going. You wonder if there is something still *them* in there, some small part of their consciousness that remembers who and what they once were, and is trying to recapture some essence of that former life. *Do they dream?* you wonder.

So you ask.

. . .

Do you dream?

. . .

Cornbread or rolls?

. . .

Red wine okay with everyone?

. . .

Did I ever mean anything to any of you?

. . .

No need to get all sugary on me, folks, just a simple yes or no.

. . .

I still love you guys, you know that?

. . .

You move into the living room, stepping around the Christmas paraphernalia, and turn off the sound on the DVD player. It's time for Christmas music. This year, you stole a multi-disc player, one that reads MP3s, and you've set up the discs so that you will have 24 hours of continuous Christmas music. Dad used to love to sit in the kitchen with the lights turned down and listen to Christmas music while he had a beer or two. You've got several cases of his favorite beer. One bottle sets open next to his favorite mug. For a moment earlier, he stared at it as a shadow crossed his face, as if he knew this were something he ought to remember. Mug and bottle are still on the table.

How do you like the new refrigerator? I got it a couple of weeks ago. Moved it all by myself. Damn thing can hold a ton of food. Do you like it, Mom?

. . .

Hey, why do you suppose doctors never use the word consumption anymore? No, now it's TB. I think consumption's a fine word, you know?

. . .

I found the old photo albums. They're right there on the coffee table. Maybe you want to look through them later? That might be fun, don't you think? All of us flipping through the images, the years, the memories. Been a while since I took a trip down Amnesia Lane. Sound good?

. . .

Sorry, I didn't quite catch that.

. . .

That's okay, you can tell me later.

You turn around and damn near drop the salad bowl because your little sister is standing right there in front of you, just . . . staring.

Jenny?

. . .

Jenny, is there something you want?

. . .

What is it, Sis?

. . .

Please say . . . *something*. Grunt. Sigh, snort, *anything*.

. . .

You close your eyes and swallow back the feelings that are trying to come to the surface. You knew this year would be no different. Christ only knows what Jen wants in here, what she remembers. You just know it's got nothing to do with you. You step around her and put the salad bowl on the table. Jen does not move. The oven timer sounds: the turducken is ready to go.

Dinner's ready!

. . .

You sit. They sit. You eat. They don't. On the disc, Greg Lake is singing about how he believed in Father Christmas. This is your favorite Christmas song, even though if you think about it, it's a damned depressing one— but then so is Elvis's "Blue Christmas," so why overthink it?

The turducken is delicious. The mashed potatoes are just right. The rolls are great. And the homemade pecan pie is the perfect way to end the meal.

You go to your usual place on the far right-hand side of the sofa and watch the tree lights blink, watch the banked fire blaze, watch Jimmy Stewart run through dark streets. You pick up one of the photo albums and open to a random page. That was you, once. That was your family, once.

The pain is getting pretty bad. You've been sticking with the Demerol for the last couple of days because you wanted to be lucid enough in case something happened—a word, a gesture, a touch, something, anything.

The rest of the family take their traditional places. You look out the window and see that it's begun to snow. Good God, could there ever be a more perfect Norman Rockwell-type of Christmas scene?

You make yourself an eggnog and Pepsi. Everyone used to say how disgusting that sounded, so when you'd make the drink for your friends and family when all were still alive, you'd never tell them what it was until after they'd tasted it. Once tasted, everyone loved it. Your legacy. Could do worse.

Afraid I'm not feeling too well, folks. Haven't been taking my meds like I should.

. . .

Isn't anyone going to scold me for that?

. . .

You stare at the unopened Christmas presents under the tree. It's been so long since you've wrapped them you've forgotten what's in any of the boxes, only that they were gifts you gave a lot of thought to, hoping that they'd make everyone smile.

You go into the kitchen and remove several 4 mg vials of Dilauded from the refrigerator, make yourself another eggnog and Pepsi, and grab the bottles of Percocet and Demerol.

Back in the living room, in your traditional place, you lay out everything, then discard the Percocet and Demerol because they seem like overkill. Overkill. Funny-sounding word, that. Considering.

You draw the vials of Dilauded into the syringe until it is full. You almost tap it to clear any air bubbles, then realize what a silly thing that would be.

This has been a nice Christmas, hasn't it?

. . .

It really means a lot to me, that you still come here and help with all the decorating.

. . .

You look at the television. Jimmy Stewart is now back in the real world, and everyone in town is dumping money on his table. Donna Reed smiles that incredibly gorgeous smile that no other actress has ever managed to match.

Bach's "Sheep May Safely Graze" begins to play. The perfect song to end the day. To end on. To end. You slip the needle into your arm but do not yet sink the plunger. There is a passing moment of brief regret that you threw out the gun, because you know what that's going to mean. But maybe you won't remember, and, in not remembering, there will be no caring, no hurt, no regret or loneliness.

You look at each of your family members one more time. None return your gaze. They look either at the tree or the fire or at the snow outside.

Merry Christmas, everyone, you say.

. . .

You slowly sink the plunger. If your research has been correct, once the syringe has been emptied, you will have at best ninety seconds of consciousness remaining, but you can already feel yourself slipping down toward darkness before the plunger has hit bottom. But that's all right.

You have enough time to pull the needle from your arm and lay back your head.

Bach fades away, and is followed by "Let There Be Peace on Earth." You're surprised to feel a single tear forming in your right eye.

Do you like . . . like the music, Dad?

. . .

Shadows cross your face, obscuring the lights of the tree. You blink, still slipping downward, and see that your family is surrounding you. Looking at you. At *you*.

You reach out one of your hands. It takes everything that remains of you to do this.

. . . , you say.

. . . , they reply.

And your family, with the light of recognition in their eyes, as if they have missed their son and brother for all of these years, takes hold of you, enfolding you in their arms, and the best Christmas you've ever known is completed.

The Blue Word
by Carole Lanham

At Salvation House, you had to be an upper classman to play *Leaves of Destiny*. I don't know who made up that rule but we were very strict about it. If you were in Grade Two or Grade Six or Grade Eleven and could be trusted not to fidget, you could sit in a folding chair and watch. The girls, I'm proud to say, were better at this than the boys. The game had ancient roots that were entirely non-Catholic, yet the sisters permitted it like they permitted *Buck Buck* or *Bilboquet*. Every year they pretended not to spy when the Grade Twelvers cloaked themselves in white and passed around the Bible. Their whispers behind the curtain were as much a tradition as any other part of the game.

The students attended to *Leaves* more sacredly than prayer. I watched with held breath every year, looking forward to my own turn more than I looked forward to anything else in my life. One winter night when branches could be heard snapping under ice outside, my time finally came.

Eyes shut, I held the book on the upturned palm of my left hand (as is the official way) and picked a place with my right. Thousands of other destinies whispered by in a flutter of tissue pages. My finger sought the one that was meant to be my own. "Here," I said, stabbing blindly and picking out a verse.

The girl to my left had just chosen something lovely from Exodus about sashes and headbands, and the girl before her had fingered *four cups made like almond blossoms.* The almond blossoms made everyone gasp. I had every hope that my own choice would be something equally special.

Golden teardrops of honey dripped down the walls of my imagination as I drew the big moment out. Cherubs circled around my brain. A new limb surrendered in the dark, popping like a knuckle. I opened my eyes, ready to behold my future.

Dead flies cause the oil of the perfumer to send forth an evil odor; so does a little folly outweigh wisdom and honour.

Even the nuns laughed. It turns out I'd waited all this time for folly and dead flies.

After the game, I couldn't help but feel anxious when confronted with foul smells. I was on the look out for flies everywhere I went. Two weeks before graduation, the rank whiff of destiny found me at long last.

We were asleep when the first projectile came crashing through our burning roof. I thought it was a boulder at first until it splattered against the linen cupboard in a firework of red droplets. More fireworks followed. The monsters were catapulting things at us from outside the school walls.

"Looks like pork," my best friend, Corinthians, said, squatting by the mess to give it a closer look.

Meat might sound like odd ammunition but we were used to variety. Never mind that there was no shortage of proper stones to sling, the monsters seemed to favor more indignant things. We once got hit with some rather nice running shoes, which came in handy after. Another time, it was old doll heads. I only cared that the ammo this time around was sure to leave blood stains.

Burning bits of ceiling began falling faster than meat. Deuteronomy's head caught fire. Before she could let out a scream, the bells started playing *Jesus Wants me for a Sunbeam*. Sister Sabastienne ran into the room. "Safety Positions, children!"

I was the one to smother Deut's blackened skull, though she never thanked me for it. "Damn you, Esther!" is what she said after I finished hitting her with the pillow. The room was filling up with smoke and pork so there was no time to bother about that.

"Buckets," Sister said.

Usually the bells signaled a drill. Every so often, the alarm meant something more. I'd been *Second Girl* on the brigade since I could stand on two feet. We formed a snake down St. Jhudiel's Hall, passing water to Sister Edwige on her ladder. "They've broken through the keep," Sister Edwige reported, for she could see the monsters from her perch and was never one for shielding us from the truth like some of the others. "One of the guards is down!"

Salvation House was located inside the walls of Castle Montségur on a cliff in the Pyrenees. Before chalk boards and desks were added, people used to pay for historical tours. Archeologists once searched the site for a manuscript called the *Book of Love* that had been hidden in the castle years before. The book was made of palm leaves soaked in peacock blood and was said to contain revelations confided by our Lord Jesus Christ, the words of which were so powerful, they need only be heard and all hatred, anger, and jealousy would vanish from the hearts of men. Anyone who touched the book would be attracted to the leaves of their destiny within, hence our little game. We'd spent many an hour poking about dark cervices looking for the thing without any luck. Fortunately, a regular Bible worked much the same as substituting a 5 franc coin will make do for a missing tiddly-wink.

Jesus' most consequential words were not the only feather in Montségur's cap. A stele by the Pepsi machine marked the spot where a group of religious zealots had been killed in a bonfire centuries ago:

IN THIS PLACE ON 16th MARCH 1244
MORE THAN TWO HUNDRED PEOPLE WERE BURNED.
THEY CHOSE NOT TO ABJURE THEIR FAITH.

Most of what I knew about the zealots came from teenagers hoping to scare little kids. It wasn't all made-up stuff though. Junior Wing sometimes smelled of smoke, even when we weren't being pelted with flaming arrows. There's a cry people make when their skin is blistering off their bones. I shouldn't have known what that sounded like, but I did. I'd heard it many a night. Sister Sabastienne said it was just the wind because she wanted us to smile all the time. But everyone knows that wind does not whimper as though its tongue is being boiled in the bowl of a dying mouth.

After the Devastation, guard towers were built around the keep. The Routiers attacked anyway.

"Routier" was the nice name the sisters used for those who lived beyond the walls. Corinthians saw some once when she was helping paint the belfry. She said the creatures were hideous, with arms as thick as bread loaves and fat, bloated cheeks. I asked her what their skin was like because we'd all heard so many rumors. Some of them were puffy and pink, she said. Some were puffy brown. Their skulls were covered with thick wild hair. They moved in snarling droves.

Even though our student population was composed of orphans, only the best and brightest were allowed to live at Salvation House. The monsters did not like us because of this. We had to have bars on the windows and locks on the doors. They were more vicious than ever on the night of the attack. As if smelly meat was not insulting enough, a fiery arrow hit Sister Sabastienne in the shoulder. "Be strong children," she told us as she went down. "Do you remember who you are?"

"The Blessed," we said in one clear voice, saying it like you say "Amen". We said these same words every day. Sometimes Deuteronomy mumbled them in her sleep.

Being *The Blessed* was not something to be vain about but the sisters said it was important to remember how fortunate we were, especially in these difficult times. The countryside was full of heathens who thrived on violence. They lived without the hope of finding a *Book of Love*. There were precious few who had any destiny at all.

Instead of God, the Infected worshipped flesh, craving it like air. I'd heard a thousand history lectures, but I would not be seeing things for myself until my Leaving Ceremony.

"Must protect the children," Philemon said, swinging his protection stick. With his shadowy eyes and paper-white skin, Philemon was the most beautiful of the beautiful. Given the high standards at our school, this was no small thing. When the arrow hit Sister Sabastienne, Philemon hurled his stick through the hole in the roof and let loose a warrior cry. Later he would be bawled out for losing his stick, but the act seemed magnificent to us. Salvation House was a hive of self-preservation. Although the guards would shoot Routiers when forced, the rest of us spent every attack the same way—dutifully keeping ahead of the flames. There was no thought of fighting back. Until this night.

To see Sister Sabastienne bleeding on our hand-embroidered *Let the Children Come to Me* rug was more than we could bear. Had we all been holding our sticks instead of buckets, we'd have let loose a shower of spears on the backs of those ugly monsters! Salvation House had taught us to love, yet I felt a dark finger of hatred beginning to poke around inside of me.

For a minute, I forgot the biggest rule of all: *A grateful child counts her blessings and remembers to keep the peace.* In two weeks, my class would be entering the out-world for the first time ever. Usually this thought delighted me beyond description. Now I experienced something terrible in my soul. I thought it might be *terror,* but I couldn't be sure.

Oh, I'd sat up many a night with a pumping heart listening to ghosts choking in the throes of burning death, but fear, for the most part, was not allowed. At Salvation House, no one was afraid of the dark because there were nightlights everywhere. The same could be said for crawling things. Spiders were stamped out the minute they were spotted so there was no need to get hysterical. Thunderstorms were angel burps, and lockers took up the space under a bed where otherwise vile beasties might have lain in wait. If only the sisters could have gotten their hands on the ghosts, they should have found themselves flushed down the pipes with the rest of the potentially scary stuff. Even Routiers normally caused no more damage than a missed hour of math.

Now, I was shaking at the thought of living among these monsters with no guard towers in between us. That hateful finger of fear ran up the stalks of my organs to wedge securely in my throat. We'd all seen the charts in first hour World Preparation. Small tribes of the diseased still roamed the nether-reaches of almost every country, their symptoms only temporarily suppressed by illegal doses of Lariathol. "But don't despair, children," Sister Edwige had told us. "Elimination rates are up ten percent this year."

As I wiggled my house slipper free from the oily splat of an exploded ham butt, I tried to think on the bright side. I imagined the private room I would live in at Job Corp while receiving my training. I had such high hopes for the place, in fact, I'd colored in three boxes on the Placement Form even though it said to pick only one: DOCTOR. WIFE. MOTHER. At the time, Sister Sabastienne praised me for having such big dreams.

After I worked my slipper loose, I hid my face in my hands and cried. I could tell the meat was never going to wash out of the fluff.

Once the danger was over, Sister Sabastienne was carried off to hospital and I was given nursing duty. Corinthians got clean-up. While she swept and scrubbed and tossed out burnt pillows, I patted a cool rag on Deut's sore head and tried not to listen as Sister Sabastienne's arrow was being yanked out. A couple of people slipped in her blood so this gave me more patients to look after. I still heard too much.

Sister Arnaude, who ran the ward, and Father Barthelemy, who ran the school, stood around in the blood debating whether to send out for help or not. In the end, they decided to patch Sister Sabastienne up and give her lots of medicine. Not the little red Keep Well pills we all took in order to stay disease-free. This medicine looked like water and it went into her arm through a fat needle. The water-medicine was to stop the pain. "Does it really hurt so bad that she needs a needle stuck inside her?" I asked Sister Arnaude.

Before she could answer, Sister Sabastienne jerked fitfully and spoke for the first time since they'd pulled out her arrow. "Hurts like a son of a bitch," she said.

That's how I found out that the water-medicine made Sister Sabastienne willing to answer any question, even if the answer wasn't something that would put a smile on your face.

The way the sisters taught about *The Great Devastation* was enough to put you to sleep for good. Somehow, it didn't feel that important.

WHAT YEAR DID STRASBOURG FALL? WHAT ECOLOGICAL CRISIS IS BLAMED FOR STARTING THE OUTBREAK? HOW MANY PEOPLE DIED WORLDWIDE?

It was just a lot of numbers and old stuff that happened a long time ago. We couldn't fathom what had been lost because we'd never seen the world as it once was, or what had been left in its place. Only one part appeared to apply to us.

IN ORDER TO PRESERVE THE INNOCENT LIVES OF THOSE ORPHANED DUE TO THE GREAT DEVASTATION, SISTER NATHALIE MARYSE NEGOTIATED WITH NEW WORLD GOVERNMENT TO SET UP A SAFE HAVEN FOR THE BLAH BLAH BLAH BLAH BLAH . . .

I was in my last semester of *Honour and Duty* after twelve long grueling years. I'd spent two years in *Brotherly Concepts* and a year in *Out-World Ethics*. It was only in the last hour, I'd managed to muster a proper interest in the events of the past. Still, I might never have begun the secret interrogations had Corinthians not shown me the rock.

She came across it while mopping our room. One of the Routiers had thrown a stone with four words written on it in blue paint and it ended up under Corinthian's bed. "What do you think it means?" she asked me.

"I think we should ask Philemon," I said.

Philemon could finish a book in less than a month and he had a very talented tongue. He could say *six thick thistle sticks* as fast as you please without getting twisted up at all. When we gave him the rock, he tapped his finger on the words as if he could wake up the letters and make them explain themselves.

"HUMBIES?" he said. "Never heard of it."

That afternoon, I was pouring tea for Sister Sabastienne when she began to twitch. "Back, you God-damned demons!" she said. I put the tea cup down.

Hmm, I thought.

"Is it the Humbies, Sister?" I asked, taking hold of her hand.

I recalled the noises I'd heard during the attack. The mush-mouthed fury of the monsters was a language I could not understand.

"Don't call them that," Sister said when she heard me say the blue word. "It isn't right. They're God's creatures too. Don't call them by that *name*."

"What should I call them then?" I asked.

Her tongue punched against sealed lips as if she wanted to let something out.

"Say it!" I urged. "What should I call them?"

Two words rushed out with the force of a cough. "The Blessed," Sister Sabastienne said.

I took the rock from my pocket and considered the words again.

DEATH TO ALL HUMBIES

"Well?" Corinthians asked me later. "Does Sister Sabastienne know what Humbies are?"

"Yes."

"And?" she said, clapping her hands, so sure it would be something fun.

"Humbies are *us*."

They let me sit up all night and keep an eye on things because Sister Sabastienne was so restless. I was to call first thing if there was trouble. I used the opportunity to ask more questions.

"Why do the monsters call us Humbies?" I asked. I thought she was delirious but she opened her eyes and looked at me, very surprised.

"Where did you hear that word, Esther Six?"

I knew she was upset because she used my full name. Unlike Sister Edwige, who always just called me Six, Sister Sabastienne only used our last names when she was really worked up about something.

I showed her the rock.

"Oh dear. How many children have seen this?"

"Plenty," I told her, and it wasn't really a fib. "Everyone is demanding to know what it means.

Sister waved the idea away. "Routiers never speak sense. It doesn't mean anything."

Hearing her lie hurt my heart in the most shivery of places. I left the ward with the intention of taking a nap but I knew I wouldn't be able to sleep. I hadn't slept in weeks.

Before the attack, my sleeplessness was due to excitement. Every June 1, for as long as I could remember, I'd raced to the departure platform to watch the graduates enter the *Leaving Car* and descend to their new lives. It was important to get there early for a good spot so you could get a last look as the glass elevator bore them away: first feet, then knees, then shoulders, then smiles . . . Rumor had it, there was a champagne toast waiting at the bottom, but that was a private affair. For the rest of us, the *Leaving Car* was the end of it.

Oh, the graduates still visited us, but only in memories. The yellow wall that led to the platform was plastered with snapshots of their faces. There was Genesis Twelve from a few years back, her picture slightly crooked. Genesis had been voted "Class Clown" and in her picture, the blue ties of her uniform were tied in front instead of in back. Lips puckered, she was blowing a giant bubble that painted her face every color of the rainbow. My friend Proverbs was in the photo next to Gen's. Proverbs had been frozen in time jumping across the Finish Line in a sack race. The shriek she shrieked when she hopped to victory was so loud, it was still echoing around our school a year later. I was especially fond of the photo of the first Mark One, though I'd never met the boy. Before Philemon got handsome, I'd planned to look him up in the out-world and see if he wanted to get married. He was juggling little red balls in his photo and I thought he might be willing to teach me how to do this after we became friends. I'd fallen into the habit of patting his picture every year, as if to say, "See you soon." Corinthians reminded me that the first Mark One would be an old man now.

This year it was going to be *our* year. Soon, our pictures would be joining the others on the wall. It would be our turn to step into the car. Maybe one of the younger students would pat my picture when they passed by? Just thinking about the big day made me dizzy with longing.

But that had changed.

I tried to sleep but I kept hearing a buzzing in my ear. Flies circled as though I were a hunk of meat. Before I knew it, the wrinkles in my blanket had all transformed into bread loaf-sized arms reaching out for me. Moaning Routiers stalked the twisty tunnels of my mind, their breath reeking of rot. DEATH TO ALL HUMBIES. When sleep finally came, it took me in spasms.

Ten minutes later, I was jarred awake by the sickly dings of *Jesus Wants me for a Sunbeam*. Everyone else was in the Honour assembly and got to see it, first-hand, when the bullet chipped the chapel window. Me, I covered my head with my pillow and waited for a flaming arrow to strike me someplace bad.

The blue word soured everything, turning my last days at Salvation House into a nightmare. Instead of wrinkling my nose at the Wednesday menu and thanking God that I would soon be free to eat what I liked, I felt tears prickle at the back of my eyes as if the potent stench of liver sorbet was the perfume of my long-lost mother. One afternoon, while grumbling about the shower line that wrapped from here to there and back again, it hit me like a lightning bolt that this was the very place where my friends and I always laughed the hardest. And who would sleep in Bed 45 after I was gone? I'd begun to worry about this non-stop.

I hoped it would be someone who would hang her class ribbons from the grill and keep her shower cap on the post. I hoped too that she would leave Philemon's name on the wood where I'd painstaking-ly chiseled it with a pen nub. I'd not sanded off the things I'd found there. There was still a reminder to leave a candle burning on the win-dowsill in case the Virgin Mary passed by, and I'd long ago made my peace with the words YOUR FEET SMELL that someone had taken more time with than I had with my true love's name. The plastic pearls of a stranger were knotted around one leg. I'd kept those too. I hoped whoever came after me was clever enough to store secret things in the little dip under the mattress. Not every mattress had one.

I was going to miss Bed 45. I blamed this on the blue word.

After the pork bombs, Salvation House suffered from a fly infes-tation that proved tormenting for all. I was worried about my destiny, of course. Others routinely mistook the flies for mosquitoes. Sister Arnaude proved particularly squeamish. Father had sprayed the ward ten times but the flies kept re-appearing. One morning, a fly walked across her cheek, and she jumped around flapping her arms and swat-ting angrily. Because Father was saying mass at the time, she put a key in my hand and said, "Fetch me the bug traps."

I'd been inside Father's office a few years earlier when Corinthians and I were playing angels in the *le Réveillon* pageant. Sister Edwige had stopped off for masking tape to fix my torn wing and I took in as much as I could; hoping to see something that spoke of a secret, and I did. There were filing cabinets with keyholes under every drawer handle. There was an envelope next to the masking tape marked SECURITY CODE. There was a phone with a red button labeled

PRIVATE LINE. I lived a life without any keyholes so I'd found this very mysterious. When we were leaving, Sister Arnaude bumped a shelf with a plate collection on it. The plates had belonged to Father Barthelemy's mother and a couple of them broke. While we were cleaning up, I pocketed a piece of china with Bertha of Burgandy's head on it. It was going to be thrown out anyway. I hid the head in my mattress dip.

When Sister Arnaude gave me the office key, it was like a lit firecracker inside my fist, but I acted nonchalant. My face said, "I'm here on official bug business."

Pretending not to see the tremendous stock of traps in the corner, I started to search. There was a book on the desk with a sticky note on it. CHOOSE PHOTOS. I recognized the book at once. The sisters had been pasting pictures in it since the doors opened on Salvation House. I was in the book wearing a taped wing.

Next I found a newspaper clipping. At the top was a photograph of a bride, but her fluffy veil made it hard to see her. Someday I wanted to marry Philemon and wear a fluffy veil just like the one in the picture. Philemon seemed agreeable.

The previous New Year's Eve, when I was getting more cups for the punch and Philemon was getting more ice from the freezer, we'd both stopped in the middle of the kitchen and looked at each other. Before I could think, he slid his hand through the tufts of my hair, daring to touch the bare places in between with his ice-cold fingers. No one had ever touched the skin on my head before and I was sure we'd get detention but it made me feel unspeakably happy and light. When Sister Sabastienne walked in, we were standing in a puddle of melting ice cubes.

Sister reminded me that I was to save such things for after graduation. Luckily, she let it go at that. I never forgot how nice it was though. I hoped to touch Philemon's head after we were married.

Under the bride was a recipe for something called *Tex-Mex Chili* and an article about our school.

Amid a fresh burst of public outcry, Salvation House releases a new report claiming to have saved the lives of over two hundred cross-bred children since the Devastation.

Hmm, I thought.

I finished reading the article in a bathroom stall, but the facts were all confused. The newspaper said that Salvation House was a *lock-down center for children of mixed heritage.* I was suspicious that the reporter was a jealous Routier.

Despite opposition, the government maintains that the need for such a facility is strong. The Minister of Health and Solidarity met with outraged citizens in Dunkerque this week to address concerns.

"Whether or not the law prohibits marriage between the well and the infected, Hydrids continue to be born," Boulanger said Tuesday. "The question is, are we as a society prepared to kill innocent babies because of parents who disregard the law?"

The article spoke of a place called *Salvation Out-Reach* where mothers could receive prenatal care and make a fresh start by turning over their children to the proper authorities without fear of prosecution. *While military forces seek to eliminate the lingering threat, a small segment of those suffering from Greenhouse Maleria have managed to get their hands on illegal doses of Lariathol, making their condition harder to detect.* The article cautioned people to be responsible and ask for a complete medical examination before partnering with anyone. *But carelessness is not always the culprit. While authorities continue to warn about the selective pressure Greenhouse Maleria puts on the human genome, there are still those choosing to engage in relations with the infected.*

Meanwhile, a group calling themselves S.A.V.E. (Students Advocating Victim Elimination) has been responsible for numerous outbreaks of violence in the capitol city since November. An unidentified spokesperson for the group announced plans to begin targeting Salvation House itself if lawmakers will not hear their plea. S.A.V.E. is demanding legislation that would put into place the same elimination protocols for cross-species that exists for the infected . . .

Opening a folded flap next to these words, I came face to face with a picture of one of the monsters. I nearly threw-up. It was all the more awful in that the creature was a freakish distortion of a person.

The arms and legs were in the normal places but they looked huge, as if its skin was really thick and there were no bones to speak of. The face was puffed up with fat, like the sisters', and the eyes were slitty and mean. There was hair in unnatural places too—under the nose, on its chin, all over its giant head. Worse still, the thing had not been de-teethed. Corinthians never said anything about seeing teeth. The sisters all suffered survivor effects from the *Devastation* but at least they didn't have teeth. In the picture, the monster was wearing a shirt that said: ABORTION IS THE LAW.

Abortion?

This black word proved just as strange as the blue one.

All told, I was two hours getting through the whole article and still couldn't wrap my brain around it. For me, it was like hearing someone claim that the grass was red instead of green, or that Christmas would not be coming in April, August, and December. The last part was the most troubling of all . . .

Salvation House prides itself on giving life to the innocent, offering Hybrids some-thing that could not be safely offered otherwise: Eighteen years.

Everyone knows that honour is a citizen's foremost duty. Without it there would be chaos. Disregard the rules, and you may as well be a Routier. When I showed the article to Sister Sabastienne, she reminded me that I had been trusted with a job and that I had not lived up to that trust. She put the clipping in her nightstand, fully expecting me to shut-up honourably, but it was too late for that.

The article spelled things out reasonably well but I still had questions. "Why?"

Sister Sabastienne took a deep breath. "In a few days, you're going to graduate. You'll have all your answers then."

For Christmas one year, Philemon had given me a drawing he

made of a hawk soaring past his window. SOMEDAY it said. Someday was almost here. That didn't stop my need to know.

"Why didn't you tell us we're part human and part . . . zombie?"

"Don't use that word, dear."

"Humbies."

She clapped her hand over my mouth. "You are *The Blessed*, do you hear me?"

I pushed her hand away. "Are we really brighter and more beautiful?"

"To us, you are."

"To you? To the fifteen nuns who live here and Father Barthelemy? But not the rest of the world?"

"This is why we don't keep newspapers."

"To deceive us?"

"To give you peace in a troubled world. There are different truths, Esther. You know as well as I do that there is great joy to be found in our special family. Why should this be any less true than what goes on out there?"

Sister had not been able to sit up for three days but she sat up now. "I want you to understand something. We've taught you about duty and honour and the importance of considering others. Like all people, you've found these things to be tested in your life, but never more than now. Salvation House exists on shaky ground. There are a lot of people waiting for us to slip up so they can pull the plug. If ever there is an escape or a revolt, Salvation House is to be shut down permanently."

"An escape? That makes it sound like a dungeon."

"Not a dungeon. A sanctuary. It is in everyone's best interest that you live within these walls. We have revealed and concealed different parts of history for a reason. Everyone must be content."

"So you withhold the facts to keep the peace?"

"We tell as much as we can. It was originally proposed that we not teach anything about *The Great Devastation* but we wanted to prepare you for the Routiers. It is difficult to untangle ourselves completely from the out-world."

"And if I won't keep quiet?"

"Then you will kill Salvation House."

I bit my lip. I had one more question and it was a big one. "The newspaper said we get eighteen years, as if that's all there is."

I could see it in her eyes as clear as a crack in a marble. Pity.

"It can't be," I whispered. *World Preparation* had been preparing us for a truth that did not exist! "We don't leave, do we?"

Sister was biting on her fist now, tears pouring down her face. "Let it go, Esther."

"What happens?"

She didn't want to tell me. She wept and begged but I was without honour now. "What happens to us after we step into the *Leaving Car?*"

She wiped her eyes with the back of her hand. "Heaven," she said.

The bargain had been struck long ago. The world could not afford a third species, a mix of the mixed. When our years were up, they promised us a graduation party and put us in a car filled with gas.

Sister tried her best to put a cherry on it. "The average life expectancy out there is sixteen to twenty years. Eighteen is a good long life. It's better than killing babies."

Babies.

I saw my baby daughter then, the one that cooed in my imagination. "But how can I go through with this, Sister?"

"Think of that champagne toast," she said. "Think of your dreams. You're feeling sorry for yourself right now and all that you will never have, but remember this: a lot of people out there never get a real Christmas or a warm bed or good health or love. Most of them never know the luxury of having any dreams at all."

I didn't know if honour was really about honour anymore or if it was just another protection device like the *Bucket Brigade*. For the first time, I pictured shimmying down the bell rope and making a run through a forest I'd only seen from afar. It wouldn't be easy. I'd have to try and survive in a world that I knew less about this week than I did the week before. But at least I would be free. Free to learn the truth and turn nineteen and have a baby.

They would shut down Salvation House, of course, but the place was a lie anyway. I'd be doing everyone a favor by exposing the truth. And sure, the other children would die and the program would end, but they were all dead anyway. Corinthians, Philemon, Deut . . . all of them caught up in a dream that would never be.

But wait!

I could take them with me. Well, I could take Corinthians. I could take Philemon. I pictured us charging Father with our protection sticks and making him let us out. Who did they think we were, anyway? They couldn't keep us down with honour. Buy us off with Christmas! Why should I step into that elevator and let them silence me? It was a bonfire for the faithful all over again, a bonfire they had been slowly luring us into since the first minute we drew breath.

I began practicing different ways to tell Corinthians. *You remember Gen Twelve and the first Mark One? Well, both of them are dead . . .*

I found her in the Craft Room pouring honey on strips of yellow paper. She was making flypaper for our *Leaving Ceremony*. "No bugs allowed," she said. I'd never seen her look so happy.

Terrific.

"Guess what?!" she said. "Don't tell anyone, but we really do get to have champagne for the toast. Sister Sabastienne said we could."

"I'll bet she did," I said. I was sad and furious and ready to scream. A big part of me still wanted to see what Corinthians saw when she thought of graduation. Instead, all I could see was running through the trees into a world that didn't want me, while the one that did went up in flames at my back.

But I had to tell her. There was something wrong when a lie was made to be more honourable than the truth.

"Ew!" Corinthians said, holding up the honey paper. "I've already caught a fly."

It wiggled and kicked, its wings stuck in the sugary glue. She said, "Dead flies cause the oil of the perfumer to send forth an evil odor;

so does a little folly outweigh wisdom and honour."

"You memorized it?" I said.

"Of course. It's your destiny."

"Listen to me, Corinthians, I learned more about the blue word you found on that rock . . . "

"Did you memorize mine?" she asked

The poor girl. All she cared about was a stupid destiny that was never going to be.

"Mine is nice," she said. "Their wings were joined one to another. They didn't turn when they went. They went everyone straight forward."

With that, my best friend Corinthians, whom I loved with all my heart, set aside the flypaper and began to blow up balloons.

We lined up girl-boy in the yellow hall, everyone laughing about the new pictures on the wall. Corinthians said her nose looked big but I could tell she was thrilled. We were in a picture together, scooping handfuls of bonbons and Orangettes out of our shoes on Christmas day. It was a nice shot. A good memory.

We'd spent this morning putting our things in boxes with our names on them. I wondered if my new espadrilles and my *Best Speller* ribbon would end up as someone's hand-me-downs, or if they would be burnt up in the furnace. We put our protection sticks in the athletics closet to be passed on. I folded up the picture of the hawk and left it with Bertha of Burgandy's head in the mattress dip. I said goodbye to Bed 45.

The younger students started jumping up and down as the *Leaving Car* cranked to a stop. "This is it," Sister Edwige said.

I glanced at Sister Sabastienne. She swished a fly off her nose and looked away.

The day before, she'd taken me aside and promised it would be quick. All I had to do was step in the car and I wouldn't feel a thing.

"So . . . what will you do, Esther?"

"I don't know."

The door to the *Leaving Car* slid open and everyone smiled and piled in. It wasn't too late to have my say. At that moment, every eye in the school was on me.

I knew their faces, each and every one. I knew them because they were me. I knew they would follow us as far as they could, wildly waving when the doors slid shut.

The doors slid shut. Everyone waved. I reached for Corinthian's hand.

Closing my eyes, I thought about the champagne waiting for me at the other end.

Fleeing, on a Bicycle with Your Father, from the Living Dead

by Ralph Robert Moore

You hear Tess arguing with your father.

Walk through the doorways to see what it is this time.

She's at the back door. The door is swung open, inwards. She's crying, face red, looking up at your father. She sees you, breaks into new tears. "He won't let me get the dog!"

You head over, past the kitchen counter, looking at your father, his face set, features squat and harsh, an older version of yours, just as Tess' face is a younger version.

Tess, down around your father's pants pockets, points her short right index finger at the screen door. "See?"

On the small patio off the back door, a cocker spaniel, lying on its side on the concrete, breathing hard, tongue spilled out, huffing. Red pucker in its side. Someone shooting during the night must have hit the dog by mistake.

"We can save him." You face your father. "Make sure the bullet went straight through, or dig it out, feed him, give him some water. Keep him in the garage."

Tess jumps up and down.

Your father shakes his head. "We barely have enough food for ourselves."

Tess' eyes crumple at the finality in the voice. She presses her face against the screen door, blonde eyebrows way up on her forehead. "Look, look! There's ants crawling on him! They're going to kill him!"

And there are. A brown trail going up, tiny movements, across the breaths of his muscular abdomen, towards his snouted head. That's where they go first, the eyes. To blind. Disorient.

The spaniel's head twists around on its shoulder, floppy ears, moist brown eyes staring up, blinking, tongue out.

You reach for the aluminum latch.

Your father's hand stretches down, pushes against the door, keeping it shut. "I forbid you to bring that dog inside."

"At least let me get the ants off him."

He snorts. "As soon as you brush them off, they'll start climbing on him again."

The next morning, Tess is sobbing.

She pulls you by your big hand over to the back door.

You don't want to look out, but you do, for her sake, so she doesn't have to hold whatever she saw all to herself.

The dog is dead, mouth frozen, ants crawling in and out of its eyes.

Watching it being carried away, underground, one little upraised red dot at a time, you notice a metal tag around his neck.

He used to belong to someone.

It's a brand new day.

You wake up with a hangover.

Dark-haired on your pillow, white sheet down by your stomach, you go through your morning ritual, closing your left eye, your right, flexing your right hand, your left.

The warmth of the sun glows between the boards nailed over the bay windows, stripes of brightness across the gold carpet, surprising you again the sun still exists in this world.

You use the toilet off your bedroom. Don't bother to shower or brush your teeth.

Shuffling down the short carpeted hallway, from bedroom darkness to the brightness of the kitchen, your eyes squinting, you see Tess at the stove, standing on a stool so she can stir. She turns around in her pink dress to make sure it's you, blue eyes wide, long chef's knife in her hand, short fingers wrapped around the black handle.

"Hey, Peanut."

She goes back to clumsily stirring the beans. "Dad didn't come home last night."

You rub the top of her blonde head with your right palm. "He probably got drunk again. I'll go over to the waterworks. Want some help getting down?"

"I can do it." Standing near, hands up, you watch as, with a child's pride, she lowers her questing left shoe off the stool, right shoe.

She carries the big, tilting skillet over to the kitchen table, carefully spoon-pushing the brown beans over the black curve of the skillet, so they land as dozens of asterisks on your two plates.

You lift a forkful of barbeque beans to your mouth.

"Mmmmm!"

Her eyes widen. "Really?" She looks away, flirtatiously, looks back. "Are they good?"

"Great! Best yet."

"I didn't fuck them up like I did the tuna salad?"

"I shouldn't have used those words. The tuna salad was fine. I was just . . ."

"I added black pepper this time."

"This is great!"

"Okay." Her face lowers, beam of pride across it, as if by lowering her features, you won't be able to see her pride. She scoops her spoon into her own plate of beans, with greater confidence, lifts the spoon, little red lips opening long before the spoon swings over to her mouth.

"Did I get really angry again last night?"

She looks at the silver spoon buried in the next lift of beans, small shoulders lifting. "A little bit."

"Was I mean?"

"No." She rearranges the salt and pepper shakers so they're side by side on the table.

"I drank more than I planned."

She bobs her small head over her plate of beans. "That's okay."

You put your right eye to the front door peephole, stand back, unlock the door.

Outside, it's a cold afternoon, you feel it on your face, it feels good, birds chirping in the hedges.

You take a stroll across the damp front lawn, past the chocolate mounds of fire ant hills, turning around in your pajamas, looking back, at the dark green indentations of your footsteps on the lawn, at the house. All the boards are still up on the windows. Nothing to repair.

Down the street, a neighbor in a long blue bed robe is mowing his lawn. You return the high, distant wave.

At the curb on the opposite side of the road, a corpse is lying across the storm drain. The same corpse that's been there the past few days. You can tell by his clothes.

You go back inside, lock the front door, put the bolt across.

Tess is sitting at the cleared kitchen table, striped sunlight on her hair, doing math problems she downloaded from the Internet. "I'm trying to trisect an angle!"

"That's good. I'm going to take the car and check on dad."

She looks up from her white sheet of paper, young face, yellow pencil in her right hand. "Did you see my friend?" Her blue eyes swivel to her left hand, balled on the tabletop.

You walk over. An orange and black ladybug, like a little painted turtle, sits on her small, smooth knuckle.

"Cool. Did you give it a name?"

She shrugs. Looks up at you. "How come God made things like ladybugs and butterflies, but then he also made things like spiders and cockroaches?"

You glance at the sunlight infusing the boarded-up windows. "He made one group when he was happy, and the other group when he was sad."

You see on her face the cheekbone-tightening effort to think like an adult. "Which group did he make first?"

"I don't know. Maybe the ladybug and butterfly group."

"Are you taking the gun?"

"No, you keep it. I'll be back before dark."

"Take some money with you, Nate."

You hold up some of the new six dollar bills.

She sits up in her chair, proud. "While you're out, I'm going to make a lemon meringue pie for us."

You stoop over behind her, with your uncombed hair, give her a hug. "Do I love you?"

Rolling back her head, so that you feel the strength of her neck muscles in your embrace, she gives you an upside-down, pearl and pink smile. "Sure do!"

You back the car down the slope of the driveway, swing out the driver's door, rattle down the white garage door, tiny dark snails attached to the paint, yank up on the aluminum handle to make sure it's locked.

Across the road, the corpse is still sprawled face-down on the storm drain. You stride over, looking up and down the street. His right arm is extended out, hand holding onto a tall yellow and green dandelion weed growing in the space between grate and pavement, slowly pulling it out, probably has been for the past hour or so, with that exhausted slowness they get during sunlight.

At least he hasn't made it across the street, ringing the front doorbell for hours, like many corpses do, which is now illegal.

You give him a hard kick in his ribs. His face lifts, blood around his mouth, like melted chocolate, dark circles under his eyes.

"If you're still here when I get back, I'm going to lift your head, place it on the edge of that concrete curb, and bounce my baseball bat off your temple until I split your skull apart. Do you understand me?"

The dark-furrowed eyes squint in the sunlight. "Please go away."

"I'll slap and slap that baseball bat down on your fucking head until your ears are a foot apart. Do you understand?"

He lowers his face back down onto the grating, away from the bright sun. "I really, really want you to go away now."

"And if the police investigate, if it turns into a civil rights thing, I'll just say you tried to bite me."

You walk back across the street, get in your car, slam and lock the door. Back out of the driveway, upper body twisted around, forearm resting on the top of the driver's seat, consider for a moment running over the corpse, who's getting bigger and bigger in your rear window, but it might fuck-up your car.

The roads are easier to navigate since the last time you were out. You see two guys in a tow truck, rifles slanted across their backs, moving abandoned cars, front and side windows smashed inwards, up onto adjacent front lawns. So it does seem like progress is being made, despite all the negative criticism in the press from the Democrats.

A few miles down State, you run into an army roadblock. Flimsy sawhorses arranged across the road. There isn't much traffic, so you only wait behind your steering wheel five minutes before one of the soldiers walks up to you.

His green uniform is torn, blood on it. "Afternoon." Broad smile, but he doesn't stand too close to the opened driver's window.

"Hi."

"Mind if I ask where you're going?"

"Picking up my dad." When the soldier keeps staring at you, bloodshot blue eyes, you add, "He's at the waterworks."

The soldier nods, looking beyond you into the backseat, glancing down at the floorboards on the passenger side. He refers to the opened, spiral-bound manual in his hand. "What's thirteen times three, minus two?"

You put a hand on your forehead. "That's . . . thirty-seven."

It's been a while since you've been out, so you decide to stop by Pete's place, just to have someone to talk to.

Pete lives in a bad section of town, but you don't see any corpses.

You park out front, next to the burnt-out husk of a pick-up truck, wheelchair in the bed, lying on its big-wheeled side. Get out of your car, beep it locked, stroll quickly across the quiet sidewalk to the column of names by the building's door, press Pete's little metal button.

After a minute of buzzing, you hear Pete's voice come through the horizontal grates of the speaker. "Yeah?"

"Nate."

"Hey! Nothing personal man, but, you know. If A is greater than D, and Y is less than D, is A greater or less than Y?"

"Greater."

After you get buzzed in, you walk up the three flights to Pete's apartment, taking each corner in the stairway at the far wall.

Pete steps back after unlocking his door, skinny in a purple t-shirt, pot belly, brown eyes. You're always surprised when you see Pete. He was a real force in the early, scary days, fighting fiercely beside you, punching faces above the headrests of the cushioned chairs to get out of the movie theatre, but now, he looks thin, wasted. He holds out a smoldering joint. "Want a hit?"

You shake your head, look around at his rat's nest. "I have to keep my head clear. You have any booze?"

"I only smoke pot now. It's a renewable resource."

"The thing about booze is, it lasts forever. It's its own preservative. Even if they never make any more, there's enough in stores and homes to last us the rest of our lives."

Pete stands in the middle of his trashed living room, swaying slightly, eyes squeezed almost shut. He sticks the nailed tip of his index finger in his ear, wiggling it, making a face. "I think an insect crawled in my ear. I feel it shifting around. Sometimes, there's a flutter high up in my right nostril. There must be a passage between the ear and the sinus cavity. Did I tell you this last time?"

"I don't remember."

"Well, it's still there."

"You should try to find a doctor."

He snorts. "A doctor's not gonna bother. Fuck it. You can get used to anything over time. Plus, I downloaded this HTML editor? But now it doesn't work. It keeps fucking up. I e-mailed the creator, that was like a week ago, he's in Philadelphia or some shit, and he never responded. I think he's dead."

You look around Pete's dirty living room. "I'm thinking of moving to Norway. It's got lots of snowy mountains, blue inlets, islands, farms. You can fish right off your back door. Just drop a line down. Salmon, lobster, crabs. There probably aren't that many corpses. Too cold."

"Do you want to see what I found the other day?"

"Yeah. You don't have any booze?"

He staggers over to his thrift store couch, reaches under with both hands, pulls a long box out, grinning up at you.

You tilt your head to read the top. "Monopoly!"

"Fucking right. Wanna play?"

"I would if you had booze."

"Smoke a fucking joint! What's wrong with you?" He struggles to get the lid off, splitting one cardboard corner, sets everything down on his coffee table. "Just look at this."

It's the Monopoly game board you remember from childhood, with the big, red-lettered *Go!* square, the jail, the rectangles in the center of the board for the community chest and chance cards.

"Look at this, Nate. All the little green houses, red hotels."

You read the different street squares around the board, each set of squares with a uniform color bar at the top. Mediterranean Avenue, St. James Street, the Boardwalk. "Jesus."

Pete lowers some of the green houses onto the different properties. He's got tears in his brown eyes. "Look how safe the streets are, man. So clean. And the houses don't have any windows. They're impregnable."

You want to stay, but it's getting late. "Next time. I'll bring a bottle with me. We'll play all night."

"Why do you have to go?"

"I have to get my father."

"He's drunk again? How's Tess?"

"She's good. Doing really well."

"Your dad is a piece of shit, man. Sorry."

You pick up one of the red hotels, turn it over in your fingertips, admiring its clean lines. "Is that girl still around?"

"Who's that?"

"The girl who'd let you have sex with her for six dollars."

"Oh! No, she's dead."

"Really?"

"Yeah, it was, what, a few weeks ago? They got her coming up the stairs."

"You didn't help her?"

"It sounded like there were a lot of them. About half an hour before, I heard this loud screech, like brakes, about a block away. So there must have been all these people who died in a car crash. You know yourself, they're a lot more energetic when they first die. I called 911."

"That'd creep me out. I'm used to seeing strangers. I'm not sure I'd want to see someone I actually knew."

"They need to revise the laws. I mean, I know they're still human, they've got rights and shit, but, fuck. They got AIDS under control, and that's supposed to be incurable. Why can't they control this?"

You drive across town, searching for liquor stores or homes recently abandoned.

On twenty-third street, you come across a restaurant, shards of glass on the sidewalk.

You park your car, get out with your baseball bat.

Inside, overturned tables, large splotches of blood on the floor.

You go behind the counter. Hit the cash register, stand back as the tray opens. Snatch up all the paper money from the metal rectangles, fold it, jam it in your pocket.

Underneath the wooden counter, a huge supply of booze.

You get down on your knees, pull out six unopened plastic jugs of vodka.

Gather them up in your arms, walk towards the front door, upright baseball bat wiggling.

A figure appears in the store's front doorway.

Fuck!

"What do you think you're doing?"

The figure advances inside the restaurant, black shoes walking over the purple bloodstains on the vinyl, both elbows bent, pointing a shotgun.

You can't hold up your hands, since they're loaded with the vodka bottles and your baseball bat. You raise your head instead.

"Hey."

The figure comes closer, shotgun still aimed at your head. You can't take your gaze off the two eyes of the shotgun's barrels, like being unable to look away from the stare of a snake. You see the blue of his uniform, realize he's a cop.

"You think that's right, to loot this place? That's not very nice."

"I just want this booze. I'll pay for it, if that's the issue."

The cop lowers his shotgun. "How you gonna pay for it?"

You stand still, arms full of the jugs, your baseball bat. "I'll pay for it with cash, man. Six dollars a bottle."

"Yeah?"

"I'll pay you. You can try to get the money to the rightful owner. I have the cash in my pocket."

"I don't need cash."

"So what do you need?"

The cop steps further inside, shotgun held down. Forehead, nose, lips in the light. "What I really need is a blowjob."

There's no booze left in the house. You finished it last night.

"That's what I really need."

"I get to leave with this booze?"

He carefully lays his heavy shotgun down on one of the tables, across dinner plates, black flies lifting.

Unzips the copper teeth of his blue pants.

Pulls out his pale cock.

It's limp.

You park in the large, chainlink-fenced lot of the waterworks, almost all the slots empty, so you can pull right up to the front, under the skyline shadow of the huge building.

You walk along the gray metal catwalks, steam rising from three stories below.

A fat man with green Magic Marker horizontal lines on his forehead hails you on one of the meshed ledges. "Nate, right?"

"Yeah."

"Looking for your dad?"

"Right."

"He's in the manager's office." He raises his right arm, points across the metal canyon.

You find a cross-walk a hundred feet down, shoes echoing above the churning turbines underneath. Backtrack to get to the small, lit office.

Your dad is sitting behind a desk, talking on the phone.

Ear cradled to the black phone, he jerks his head up in acknowledgement. His sharp blue eyes direct you to an empty chair on the interviewee side of the desk.

You sit down.

"I have to go. My son's here." He puts the phone back down on its base. Looks at you.

"You didn't come home last night."

"I decided to sleep here."

"Tess is frantic."

His face, black and white hair swept back, black eyebrows, severe blue eyes, big nose, ruddy skin, jowls, shrugs. "I have a lot of work. We've all got a lot of work now."

"So I'm here to take you home."

His pale lips turn down. "All right. Let me tell them."

The two of you walk side by side down the catwalks to the rear of the waterworks. He's shorter than you, by a head, and as usual, smells. Not so much of booze, as of someone who stopped showering.

Out in the parking lot, a corpse in a white polo shirt, naked from the waist down, little cock riding on an immense bush of black hair, has pried the hood of your car up, bent the metal back, chewing the black cables inside, mouth bloody. They love electricity.

"Fuck!" You storm over to the corpse, shove him sideways, so he falls to the ground. Kick at his raised hands, step around on the black pavement behind his head, kick the toes of your boots against his scalp.

Your father pushes your shoulder. "Don't do that."

You catch your breath, looking down at your shoes, realizing you need to find a lawn where you can rub off the blood. "Why shouldn't I? He's dead."

"Don't forget, I'll be dead someday too."

"He just fucked-up my car. You don't care, because you don't have a car. You don't have anything."

He looks around the parking lot. "I have plenty."

"You don't have a wife."

He turns toward you, face wrinkled on its skull. "What the fuck did you expect me to do? They were coming from everywhere . . . " He starts coughing, bending over.

"And you turned and ran with a yellow streak down your back. Saved your own fat ass. Where is she now? Is she just stumbling around somewhere, blood all over her?"

His face clenches, white foam on one side of his lower lip. "Shut up! Shut up!"

You both stand by the ruined car, the blubbering corpse on the pavement, not talking, breathing heavily. Finally, you glance at him, glance down at the corpse, glance at the faraway entrance to the lot. Get your baseball bat from the front seat. "Let's start walking."

He looks up at the gray and banana sky. "It's getting late."

"I don't give a shit. Tess is waiting for us. She's baking a lemon meringue pie."

He follows by your side, face still splotchy from getting angry.

After half an hour, you come to Inwood Avenue, the main business district in this area of town.

The majority of the shops are deserted, front windows smashed, one or two of them burned, but the others are open for business, huge white squares taped across their windows, big blue and red words announcing sales, a grocery, clothes store, greeting card shop now turned into a gun and ammunition center, clinic. Below street level, accessed from concrete steps leading down past a candy cane pole, a barber shop, the two black-haired, white-aproned proprietors sitting in the lower level brightness in the customers' leather chairs, reading newspapers.

All the shops have their outside lights on, bleaching sidewalk, although the sun is still out, low in the sky.

Most of the people strolling along the sidewalks have guns or rifles in their hands. You see a pretty girl hurry towards her car, shopping bag in one hand, revolver in the other. There's always a pretty girl, no matter what the situation.

The few corpses are lying in the gutter, slowly swinging their heads around, looking upside down at the pedestrians.

Your father pokes your back. "There's a gas station on the corner. Let's see if we can rent a car."

"Do you have any money?"

Resentful blue eyes looking sideways at you. "Don't you?"

The station owner is inside, sitting behind the counter on a tall stool in his red pajamas, brown grease on his face, shotgun across his lap.

You smile. "You have a car to rent?"

He shakes his head. "I got a bicycle. Two-seater. Let you have it for forty-two dollars."

You turn over eight sixes.

The owner swings his shotgun up, aims it at your face.

You take a step back, hands in surrender.

Your dad raises his black eyebrows. "Whoa, whoa!"

The owner slips his ass off the stool, pointing the shotgun from you to your father, back to you. "If one is really five, what's thirteen?"

You keep your hands raised. Concentrate. "If you mean what would thirteen be under the new numbering system you're proposing, it would be seventeen or sixty-five, depending if you're adding four to each number, or multiplying it by five. If you mean what would thirteen under your new numbering system have been under the old numbering system, it would be eight."

The owner gestures with the snout of his shotgun at the yellow bills you put on the counter. "So what's six times eight, hot-shot?"

You recalculate. "Forty-two. I should have given you seven sixes, not eight."

"Fucking A. I had a guy in here two nights ago, talked to him for ten minutes about all the rain we've been getting before I realized he was a corpse. Sometimes they don't even know themselves."

Your dad, trying to defuse the situation, nods his head. "I've seen corpses run away from other corpses, terrified, thinking they're still alive. I've even heard of some corpses who live in houses, behind boarded-up windows."

The owner comes out with the two of you, crossing the chilly late-afternoon air to the gas pumps, unchains the two-seater bicycle. "The back tire loses air. I got it all pumped-up, but it probably won't last more than a few miles. That's why I sold it so cheap."

You turn to your dad. "Get on the rear seat. I'm riding in front."

The two of you wobble out into the sparse evening traffic, four knees lifting.

Start down the dark suburban street.

Darkness rises from the ground quicker than you expected. As you bicycle farther from the populated business district, coasting down the slope of a tar road, shoes motionless on your four pedals, tall maple trees on either side, their winged seeds in the gutter, the overhead lights of the street pop on.

Four more blocks down the deserted road, you see an elongated black shadow stagger across an intersection.

The next block, three corpses stand in the middle of the road, spreading their arms out sideways from their shoulders, like cut-out paper dolls, stumbling left and right to block you, howling. There must have been another outbreak, somebody getting careless again. Fuck.

You fake right, twist the handlebars left, pumping fast to get past their waving arms. Whipping your head around, you look back at your dad, who's sitting back, burst vein cheeks, like he's on an exercise bike.

"You think you can you pump any faster?"

He nods, face red, black eyebrows down.

Steep slope of lawn on the left. You try pedaling furiously up it, but the two-seater bike wobbles in the wet grass, crashes sideways into the stone wall at the crest.

You both tumble off your handlebars, landing on your sides.

Down in the dark street, the corpses, heads swiveling on boneless necks towards the noise, shuffle their bodies around, shoulders dipping, get down on their hands and shins, start crawling up the sloped lawn, elbows and knees lifting.

Your father is on his side, harsh, black-eyebrowed face wincing.

You get down on your haunches. "Dad! You have to get up."

His left pants leg is torn below the knee, exposing his calf. Long, vertical red slash through the dark hair of his calf.

"Okay. I'm coming." He rises to his feet, wrinkles deepening from his eyes. "That fucking pedal cut into me when I was thrown off."

You put your hand up into his moist left armpit, pushing him forward. "We have to go. Right now."

He shakes his head, black and white hair sweaty bangs across his forehead, making him look younger. Sees, below, the lifting knees and elbows, getting closer, starting to fan out, surround. "Okay. I get what you're saying."

The two of you start down the slope, passing between corpses shuffling four-limbed up the slope. Your dad rolls his blue, blood-shot eyes sideways towards you. "Look dead."

The two of you stiff-limb down the slope, past the bent backs of corpses, elbows and calves lifting, crawling uphill.

It looks like you're going to get away, still one more time, but as you pass the final crawling corpse, it lifts its shiny red face, tilts up its nose, sniffs.

Opens its bottomless mouth.

Howls.

The corpses on the slope rise up under the dark sky, torn and bloody clothes, shuffle around, arms out sideways for balance, start shambling down the slope, in your direction.

You help your dad out onto the hard pavement of the street, hand still in his warm armpit, move him along the yellow lines in the street's center.

Around you, in the dark hills, howls rise.

The two of you hobble towards the next thoroughfare. A car goes by, bright headlights. You wave with your free hand, but of course, it doesn't stop. You wouldn't.

"Nate, I can't walk. My left leg keeps giving out."

Up ahead, there's an abandoned drive-in theatre. As you shuffle with your dad towards it, you turn around under his weight, look behind you.

Corpses cross the dark road under the moonlight, swaying in your direction.

The large white sideways rectangle of the drive-in screen gleams against the backdrop of treetops, brown and purple sky.

You drag your dad over to the nearest abandoned car with unbroken windows. Your knees are aching, heart beating too fast.

You open one of the back doors of the car, help him to fold himself in, onto the back seat.

Go around the rear of the car, get in on the other side of the back seat.

Push down all the door locks. Roll up all the windows.

Drape your stomach over the top of the driver's seat, feel with your right fingers along the steering column. No ignition key.

"We'll hide here until your leg feels better. Keep yourself as low in the seat as possible. Try to squeeze down near the floorboards."

Your father shoots you a sharp look. "There's no way I'm going to be able to squeeze down near the floorboards, Nate."

"Just keep yourself as low as possible. And don't talk so loud."

After a few minutes, both of you squashed down as low as possible in the back seat, he says in a quiet voice, "Do you remember when I used to take you to the airport? When you were a kid? We'd sit in the car. Watch the planes land and take off."

"Vaguely."

"That was a different world back then."

"No shit."

"After they got your mother, I went back to look for her. To kill her."

You don't say anything.

"I don't think I was a coward. If I was, it was just for a minute."

You don't say anything.

You both crouch down, not talking, for an hour.

Your dad clears his throat. "I think they probably moved on."

A shadow moves across the side window of the car.

Fuck.

More shadows, their gray overlapping.

Fuck!

You glance up, fearfully, at the side window.

Profiles move by, hair mussed, bullet holes in their faces, noses blown off, from the early days when it was thought you kill the dead by shooting them in the head.

You see your dad's half-lit face crouched down by the back seat cushion. In the side window above his head, gray and white flesh presses, flattens, red in the center.

An old woman's breast.

You stare at your dad's eyes. Push your open lips forward, in a *Shhhh!* warning.

The corpse lowers the right side of her face against the window, blood smearing against the glass, eye rolling down.

Black and white tufts on the top of your dad's head are illuminated in the moonlight.

You bug your eyes at him. Don't move. Don't breathe.

The corpse puts her big white palm against the glass, gray whorls and pale pink lifeline. Her lipsticked mouth moves. "I see you." She bends her head back, lets out a howl.

Her yellow teeth scrape down the glass.

Your dad hunches his shoulders further down.

You mouth at him. Don't move.

"I see you. I see your head!"

The locked latch above your dad's hair shakes violently.

He hunches further down, eyes terrified.

Above your dad's head, the safety glass of the side window falls inwards, diamonds landing on his hair. The woman thrusts her jowly face through the shattered window, big arrogant hand reaching down.

Your father's face is quickly surrounded by her white fingers, pulling his body up out of the back seat, his eyes blinking, mouth clamped in pain, wrinkled backs of his hands trying to pry the strong wrists away.

Her lipsticked mouth turns down. "I'm sorry. I don't want to do this. But I'm going to do it."

Your dad's head is pulled through the window. You grab his calves, glad to still feel life there, try pulling him back into the car, but there are too many forearms under his jaw by now, unshaven Adam's apple bobbing furiously, and the dead are strong.

You unlock your side of the rear door, fall out.

Run a few feet away, stop, look back.

Corpses are circling him, hands out, ready to block any run to freedom.

A metal drive-in speaker pole lies on its side, knocked out of the concrete, pale pink bubblegum stuck to its gray sides.

You hoist up the pole.

The corpses close in, touching your dad on his shoulder, between his legs, his ass, distracting him, making him whirl left, right, as they cramp closer with their encircling arms.

A man with three bullet holes across his forehead reaches out, grabs, like a priest, your dad's hand.

You swing the heavy pole at their heads, banging them back. They wave their arms sideways, regain balance on the backs of their heels, stumble forward again.

Your dad, knocked down, looks up at you with scared eyes. "I'm still alive, Nate."

His head vibrates, shoulders lifting, knees jerking.

That's the thing. They always think they're still alive.

You smash the end of the metal drive-in speaker pole down into his chest, like a sword, ribs cracking apart, smash it straight down through his heart.

Those bloodshot blue eyes that stared at you all your life go flat, like a fish. His body relaxes back onto the ground, arms spread, motionless.

Now it's too late for him to ever say, I'm sorry.

The corpse that was outside your house, huddled on the storm drain, is gone.

You bang on the front door.

Tess' frightened voice, through the door, asks who it is.

"Nate."

She opens the door, steps back, big black gun in her right hand. "Are you okay?"

You shut the front door behind you, bolt it. "I'm fine."

Her large blue eyes look back at the locked front door, at you. "Where's dad?"

"He's been reassigned. He's doing such a great job, they transferred him to New York City. That's why he didn't come home last night. We probably won't see him for a while. He's promised to write postcards."

She steps back, big blue eyes alarmed. "Why is there blood all over your clothes?"

You stand under the front hallway light, combing your long black hair with your fingers. "There just is."

It dawns on you the vodka you stole is still in the trunk of your car, which is at the waterworks, and there's no booze at all in the house.

"I made my lemon meringue pie."

"Did you?" You force a grin on your face. "Let's see!"

She leads you happily through the doorways to the kitchen.

There's a pie on the counter. It looks like it's been sitting there for hours.

There are no eggs anymore, so no egg whites that can be whipped to form peaks that turn golden in the oven. Instead, she's poured canned evaporated milk over the lemon gelatin.

You stand back in admiration, look at her.

"Did you make this all be yourself?"

She bobs her head happily. "Sure did."

"It looks great."

"Did I fuck up?"

You rub the top of her blonde scalp. "No. Don't keep bringing that up. I'm not mad, but if you keep pushing me, I can get mad. Then it's your fault."

"Do you want me to cut you a piece? Did you have dinner?"

"Hmmm? No, I didn't."

She stands matter-of-fact in the middle of the kitchen floor. "I forgot to ask."

You smile. "Ask what?"

She hangs onto the gun, blinking earnestly. "If our numbering system were based on fourteen instead of ten, what would eighteen be, Nate?"

December Warming
by William Bolen

We were all sitting outside in a circle—some of us in wheelchairs, others leaning tiredly on our cold aluminum walkers, the rest of us either on the bench in the courtyard or standing stoop-shouldered against the gusting December wind—when Willard Hunt started whacking one of the zombies over the head with his shiny brass walking cane. The zombie was—or had been—Nurse Baxter; the tattered remnants of her vermillion-colored scrubs still hung from the bones of her shoulders. She didn't seem to mind, in fact she didn't notice him at all, not bothering to ward off his ineffectual blows as she shambled among our aged circle.

"Oh, stop it, Willard. That makes no sense whatsoever." This came from Kate Palmer, one of the liveliest of us all. It seemed to me that on her best days the zombies took some notice of her, but it was probably just my imagination.

"I don't like 'em," Willard mumbled. He had slumped down on the bench next to me. He was wheezing like a punctured balloon.

"Oh, no one does, Willard, but we don't waste our time beating on them." Kate wheeled her chair up next to Willard and placed a hand on his shoulder.

And she was right. We didn't waste our time trying to beat them anymore; there were just too many of them. Only a few months had passed since the changes began, but it seemed like years. And our best, our brightest, our youngest—they were all on their side now. I wondered if there were other communities like ours—islands of aged and infirm survivors, table scraps not deemed worthy for consumption by the walking dead.

I patted Willard's bony knee. "Let's just enjoy the time we have left." Kate was still touching Willard's shoulder. Looking at her nut-brown hand, tanned from her years in Florida, I felt a twinge of something I couldn't quite define.

"Listen to Ralph," Kate said, briefly glancing my way. "After lunch we can play dominos. You know you love dominos."

Willard looked ready to make an angry reply when the tinny sound of the dinner bell echoed through the courtyard. It was Miss Eliza, one of our undead, leaning against the French doors leading into the dining room. She had lost all of her toes and most of her fingers but she still managed to cook our meals each day. We moved as a group into the dining room—rolling, shuffling, and limping together like a herd of threadbare, arthritic buffalo. The irony of the buffalo analogy brought a bitter smile to my lips. I took the concept a step further. If humans were buffalo, then the zombies were like wolves, but unlike wolves, they didn't hunt the weakest of the pack—they ate only the strong, in whom the spark of life burned brightest, leaving the rest of us wandering among the hunters—rheumy-eyed zombies ourselves, faded shadows invisible to the feral gaze of their single-minded hungers.

The undead served our dinner. We watched them carefully. Whatever drove them to keep going through the motions of their former lives was deeply embedded, and this single-minded programming fostered a certain level of devotion to their tasks, but we still didn't trust them. Our lack of trust had been justified when Harold French discovered a rotting finger nestled among his shrimp fettucini. But for the most part they did okay; some of them did better than they had while still breathing.

I found a seat next to Kate. Across from us sat John Harkins and Berniece Wilson.

"Do you think he'll be okay?" I asked.

"Willard? He'll be fine," Kate said. "He's just frustrated. I can see it in his eyes. He wants so badly just to *do* something."

"Willard's banging on the zombies again?" John Harkins asked loudly, his blue eyes mirthful.

"Quiet," Berniece whispered, "he'll hear you."

Willard was sitting two tables away, eyeing the pot roast suspiciously.

"I don't think he'd mind," John said, but he lowered his voice.

Then I saw it. John looked at Berniece and she stared back at him. They gazed into each others' eyes for a few moments, and I saw something in their faces I hadn't seen since the dead had risen. Then Bernice looked away, her face flushed. John locked eyes with me and grinned like a mischievous schoolboy. In that moment they both seemed to shed twenty years.

Were they falling in love? The thought felt alien to me. It was a colored thought—love was a colored word—and the colors of my world had all darkened to muted shades of gray when my family, along with the rest of the youth of the world, had been attacked and assimilated into the ranks of the living dead.

Then the growling started. It was a guttural bleating, raw and jagged. At first I thought someone was choking, but then I saw Lenny Howard, who had been one of the janitors before becoming a zombie, standing in front of the salad bar. Head tilted back like a dog, he sniffed the air and stared down his ravaged nose at our table. Was he actually noticing us? My mouth went dry.

Kate punched my shoulder, hard, and I tore my gaze away from Lenny. She was nodding at John and Berniece. Despite the unearthly growling, they were still staring into each other's eyes.

"He sees them," Kate whispered harshly.

"How—"

"Just do something." Kate's face was pale and taut.

So I moved. I must have known, even then, what was going on, for the first thing I did was try to separate John and Berniece. I jumped up, too quickly; the pain in my lower back was sharp, unforgiving. I would pay for that later. I grabbed John's arm. He looked up at me, a lost expression clouding his face.

Lenny was staggering across the room, unmistakable hunger in his eyes. The swinging door to the kitchen banged open, and Eliza lurched through, shuffling more quickly than I had ever seen her move. She scanned the room, her milky eyes jangling crazily, then she saw us. A mournful yelp of longing escaped her desiccated lips and she headed our way.

"Move," Kate said.

Then I pulled John to his feet. Berniece started to get up, but Kate leaned across the table and pushed her back down.

"What the hell?" Bernice said. She was staring angrily at Kate.

I was still pulling on John's arm, trying to get him away from Berniece, when I heard the sigh. It was a sorrowful sound, fraught with unbearable pain. It was Lenny. He had frozen halfway across the room to our table. He shook his head from side to side like a jackal worrying at a troublesome scrap of gristle, then he turned back to the salad bar. Seconds later he had retrieved his broom and was sweeping the lunchroom, step by jerky step.

I looked for Eliza, but the only sign of her was the door into the kitchen door rattling closed.

I looked at Kate. "Did that really happen?"

She nodded, her eyes still locked on Berniece's.

Berniece smiled.

John gently removed my hand from his arm and sat back down. "Should we tell them?"

Berniece just nodded, still smiling at Kate.

John leaned across the table, looked around the room, and gestured for Kate and I to lean forward. We did, and an absurd mental picture flashed through my mind. It was like a scene out of one of those World War II POW camp movies where the prisoners, surrounded by Nazi guards, whisper conspiratorially of their escape plans. I half-expected John and Kate to tell us to meet them at the tunnel after lights out.

"They've been noticing us," John said, like it was a good thing.

"We can see that," Kate whispered back. "What's going on?"

Berniece giggled "It's because we're in love."

Kate and I could only stare open-mouthed at the two lunatics sitting across from us.

"That's why they attacked the others and left us untouched," John said.

"Because we didn't have a lot of life left in us." Berniece reached out to grasp Kate's hands in her own. "Don't you see? They treated us like shadows because that's all we were, but when John and I fell in love, they started seeing us as living creatures again."

"Well, you have to fall *out* of love, dammit," Kate whispered harshly.

They both laughed then, and shook their heads.

Kate grinned sheepishly. She must have realized how silly that sounded.

"Look," I said, "you can't keep playing this game. If those son-of-a-bitchin' things catch you unawares . . . " my voice trailed off.

Then, in unison, their voices an eerily melodious harmony, they said it. "We don't care."

I didn't know what to say.

That night, sleep couldn't find me. My back was killing me; it had stiffened up since dinner. But that wasn't the only reason I couldn't sleep. Over and over, I kept seeing John and Berniece's faces as they stared across the table at Kate and me. They had looked so earnest, so satisfied, despite the obvious danger of their actions.

I rolled out of bed. The loud grunt startled me, but then I realized the sound came from me. I pressed my thumbs into my lower back and felt the waves of pain recede.

A full moon had risen, and bright moonlight shone through my window, marking four luminescent squares on the flowered quilt of the empty bed next to mine. I still thought of the bed as Owen's, even though he had died months ago, just before the dead had risen. I wondered what Owen would have made of our world had he been alive today. Would his dry humor have withstood the madness of the undead? I missed him terribly. He had been my best friend.

I rubbed my eyes, surprised at the moistness there, and went out into the hallway, softly shutting the door behind me. Lately, I found myself prowling the halls at night more and more, unable to close my eyes and let sleep take me.

Before I knew it I had made my way to the ladies' wing. Light glowed from beneath one of the doors in their hallway. The door was Kate's. I was standing before it, debating whether or not to knock, when it swung quietly inward. Kate smiled up at me from her wheelchair. She was wearing a woolen nightgown adorned with countless yellow marigolds.

"Couldn't sleep either?" she whispered, backing away from the doorway to let me in.

"It's my back."

"Sure it is." There was a sardonic tone to her voice as she wheeled her chair into the door behind me, gracefully pushing it closed. "And I'm the Queen of England."

This was the first time I had been in Kate's room. It surprised me. Most of the rooms in the home were Spartan and cold, scarcely more than cells for the elderly. But Kate's room was different; it looked like an apartment. A marigold-patterned comforter neatly covered her bed, and fluffy, hand crocheted pillows were stacked at the headboard. Pictures of friends and family papered the walls. A marigold throw rug lay next to her bed and an expensive looking painting of a meadow brimming with marigolds was centered on the wall above her desk.

She caught me staring. "I love them. Marigolds, I mean. I used to have gardens teeming with them." She was staring wistfully at the painting, then a black thundercloud darkened her face. "I haven't seen a marigold since . . . it happened. My son used to bring me bouquets, but now . . . " Her voice trailed off and she gestured wanly at an empty vase on her desk.

A heaviness filled my throat. I didn't know what to say. The next thing I knew I had my hand on her shoulder. She lay her head down, pressing her cheek against my hand. Was that a dampness I felt? So close to her, I could smell her perfume. It was a sweet, innocent, flowery fragrance. Was it marigolds?

I was leaning down to inhale more deeply when the door swung open and Keith Young burst in. I snatched my hand away from Kate's shoulder then instantly regretted it. Why should I be ashamed?

"It's John and Berniece," Keith said. He was panting heavily and leaning on the open door for support. "This way."

We followed John's roommate back to the men's wing to John's room. On the way Keith told us that he had left John and Berniece in the room earlier. They had asked for some time alone. When we got to the room the door was wide open, and it looked like the entire population of the home was milling around in the hallway. Candlelight flickered through the doorway. Keith pushed his way through the crowd; Kate and I followed in his wake.

I don't know what I expected to see, but what I found in John and Keith's room wasn't it. Neither John nor Berniece were there. The flickering light came from a multi-colored row of candles burning on John's desk. Both beds were pushed tightly together. The blankets lay in a tangled line from the beds to the doorway. A single blue slipper —Berniece's—was wedged under the door.

Kate gasped. "They took them, didn't they?"

Keith said nothing. He was pacing the length of the room—his head was down, his eyes were almost closed. He was quietly and frantically mumbling into his chest.

"I think so," I said, having finally found my voice.

"Oh Berniece. For love? I don't know whether to laugh or cry." For some reason, Kate was staring directly into my eyes. The question I saw there, the invitation I saw there, made my heart race like a twenty-year old groom's at the altar.

I was once again speechless. Kate traced her hand along my arm as she wheeled herself back to her room.

It's now been three days since John and Berniece disappeared. My hand aches from writing all this down, but the decision I have made may be suicidal, and for some reason I feel an obsessive need to record what happened.

It's early afternoon, and for the first time since the dead awakened, I am leaving the home. I think John and Berniece were right; better that our hearts stop beating than our hearts stop feeling—that's what it means to be alive.

So I'm headed out the door to run my errands. Two of them. About a mile down the road I remember a flower shop with a greenhouse out back. I'm going to take the groundskeeper's wagon and I'm going to fill that wagon to overflowing with potting soil and every pack of marigold seeds I can find. Come Spring, I'm going to plant those seeds outside Kate's window—so many of them it will look like a sunrise every time she draws back her curtains.

Oh, I almost forgot. The second errand. On the way back from the flower store I'm going to stop at a pawn shop that has been there for forty years. I think they have a lot of guns there.

A Bite to Remember

by Jennifer Brozek

The two of them stood in the medical processing line, bragging about their respective wild nights. All around them stood the protected guard towers with trained snipers at the ready. Everyone in line ignored the towers. Quarantine zones always had guard towers and always had trained snipers. That was just the way it was in this day and age of possible (and probable) zombie uprisings. If you showed up looking disheveled and dirty, you were immediately suspect. This new world was the cleanest the human race had ever seen and personal hygiene was better than ever.

"Man, I'm tore up from the floor up." Steve said, rubbing his head. "You should've seen this woman. Smokin' hot and wild in bed."

"Yeah? Does she beat Diana?" John asked as they both took a step forward as the medical facility started processing the next person.

Steve paused, rubbing a sore spot on the backside of his left shoulder. "Not in looks, but damn, in bed, she was a fucking panic.

Teeth and nails and stamina that just would not quit." He grinned and leaned into John, "Damn near wore me out. Not that I'd admit it to her."

"And where is she, this wild woman of wonder?"

He gestured forward towards the head of the line. "Already in the protected zone. She's a secretary for some high-mucky-muck. Had to be to work on time. Left me a note. She's in the big leagues. Not like us scavengers who do triple the work and get half the pay."

John shrugged, "That's what an education'll get you." He paused as Steve sneezed. "I see you're in for the special treatment today."

"Yeah. I know. I hate colds. I hate having to explain, 'No, not bitten, just sick' about eight hundred thousand times." Steve sighed as he was waved in. "Don't wait up for me, man. I'll get there when I do." He turned forward and stepped into the first chamber of the processing booth.

He knew this routine so well he no longer remembered to get embarrassed as he stepped from the Identification Room and into the Possessions Room where he automatically stripped to the skin. He made a half-hearted attempt to fold his clothes before shoving them into the basket that would eventually be returned to him at the Final Room. He stepped from the Possessions Room to the Exam Room or the "Grin and Bare It" room in the common vernacular.

The Exam Room was where you grinned and bared it all—right down to bending over and lifting butt cheeks. Ladies got the extra special treat of lifting their breasts to allow examination under them. Steve did not even want to think about the pain of what fat people had to go through to show every inch of skin to prove they did not have the fatal Z-bite. After the last Z-terrorist, everyone went through this process. No more get bit, sneak into the protected zone and wait to die before rising again. Talk about a fucked up way to prove your religious group's point.

He stood there facing the screen with the pose of Da Vinci's *Vitruvian Man*, arms and legs spread, and waited as the front of him was scanned.

"Anything to report?" The disembodied voice sounded bored.

"I have a slight cold." Steve said and waited.

"Describe." Suddenly, the voice did not sound so bored.

"Sneezing and slight nausea. It may be a hangover." He waited and held his breath.

"Blood test ordered." There was a pause before the voice resumed that bored tone. "Turn around."

He relaxed and turned around. He closed his eyes, waiting for it to be over. Then there was a beeping sound he had never heard before. Steve opened his eyes to see a red glow shining in the Exam Room. "What? What's happening?"

Instead of answering him directly, but answering him nonetheless, the overhead alert system squawked out, "Level-W alert in Exam Room 3. Suspect bite mark in Exam Room 3."

Steve's eyes flicked up to the number above the exit to the Exam Room and saw the number '3' glowing red. He reached his right hand over his left shoulder to that sore spot and felt Jane's teeth marks there. At that moment, all hope that this was just a technical malfunction drained away and Steve prayed he would survive long enough to laugh about this with John later.

The next few moments were chaotic at best and terrifying at worst. More than once, Steve was certain he was dead. Nothing had happened at first, then the door between the Exam Room and the Decontamination Room slid open.

Normally, this room was empty. You would walk in to be sprayed down to kill most lingering skin germs. If a blood test was ordered, you would stick your hand in a hole in the wall where a sample was drawn. Then, the next door would open and you would walk from the Decontamination Room to the Final Room where you would get dressed, collect your other belongings and leave for the protected city center.

This time, when the door slid open, he could see two Zombie Squad members in full gear within. One was holding a riot shield, covering himself and his partner. The other was holding a large pistol pointed directly at Steve's head. The second threw what looked like a birdcage into the room, shouting, "Put that over your head. You have ten seconds to comply or you will be terminated immediately."

Steven did not hesitate. You did not fuck around with a member of the Z-Squad. Ever. He scrambled to it, lifted it up and put it over his head. As he did so he shouted, "It wasn't a zombie! It was a girl! We had sex! We had sex! She bit me!" Both Z-Squadders ignored him as the one who spoke to him clicked a button on a remote device. Steve's shouts of innocence were cut off by the sudden tightening of the collar of the head cage about his neck. The metal band pressed hard against his throat, cutting off his air for a moment as it automatically adjusted itself to the diameter of his neck.

As soon as it was set, both Z-Squad members entered the Exam Room. The one carrying the riot shield now had his pistol trained on Steve's head through a special opening in the riot shield while the second one grabbed his arm, frog marched him into the Decontamination Room and forced his arm into the hole for the blood sample. Then, a hidden door in the left wall of the Decontamination Room opened and he was marched down a hallway he had never seen before.

At the end of this hallway, there were six clear-walled holding cells, three on either side. Steve was unceremoniously shoved into one despite his continued protests that the bite mark was just a wild night. Once he was inside, the speaking member of the Zombie Squad said, "You'd better hope that's all it is. Otherwise, this is the last room you'll see."

The two of them started to turn away, but the second one paused and said, "There's a modesty towel on the bench."

The first Z-Squad member rolled his eyes and grabbed the second one by the arm, walking him away from the holding cell, "Jesus fuck, Rookie! They're not human until they're proven human. If he makes it out of this, you can buy him a beer but until then, that's not a human. That's the enemy. A zombie. Got it?"

"Yes sir."

"But, I'm not." Steve said. Again, his protest fell on deaf ears. He watched the two of them until they were out of sight before turning to the cell that could be his tomb.

Everything except the clear walls was a clinical white. It was a functional 8-by-8 foot cell with a smooth floor that sloped slightly downward to a large drain in the center. Otherwise, there was a basic toilet and a long bench that came out of the wall. On the bench was a white towel. He walked over to it, picked it up to look at it and then wrapped it around his waist.

When he turned back, he was shocked to see someone in a white coat standing outside his cell, watching him. He hurried to the man. "Look, I'm not infected. Really. I just had a wild night."

"First things first, Mr. Bough. Answer these questions. All I need is a yes or no answer. Do you understand?" The man was holding a clipboard.

"Yes."

"Is your full name Steven Allen Bough?"

"Yes."

"Is your age 32?"

"Yes."

"Is your identification number 4441-99-31862?"

"Yes." Steve was trying very hard to be patient but he was scared out of his mind.

"All right, Mr. Bough. I'm Doctor Taylor. I'm your assessor. You state that, and I quote, you had a 'wild night' last night. Where were you?"

"Yes. I did. It was the *Bandwagon Bar*."

He nodded. "And you claim to have gotten that bite mark from a lover?"

"Yes. It's just a love bite. The sex was rough but awesome. Really."

"Uh-huh. The name of the lover?"

Steve suddenly understood that this doctor followed the code of the Z-Squad. He was a zombie until proven human; something to be studied until too dangerous and then terminated. "Jane Sutherby."

Doctor Taylor nodded. "Thank you." He turned away from Steve.

"Wait!" Steve called out. "Wait! What happens now?"

The doctor did not deign to turn back to him. He spoke as he walked away. "Now we wait for the blood work to determine if you are infected or not while we find your partner."

Less than an hour later, Jane was in the holding cell next to him. She also wore a head cage but they had given her a modesty towel before bringing her down to this secret hallway. The way the Z-Squad acted around her said that they considered her still human and not a danger. She was here for observation only. She also did not receive a visit from Doctor Taylor so Steve had to assume she had been questioned elsewhere.

"Hey," he greeted her.

"Hey, yourself." Jane said. She hugged herself and gave him a brave smile before it disappeared again.

It melted his heart. "You okay?"

"Yeah. I think so. A little scared."

"I know what you mean."

She tried to tilt her head, a natural gesture of curiosity but the cage prevented her. She grimaced and sighed. "Nice digs you got here."

"This old place? I keep it for weekend holidays." The joke fell flat when she did not respond. He watched her. Something seemed off about her. For a woman dragged out of her office and into quarantine, she seemed very calm despite her professed fear. It disturbed him. He did not know why.

"You don't look so well. You okay?" She looked at him as she came to the wall closest to his cell. A smile hovered about her lips.

There was something malicious in that smile and, oddly, something familiar now that he was seeing her in full light, instead of the smoky dimness of the bar. His mind chewed this over for a moment before he shook it off and nodded. "I'm fine. Just a hangover from last night. Wild ride, huh?"

Jane chuckled. "Wilder for some," she said, crossing her arms over her towel clad breasts.

It was a defensive gestured he recognized. Also, there was a mean-ness in that laugh. Steve could swear that she was laughing at him. "What do you know?" He frowned at her, suspicious. He watched as she seemed to mentally struggle with herself and her reactions. Then, she relaxed and gave up all pretension of fear or kindness.

"Wouldn't you like to know?" Her voice was light and uncon-cerned but her eyes drank him in, flicking from his shoulder, where the bite was, to his face and back again.

"Yeah, I would."

She chose her words carefully. "Sometimes, Steve, the past comes back to haunt us. Especially past sins."

Again, that look in her eyes was beyond familiar. It was like he had seen her before somewhere else. "Do I know you?"

"You'd better. We did have a night to remember for the rest of our lives."

"That's not what I mean. You look . . . now that I can really see you, I know you." He struggled to put his mind to the task but, hon-estly, he was not feeling well. He had the chills, he was sweating and his head ached. He wished he could dash his face in cold water. Just at that moment, she said a name and it all came crashing down on him.

"Amy." She said.

Amy. Beautiful, sweet, dumb Amy. He was looking into her eyes right now. Only those eyes were looking out from another face. "Jesus."

"I don't think even Jesus can help you now." Gone was the sexual playmate from last night. In her place was an angry predator.

Fear gripped him by the balls. "What the fuck did you do to me?"

"What the fuck did you do to my baby sister? That's a better ques-tion." By this time, she had both hands pressed up against their adjoin-ing wall.

"Amy? She's your sister? What's she got to do with it?"

"Just answer the question, asshole. Then you'll have your answers."

He moved over to the adjoining wall and faced her. "You wanna make this about some messed up little girl, fine. What the fuck did I do to your baby sister? I dated her. Then I dumped her. That's what I did. She knew that's what was going to happen. She didn't want to go but I made her. I was done with her clinging. I made her go home."

"She never made it home."

That stopped Steve cold. "What? Why?"

"She walked in front of a train. Suicide. That same night you kicked her out of your house." Jane paused, "She was on the phone with me when she did it."

"Damn." He turned away, thinking of Amy. She had been a good lay. Not great but good. Her smile lit up a room but she was so needy—"Do you love me, Stevie?"—that it drove him crazy.

"She's dead and so are you." This last bit was spoken in more of a hiss than a whisper.

He swung back to the wall where Jane stood with a gruesomely triumphant grin on her face. "What?"

"You're dead. You're just too stupid to realize it yet."

Anger overrode the fear. He slammed a hand against the clear wall between them. "What did you do to me?" Then he paused and looked with growing horror at the sweat streak he left on the clear wall. "Dear God, what did you do?"

"You killed my sister. Now, I killed you. I just wanted to be here to watch you die."

All of the anger drained out of him. Fear replaced it. Perhaps that explained his shivers. "How'd you do it?"

Jane smiled a slow smile. "It took me a while to find you. Then, a little bit to get your attention. I wasn't nearly as drunk as you thought I was. Then back to your place for sex—which wasn't all that good, by the way—but was a small price to pay for my revenge. When you passed out, I rolled you on your side and poured infected blood on the bite mark I gave you."

"You didn't." His voice held no conviction.

"I did." Her smile was genuine. "I was very careful. Put gloves on and left right after. I didn't know how fast you'd change. I was just hoping I'd get to see it."

It all made sense in the hard light of day. He was here with a bird-cage on his head, waiting for blood test results and she was too sure. Suddenly, he was exhausted. All he wanted to do right now was sleep but that was near impossible with the head cage on. "They'll arrest you for this."

She shook her head. "No, they won't. They'll never know and I'm not infected."

"You don't think they're recording this?"

"I know they're not. All security in here is video only. The only time they can hear us is when they turn on the two way system to talk to us."

"How do you know?"

"My boss is the chief of security for this processing station. I know it inside and out." She looked him over again. "You're going to die soon and I'm going to get to watch it happen." Her smile widened into a leer of perverse joy.

He had been in the process of moving to sit on his bench but the anger seized him and he turned, running at the clear wall. He smashed up against it, jarring himself hard in the throat. "I'll kill you! I'll take you with me! I'll kill you!" He pounded against the clear wall, leaving great smears of sweat on it.

As she stepped back from the adjoining wall, the fear in her eyes was a gratifying sight to Steve. Then there was a brief sound of feed-back before a disembodied voice from above said, "Citizen 4441-99-31862 also known as Steven Allen Bough. It is my sad duty to inform you. . ."

Steve was barely listening. He screamed, "She did this to me!" He pointed at Jane. "She infected me. This is her fault!"

The disembodied voice did not pause and continued to talk over Steve's shouting. ". . . that you have been infected with the fatal Z-virus. There is no cure. You are to be terminated immediately follow-ing this announcement. In accordance with the laws of this govern-ment, this termination will be as swift and as painless as possible while ensuring that you will not rise again. Your most recent will on file will be carried out following your termination." There was a brief pause. "May God have mercy on your soul."

"No! Wait! She's the one who did this to me. Punish her! Kill her!" He kept jabbing his hand in the direction of Jane who still stood back from the adjoining wall. "She . . ."

Suddenly, there was a clicking noise and a hum from the bottom of Steve's head cage as directed charges were set off within. There was a soft *whump* sound as the explosives, honed by years of scientific study and progress, disintegrated the neck, severing the head from the body.

He lifted a hand upwards then let it drop down again. As it did so, Steve's head tumbled backwards from his body. A moment later, his body slumped forward on the ground. Jane watched as nozzles erupted from the ceiling and fire burned everything in the holding cell. She stepped back from the heat and covered her eyes. When it was done, automatic showers turned on and washed away the ashen remains of Steve Allen Bough from the floor.

Jane walked to the door of her cell and waited. Doctor Taylor walked down the hall to meet her. He unlocked her cell and released the lock on her head cage. "I'm sorry you had to endure all that, Miss Sutherby. Procedure, you know. Your blood work is clean."

"Where would we be without procedure?" She took off the cage and handed it to the doctor. "That's quite alllright. Proper protocol was followed and that is the way it's supposed to be. I'd much rather be inconvenienced for an hour than be responsible for another zombie uprising."

The Visitor

by Jack Ketchum

(For Neal McPheeters)

The old woman in bed number 418B of Dexter Memorial was not his wife. There was a strong resemblance though. Bea had died early on.

He had not been breathing well that night, the night the dead started walking, so they had gone to bed early without watching the news though they hated the news and probably would have chosen to miss it anyway. Nor had they awakened to anything alarming during the night. He still wasn't breathing well or feeling much better the following morning when John Blount climbed the stairs to the front door of their mobile home unit to visit over a cup of coffee as was his custom three or four days a week and bit Beatrice on the collarbone, which was not his custom at all.

Breathing well or not Will pried him off her and pushed him back down the stairs through the open door. John was no spring chicken either and the fall spread his brains out all across their driveway.

Will bundled Beatrice into the car and headed for the hospital half a mile away. And that was where he learned that all across Florida— all over the country and perhaps the world—the dead were rising. He learned by asking questions of the harried hospital personnel, the doctors and nurses who admitted her. Bea was hysterical having been bitten by a friend and fellow golfer so they sedated her and consequently it was doubtful that she ever learned the dead were doing anything at all. Which was probably just as well. Her brother and sister were buried over at Stoneyview Cemetery just six blocks away and the thought of them walking the streets of Punta Gorda again biting people would have upset her.

He saw some terrible things that first day.

He saw a man with his nose bitten off—the nosebleed to end all nosebleeds—and a woman wheeled in on a gurney whose breasts had been gnawed away. He saw a black girl not more than six who had lost an arm. Saw the dead and mutilated body of an infant child sit up and scream.

The sedation wore off. But Bea continued sleeping.

It was a troubled, painful sleep. They gave her painkillers through the IV and tied her arms and legs to the bed. The doctors said there was a kind of poison in her. They did not know how long it would take to kill her. It varied.

Each day he would arrive at the hospital to the sounds of sirens and gunfire outside and each night he would leave to the same. Inside it was relatively quiet unless one of them awoke and that only lasted a little while until they administered the lethal injection. Then it was quiet again and he could talk to her.

He would tell her stories she had heard many times but which he knew she would not mind his telling again. About his mother sending him out with a nickel to buy blocks of ice from the iceman on Stuyvesant Avenue. About playing pool with Jackie Gleason in a down-neck Newark pool hall just before the war and almost beating him. About the time he was out with his first-wife-to-be and his father-in-law-to-be sitting in a bar together and somebody insulted her and he took a swing at the guy but the guy had ducked and he pasted his future father-in-law instead.

He would urge her not to die. To try to come back to him.

He would ask her to remember their wedding day and how their friends were there and how the sun was shining.

He brought flowers until he could no longer stand the scent of them. He bought mylar balloons from the gift shop that said get well soon and tied them to the same bed she was tied to.

Days passed with a numbing regularity. He saw many more horrible things. He knew that she was lingering far longer than most did. The hospital guards all knew him at the door by now and did not even bother to ask him for a pass anymore.

"Four eighteen B," he would say but probably even that wasn't necessary.

Nights he'd go home to a boarded-up mobile home in an increasingly deserted Village, put a frozen dinner into the microwave and watch the evening news—it was all news now, ever since the dead started rising—and when it was over he'd go to bed. No friends came by. Many of his friends were themselves dead. He didn't encourage the living.

Then one morning she was gone.

Every trace of her.

The flowers were gone, the balloons, her clothing—everything. The doctors told him she had died during the night but that as of course he must have noticed by now, they had this down to pretty much a science and a humane one at that, and once she'd come back again it had been very quick and she hadn't suffered.

If he wanted he could sit there for a while, the doctor said. Or there was a grief counselor who could certainly be made available to him.

He sat.

In an hour they wheeled in a pasty-faced redhead perhaps ten years younger than Will with what was obviously a nasty bite out of her left cheek just above the lip. A kiss, perhaps, gone awry. The nurses did not seem to notice him there. Or if they did they ignored him. He sat and watched the redhead sleep in his dead wife's bed.

In the morning he came by to visit.

He told the guard four eighteen B.

He sat in the chair and told her the story about playing pool with Gleason, how he'd sunk his goddamn cue ball going after the eight, and about buying rotten hamburger during the Great Depression and his first wife crying well into the night over a pound of spoiled meat. He told her the old joke about the rooster in the hen yard. He spoke softly about friends and relations, long dead. He went down to the gift shop and bought her a card and a small potted plant for the window next to the bed.

Two days later she was gone. The card and potted plant were gone too and her drawer and closet were empty.

The man who lay there in her bed was about Will's age and roughly the same height and build and he had lost an eye and ear along with his thumb, index and middle fingers of his hand, all on the right side of his body. He had a habit of lying slightly to his left as though to turn away from what the dead had done to him.

Something about the man made Will think he was a sailor, some rough weathered texture to his face or perhaps the fierce bushy eyebrows and the grizzled white stubble of beard. Will had never sailed himself but he had always wanted to. He told the man about his summers at Asbury Park and Point Pleasant down at the Jersey shore, nights on the boardwalk and days with his family by the sea. It was the closest thing he could think of that the man might possibly relate to.

The man lasted just a single night.

Two more came and went—a middle-aged woman and a pretty teenage girl.

He did not know what to say to the girl. It had been years since he had even spoken to a person who was still in her teens—unless you could count the cashiers at the market. So he sat and hummed to himself and read to her out of a four-month-old copy of *People* magazine.

He bought her daisies and a small stuffed teddy bear and placed the bear next to her on the bed.

The girl was the first to die and then come back in his presence.

He was surprised that it startled him so little. One moment the girl was sleeping and the next she was struggling against the straps which bound her to the bed, the thick grey-yellow mucus flowing from her mouth and nose spraying the sheets they had wrapped around her tight. There was a sound in her throat like the burning of dry leaves.

Will pushed his chair back toward the wall and watched her. He had the feeling there was nothing he could say to her.

On the wall above a small red monitor light was blinking on and off. Presumably a similar light was blinking at the nurses' station because within seconds a nurse, a doctor and a male attendant were all in the room and the attendant was holding her head while the doctor administered the injection through her nostril far up into her brain. The girl shuddered once and then seemed to wilt and slide deep down into the bed. The stuffed bear tumbled to the floor.

The doctor turned to Will.

"I'm sorry," he said. "That you had to see this."

Will nodded. The doctor took him for a relative.

Will didn't mind.

They pulled the sheet up over her and glanced at him a moment longer and then walked out through the doorway.

He got up and followed. He took the elevator down to the ground floor and walked past the guard to the parking lot. He could hear automatic weapons-fire from the Wal-Mart down the block. He got into his car and drove home.

After dinner he had trouble breathing so he took a little oxygen and went to bed early. He felt a lot better in the morning.

Two more died. Both of them at night. Passed like ghosts from his life.

The second to die in front of him was a hospital attendant. Will had seen him many times. A young fellow, slightly balding. Evidently he'd been bitten while a doctor administered the usual injection because the webbing of his hand was bandaged and suppurating slightly.

The attendant did not go easily. He was a young man with a thick muscular neck and he thrashed and shook the bed.

The third to die in front of him was the woman who looked so much like Bea. Who had her hair and eyes and general build and coloring.

He watched them put her down and thought, this was what it was like. Her face would have looked his way. Her body would have done that.

On the morning after she died and rose and died again he was walking past the first-floor guard, a soft little heavy-set man who had known him by sight for what must have been a while now. "Four eighteen B," he said.

The guard looked at him oddly.

Perhaps it was because he was crying. The crying had gone on all night or most of it and here it was morning and he was crying again. He felt tired and a little foolish. His breathing was bad.

He pretended that all was well as usual and smiled at the guard and sniffed the bouquet of flowers he'd picked from his garden.

The guard did not return the smile. He noticed that the man's eyes were red-rimmed too and felt a moment of alarm because he seemed to sense that the eyes were not red as his were simply from too much crying. But you had to walk past the man to get inside so that was what he did.

The guard clutched his arm with his little white sausage fingers and bit at the stringy bicep just below the sleeve of Will's shortsleeved shirt. There was no one in the hall ahead of him by the elevators, no one to help him.

He kicked the man in the shin and felt dead skin rip beneath his shoe and wrenched his arm away. Inside his chest he felt a kind of snapping as though someone had snapped a twig inside him.

Heartbreak?

He pushed the guard straight-arm just as he had pushed John Blount so long ago and although there were no stairs this time there was a fire extinguisher on the wall and the guard's head hit it with a large clanging sound and he slid stunned down the face of the wall.

Will walked to the elevator and punched four. He concentrated on his breathing and wondered if they would be willing to give him oxygen if he asked them for it.

He walked into the room and stared.

The bed was empty.

It had never been empty. Not once in all the times he'd visited.

It was a busy hospital.

That the bed was empty this morning was almost confusing to him. As though he had fallen down a rabbit-hole.

Still he knew it wasn't wise to argue when after all this time one finally had a stroke of luck.

He put the slightly battered flowers from his garden in a water-glass. He drew water in the bathroom sink. He undressed quietly and found an open-backed hospital gown hanging in the closet and slipped it on over his mottled shoulders and climbed into bed between clean fresh-smelling sheets. The bite did not hurt much and there was just a little blood.

He waited for the nurse to arrive on her morning rounds.

He thought how everything was the same, really. How nothing much had changed whether the dead were walking or not. There were those who lived inside of life and those who for whatever reason did not or could not. Dead or no dead.

He waited for them to come and sedate him and strap him down and wished that he had somebody to talk to— to tell the Gleason story, maybe, one last time. Gleason was a funny man in person just as he was on TV but with a foul nasty mouth on him, always cussing, and he had almost beat him.

The Song of Absent Birds

by Mark Onspaugh

Dylan Walsh dried his breakfast dishes and put them away. He wiped down the counter and made sure the burners were turned off on the stove.

He was dressed in a blue and white plaid flannel shirt his grandchildren had sent him. He wore this with a tee shirt, jeans and heavy work boots. He pulled a jacket off a hook by the front door, and slipped it on. Although the temperature in the Underground never varied, it always felt cold to him in the winter. He supposed it was age creeping into his bones rather than a winter chill from topside.

He checked himself in the mirror before he left. It was a big day and he wanted to look his best. He had gotten his hair cut and his mustache trimmed. His hair had receded quite a bit in the last ten years, and the lines on his face were much deeper, but he figured he didn't look too bad. He had managed to get old without getting fat, and tried to keep up with contemporary styles without looking ridiculous. He had gotten a manicure, too. Marie might have laughed at that.

He smiled, then grabbed the bouquet of margarites and walked out the front door.

A little sign on the door read, "Doctor Dylan Walsh, MD, OB-GYN." Maintenance would be removing it tomorrow, but the brass had said he could keep the apartment. A perk for forty-five years of loyal service.

In the corridor, left would take him to the public tubes and transportation throughout the Tri-Sector area.

Doctor Walsh turned right.

He walked to an exit marked "Authorized Personnel Only". He punched in his code and the door opened for him with a faint click.

He stepped into the service corridor just as Mac pulled up. He was driving one of those little electric carts they all used. The front of the cart read "ZDC—Official Use Only" and a series of numbers and letters. It seemed like a lot of fanfare for a glorified golf cart.

"Morning, Doc," Mac said, his bulk dwarfing the little vehicle.

Kyle "Mac" McCready offered him a beefy hand and hauled him up onto the passenger seat. Once the doctor was situated, Mac stepped on the accelerator and they sped off.

Mac talked the entire way to the access shaft. Non-stop.

Nothing important or compelling, just stats on the inter-sector magball playoffs and the coming election. Walsh could tell Mac was trying to distract him. He'd known the young man most of his life. There was almost no one under thirty in his sector that he hadn't delivered and treated.

At an intersection Mac yielded to a flatbed vehicle carrying several figures wrapped in heavy white canvas and bound with bright yellow nylon ropes. The bundles were secured with colorfully striped bungee cords. One wrapped bundle thrashed spastically.

"B 'n' G," Mac said, grinning, "Binding and grinding." As he passed the flatbed he and the other driver, a fellow "zed-head," gave each other the waggle-finger "hang loose" greeting.

Mac had grown from a skinny little kid with freckles to a big, beefy block of a man with a head the size and color of a canned ham. The freckles were still there, though, and Walsh knew the other zed-heads razzed Mac about them, calling him "Opie" and "Howdy Doody." Jesus. Those TV characters were ancient when Walsh was a kid. He guessed that was the blessing (or curse) of a crystalline memtrix.

Nothing of pop culture got lost—just preserved, recycled, reused. Like people.

They scooted along the corridor, which smelled vaguely like machine oil and cloves. Unlike the public ways which were a riot of colors, sounds and smells and lined with shops, food and service kiosks, and ad-info screens, the service corridor was gray and unremarkable. Its smooth contours sometimes erupted in a profusion of pipes and conduits, then it became featureless again. The cart was smooth and quiet, its efficient little hum no match for Mac's chattering.

If Mac was worried about what they were about to do, he didn't admit it. Of course, nothing illegal would occur until the hatch had been breached.

They passed an access port for the grinders, and Walsh could hear the hollow thrumming as the big drums started up, waiting for the cargo now some one hundred yards behind them. He tried not to think of what happened beyond those walls. As a doctor he knew human corpses were just a collection of bone, blood and muscle. Rendering them down to their essential components before they reanimated was logical and efficient.

But as a husband and a father he wondered what might survive once life was over, what ephemeral and splendid energy might now be irrevocably linked to dead matter. Surely something had changed since the Incident. Dead was no longer dead, so what remained? What essence of a person was retained inside a zed? It was a question that had been argued since the Incident.

People still called them "zombies" in the early days, before activists claimed the term too pejorative and judgmental, ill-befitting a group that contained so many friends, relatives, civil servants and sports heroes. The more politically and emotionally neutral "zed" took its place. Thus, members of the former Zombie Retaliation Force were now members of the Zed Defense Corps. Walsh had never liked the term zombie, either, but for different reasons. He still remembered a time when a zombie was a term for a supernatural creature, someone raised from a grave to act as a servant. And "zed"? Colorless and without any poetry, which is just what the brass wanted. He himself preferred "shamblers" or "lurchers." Some called them "wanderers," but Walsh felt that was a little too romantic for a creature that wanted to feed on you.

About a year after the evacuation a new Christian sect surfaced, calling themselves the Saint Lazarus Church of the Resurrection and the Life, the Undeath and the Unlife. They were trying to resolve questions like whether shamblers had souls. Having never been one for organized religion, Walsh always felt questions of sacred versus profane were intensely private, more so now that the two seemed fused. Besides, the tenets of the Lazarus sect had never seemed particularly inspired or well thought-out to him. They seemed more of a "cut and paste" approach, borrowing from all the major religions and several science fiction novels of the 1960's. He politely refused membership and they had finally stopped leaving leaflets and donation envelopes in his office mail drop.

Two workmen were repairing a water pipe as they passed, and neither gave them a second glance. It was as Mac had said: if you seem to be on official or authorized business (he used the slang term "righteous"), then people left you alone.

Walsh's hands were cramped and he realized he was gripping the bouquet too tightly. Mac had balked at the flowers at first, saying Walsh might as well mount a big neon sign on the cart proclaiming "I AM GOING OUTSIDE!" Walsh told him he was being paranoid, that he had often taken flowers with him on his rounds.

He loosened his grip, holding the bouquet with one hand as he flexed the other. His hands had been so nimble, once. Clever little creatures that could stitch a wound or bring a child into the world. Now arthritis was making them strangers to him, twisting them into wicked shapes for cruel shadow puppets. Unpredictable and unreliable, manageable only through more and more frequent doses of various pain relievers.

Old age sucked.

There was a sudden lull in Mac's monolog and Walsh realized he had never asked Mac about their destination.

"Have you seen it, Mac?"

Mac looked at him, puzzled for a moment. "The Forest of Anubis?" he asked.

"Yes."

"Yeah," he said, nodding, "Every zed-head takes a tour of the woods. Course, it changes every year, that's what makes it even creepier. You never know how it's going to end up."

"A colleague of mine was trying to chart migration patterns of the sham—uh, zeds."

"Shit, Doc, I don't care what you call them. You should hear some of the terms we use when we're not around civs. Maggot-bags, pus-buckets, meat-puppets . . . "

"I guess you're right."

"Migration patterns, huh? Brass has talked about that kind of stuff. Thing is, they always thought they'd reach some point of diminishing returns. Old zeds falling apart, new ones being ground up and burned or recycled. 'Asses to ashes' as my old man used to say. Some point where the attrition rate of maggot-bags would outstrip the supply."

"But that's not happening."

"Fuck no. Part of it's that the damn things don't seem to fall apart. Oh, they rot plenty fast, but they seem to stop decaying with just enough musculature left to move around. Techs are going nuts trying to figure that out."

"And some sectors don't believe in recycling."

"Yeah, bunch of unlife fanatics. No burning, no grinding. They just turn their zeds loose on the surface as some kind of bullshit living memorial." Mac looked at him guiltily. "No offense, Doc."

Walsh waved him off. "I've heard there's also been smuggling, even in here."

Mac nodded, his mouth drawing in a thin line. "Top brass is really pissed about that. Here they hope to reclaim the surface and our own people are smuggling friends and relatives to the surface before the B & G Wagon arrives. T.B. says that any zed-head involved in or aiding such practices gets a one-way ticket to the Big Blender."

"I appreciate the risk you three are taking for me, Mac."

He patted him on the shoulder. "My pleasure, Doc. Besides, all you're smuggling is flowers."

They rode the rest of the way in silence, passing several access shafts until they came to one he needed.

Mac parked the little cart near a weapons locker and they were met by the guard on duty, Dana Chang. Dana had been one of Walsh's patients, as had her husband, Andy, and daughter, Delia. She smiled when she saw him.

Dana helped him out of the cart and gave him a quick hug. Her husband had suffered a burst appendix fifteen years ago and they had nearly lost him. His hands had been faithful and true in those days and worked their magic. Five years later his good hands delivered the Chang's baby.

Dana led Mac and him to the hatch, which was being guarded by a fresh-faced young corporal named Oganesyan. It didn't matter what his first name was, all newbie zed-heads were called "Chuck," as in "ground chuck". Some found the appellation distasteful, but Walsh knew it was to remind the newbs that that's all they were to shamblers topside—fresh meat.

Chuck wasn't happy about breaking the rules, but wasn't about to argue with vets like Mac and Dana. The hazing of zed-head newbs was the stuff of nightmares, with some losing a finger (or worse) or becoming infected with Zed-17 and ending up in the grinders. The brass tried to curtail it, but they knew that living underground created a lot of lethal pressures that had to be vented.

Dana had shut down the west perimeter cameras "for mainte-nance." She had also overridden the sensors so that the hatch could be opened without setting off alarms. Such procedures were not unheard of; several times a years outer cameras and perimeter fences had to be repaired. And security was a bit more lax this time of year, everyone thinking of the big holiday festival in the central quad. People feasted and prayed, exchanged gifts and decorated homes, sang and danced and lit candles, all to show gratitude for another year of survival.

Dana nodded to Chuck and he punched in the code to open the access hatch. It opened with a sharp hiss and then silently slid into its recess. Dana and Mac had their guns trained on the opening and Walsh held his breath, but nothing was there.

Dana held Walsh's flowers as he pulled on the gloves and wool hat he had stuffed in his jacket. He took the bouquet back, and then Doctor Dylan Walsh walked out of the hatch, his heart beating fiercely.

He walked out into the snow, breathing topside air for the first time in forty-five years. He took in great draughts of it, delighting in the sensation of air actually cold enough to chill your insides. His eyes teared up and he coughed, doubling over for a moment. Mac moved toward him, but Walsh waved him off, laughing.

"The air is so sweet," he gasped.

Mac nodded and grinned.

The sun shone sulkily through the haze, just enough to provide a pearlescent light. His breath puffed out in little clouds and his boots crunched through the snow as Mac and Dana led him to the perime-ter fence, a sturdy affair of steel plates welded in a large circle. It was ten feet high, fifty feet in diameter and topped with cameras and razor wire. No shambler could surmount that barrier. They reached the gate, which was secured with a heavy sliding bolt.

Dana had her tru-vu and checked the outside. She did a complete sweep and nodded. Mac unlocked the gate and they opened it far enough for him to slip through.

"You know where you're going?" Dana asked.

He knew she was actually giving him a chance to back out, to change his mind. He held up the little GPS monitor and it peeped once, as if answering her.

Walsh squeezed through the gate, and then stopped in stunned silence.

He had seen photos and film of "The Forest of Anubis" before, but it was something else to be in it.

Instead of trees there were hundreds of shamblers, perhaps thousands, frozen in place. Many stood, silent and still, their arms at their sides, temporarily suspended from their ceaseless wanderings, their insatiable appetites. The sun sparkled off their agonized and ruined faces, now crystallized and dusted with snow, terrible spun sugar confections for an unending *Dia de los Muertos*.

Each shambler had a clearance of about three or four feet around it, as if they did not want to be crowded during their period of suspended animation. Walsh wove his way carefully through the figures, forcing himself to remain calm in this Land of the Dead. He listened for the customary growl of a shambler, for their mournful, awful wailing, but there was only his own breathing.

Walsh chuckled. Seventy-five and he was still able to get the heebie-jeebies. He consulted the monitor and moved forward, hearing only his own breathing and the crunch of ice under his boots.

Then there was another sound, a strange low whistle. Walsh thought there might be a bird singing, but then he remembered that a strain of the zed virus had killed most of the birds topside.

This sound had a mournful quality to it, like blowing into a bottle or jug, and he realized many of the frozen dead had ragged wounds that went entirely through a limb or torso. The same wind which was chilling him and sending up little frost devils was also whistling through this frozen charnel house, making the corpses into a sort of hellish pan pipes, an instrument worthy of the god Hades. What madness and despair would be found in such music?

Walsh shook his head, chiding himself for being seduced by the strange and perverse amusements of this place. He had to hurry, so he walked a bit faster, trying to ignore the eerie sound and concentrate on his goal.

Come the spring, the sun would thaw them out. Their chaotic neurons would begin firing again and they would lurch, shamble, crawl and worm their way in search of food.

Mac and Dana caught up to him, leaving Chuck to guard the gate and contact them if there were any movements on the perimeter sensors.

"Welcome to the Forest of Anubis," Mac said, gesturing in an expansive manner. "Also known as 'The Valley of the Corpsicles' and 'Maggot-Bags on Ice'."

"What do you think brings them here in such number?" Walsh asked.

"Prof of mine said it's the smell of the grinders," Dana said "They smell the tang of flesh and blood that isn't quite turned. Guess it'd be like good barbecue to us."

"I heard it was sound," Mac said. "The maggot-bags are like dogs, they can hear all kinds of shit we can't. Somebody else said they can see emanations from power sources, some kind of adaptation to find living people."

"It's a marvel that people just . . . let them be," Walsh said.

"Believe me, Doc, if they could get the funding, they'd have us out here every year with some porta-grinders making pus-burgers."

"Or at least expending a few thousand rounds for head shots," Dana added.

"The newbs do come out here for target practice," Mac said. On seeing the alarm on Walsh's face he quickly added, "No one goes as far as we're going, Doc. It's okay."

Walsh nodded, relieved.

The three of them hiked about a quarter of a mile, watching the ground for crawlers who had frozen low to the ground. There was no danger of attack, of course, each was frozen solid, about as dangerous as a leg of lamb just out of the freezer. However, tripping over such an obstacle might mean a serious injury for an old man like him. He did not want Dana and Mac to have to carry him back to the hatch.

Most of the undead they passed were dressed in rags that had long ago faded to colorless tatters or were soiled beyond recognition. Still others were completely naked, their clothes no match for the punishment of endless wandering.

And there were those whose role in life was still recognizable from their costumes or uniforms—people released or smuggled into the open by grieving families or well-meaning friends.

They passed soldiers and cops, joggers and toddlers, business types and the elderly.

Here was a Scotsman, dressed in the proud kilt and tartan of his clan, his visage something out of *Macbeth*.

Here a nanny with a stroller, its occupant like some grotesque doll, its lips a clown smear of crimson.

Here a naked young man, frozen in an attitude of lithe grace, a latter-day David save for a missing hand and ribbons of flesh hanging from a ravaged abdomen.

Here a group of little girls, still in their school uniforms, their pigtails and pixie cuts belying faces of demons and ghouls, carved now in ice and frost like Norse trolls.

Here was a zed-head pinned under a sno-mobile who had been set upon by others as the temperature had dropped. Come the thaw he would join them, all previous hurts forgotten as they searched the countryside for living flesh.

The forest was a good square mile, packed with nightmare growths that would move on in spring, Shakespeare's Birnam Wood made flesh.

Every race, every variant of humanity was represented in a great sculpture garden of flesh and ice. A spectrum of hues dialed down to varying shades of blue-gray.

Dana checked her tru-vu and pointed, but Walsh had already spotted her.

Marie.

His heart quickened because, unlike the others, Marie had a hand out, as if beckoning to him. Walsh hurried to her and Dana and Mac hung back a respectful distance.

Even under the patina of ice and snow he could see she had not changed in forty-five years. He had become old, but his Marie was still twenty-five, her flawless skin now rendered like a work of fine crystal. Her hair was still as fine and blonde as when it had smelled of flowers and cinnamon.

She had been so beautiful, so young.

It had been seven years since the Incident. Their first and only son Taylor was a healthy little boy five months of age. They had been scheduled to evacuate to the Sector 25 complex, and Marie had fallen in the tub. She had died instantly. To this day he had cursed the irony of surviving an apocalypse only to be killed in such a banal way. People with shamblers or potential shamblers in their homes were legally bound to destroy them by decapitation and burning before evacuating.

He couldn't do it.

Apparently a lot of people couldn't. The size of the forest attested to that.

He had taken their baby and left Marie dressed in her favorite sun-dress, one that had been a gift from him early in their courtship. Knowing she would soon wake to a strange world, he had secured a GPS cuff to her ankle. He had then kissed her goodbye, his eyes blurring as he got onto the bus, their baby wailing in his arms.

Every night he would check the tracker's monitor for some sign of her. When Taylor grew older he joined his father. They placed the monitor between them on the kitchen table like some oracle, and waited for a pronouncement on the fate of Marie. As they waited for a signal, they wondered where she might be, wondered where her travels might take her.

They had dreamed of exploring the world as husband and wife, and Walsh thought that desire might be in her, still. Of course, the fact that she might be looking for him, some steadfast memory driving her too-cool flesh in restless search had caused him many a sleepless night. Had he doomed her to a futile, meandering existence?

Walsh had never remarried. As long as he knew Marie was out

there somewhere he had worn his ring and stayed true.

Taylor had grown into a fine man and left to raise his own family in a nearby sector. He was a supervisor in hydroponics and had long ago stopped wondering about his mother. To Taylor, the important part of her was in heaven, the rest an empty shell of which he had no real memory. If his children had ever wondered about their grandmother, they had never asked Walsh.

Walsh stopped checking the monitor about fifteen years ago. He had first put it in a drawer, then in a box that contained their wedding album and a light blue sweater Marie used to wear, the scent of her long faded, except in his memory.

Three months ago, the peeping of the monitor brought him out of a deep sleep. He had awakened thinking he was hearing a clock radio alarm he had owned as a boy. He stumbled to the closet and gazed at the monitor in wonder and guilt.

He had given up. She had not.

Now they were together again, meeting in this impossible place where the dead waited for the sun to free them.

"I brought you some flowers," he whispered, "Margarites, your favorite." He tried to place them in her hand but they fell to the ground. He chided himself. She was not some doll to pose and make pretty. "I'm sorry," he said.

He took off his gloves and stuffed them in his coat. He ran quivering fingers over the sweet curve of her cheek, the pads of those fingers freezing slightly on her generous mouth and stinging as he pulled them free. Would she taste him come the spring thaw? Would it spark some atavistic memory, some inchoate longing?

He ran his fingertips lightly over her left breast, its size and shape halted by viral alchemy and freezing temperatures in the youthful contours of their courtship. He worried now at her being so scantily dressed, the sundress sheer and lightly patterned with light yellow margarites over a field of pale blue. A blue now faded to match her pale flesh. He tried to ignore the blood stains down the front, daisies turned to macabre roses, and the fact that much of the dress was torn and tattered. His Marie would have been appalled by her own appearance, and for a moment he feared she might be embarrassed.

In life, she had worn the dress on a picnic in Griffith Park. They had found a little knoll under a huge oak. The park had been full of sound, the music of a carousel, the distant laughter of playing children and birdsong in the trees. So many birds in those days! Finches, wrentits, mocking birds, jays, thrashers and quail. Even the hummingbirds and crows had added to that marvelous cacophony of life. He and Marie had eaten fine old cheeses and artisanal breads, crisp red apples and luscious, juicy plums. They shared a bottle of wine he had been saving, and he toasted her beauty and the sheer joy of being with her. Then Marie had slyly revealed that she was wearing nothing underneath her pale blue sundress. Out from under the shade of the old oak the sun had shown through the light fabric, illuminating her soft curves, the cleft of her sex, the rosy pink of her nipples. They had made love near the site of the old zoo, a place no longer frequented by visitors and echoing with the ghosts of creatures long extinct. Her eyes had widened slightly as he had entered her, and then a knowing smile touched her as their rhythms matched, their breathing becoming that of a single creature.

Though he had dressed her in that same sheer and ephemeral confection, he had also modestly clothed her in a simple white bra and cotton panties. She might be lost to him, but he could not shake such ingrained feelings of propriety. Those feelings resurfaced when he saw that she still wore the lingerie. It was silly, but he was glad his sweet wife had not roamed the Earth naked and bloody, some perverse Venus bringing nothing but wailing and terrible teeth.

Marie had often gone without makeup, and he had not applied any to her before leaving. He wouldn't have known where to begin. He had brushed her shining hair and pulled it through a scrunchy into a ponytail. She lay there, looking much like she had on that picnic. He held his tears until he and Taylor were on the transport, and then could stay them no longer. He thought he might never stop weeping.

Now there was an ugly gash on her left bicep, and he wondered if it caused her pain. The wound was bloodless, and the physician in him surmised that she must have caught her arm on a projecting bit of rebar or a shattered door jamb.

Wandering was not without consequence for his Marie.

"I'm sorry," he whispered, old tears reappearing with surprising swiftness. "I'm sorry I have been away from you all these years."

She stood there, her face neither forgiving nor reproachful, no tears of happy reunion or festering resentment. If he stared long enough into her frozen face, he was sure some trick of the light would lend her the appearance of animation like those old wax figures, but he knew better.

She was dead.

And yet . . .

In such a time where death brings no rest, might not the mind itself be active? Might old pathways fire, however sporadically? Might not old memories bloom like temporary fireworks across the scarred and barren mindscape?

Might not the girl he had first seen under a tree bursting with cherry blossoms be there still?

It was a question that might never be answered, and his time was short.

He told her of their son and his family. That their eldest granddaughter had a child of her own, one named Marie in her honor. He told her of his work, his patients, of the trials of living underground and how much he missed her.

He told her how he loved her, and that he had decided—

"Doctor Walsh?"

He turned, the sound of a human voice and his own name like foreign things, syllables of a long-dead language.

Mac regretfully pointed to his watch. "We gotta get back . . . changing of the guard."

He nodded, thinking of what waited back in the Underground. Years of retirement spent with other seniors. Perhaps some teaching or lectures, he might even write a book.

And then, the grinders. No bells tolling in the Underground, just the massive drums studded with metal teeth, their hollow booming the mechanical equivalent of the wailing topside. There was no one who would smuggle the corpse of Doctor Dylan Walsh to the surface. His children were too pragmatic, products of living in confinement with chaotic and ravening storms outside the gates. Storms that might literally consume them if they did not live practically.

What happened next had only been a vague contingency when he had gotten up that morning. A silly pipe dream that his logical side had nearly forgotten, for it was foolish and selfish and risky, particularly to his young friends.

But sometimes an old heart can be surprisingly strong against a mind grown weary with too many years of memory, too many years ahead of emptiness.

He turned and pretended to kiss Marie's cheek, placing the gel capsule in his mouth and crunching down on it. He then motioned to Mac and Dana. Something in his face caused them to hurry to him.

"I thank you both for bringing me out here," he began.

"We owe you a lot, Doc," Mac said. Dana nodded.

"I have just ingested a lethal amount of Harrowcept," he told them, and watched their faces move from incomprehension to horror.

Mac moved to pick him up and Walsh waved him off.

"Mac, you know this is where I want to be. Where I should be."

"They'll look for you, Doc."

He shook his head. "I'll be frozen before reanimating. No one is going to expend the resources to bring one old man down to the grinders."

They looked doubtful, and he could see the guilty looks as they consider the ramifications to their careers.

"I'm sorry, I know this will complicate things for you," he admitted.

"No worries," Dana said. "We . . . we don't know anything."

"Yeah," Mac agreed. "Your disappearance will be a mystery to us, should anybody ask."

"And Corporal Oganesyan?"

"We'll take care of Chuck," Mac promised.

Dana kissed his cheek. He couldn't feel it. The Harrowcept was weaving a net of numbness over him.

Mac gave him a rough hug, wiping a tear from his eye. The two made their way back to the gate, looking back at him several times. It was difficult to wave, so he saved his energy.

As the gate closed, he placed his arms around Marie's waist, her extended arm providing just enough support to hold him up. He placed the flowers between them, hoping some of their brightness might attract her eyes when sight returned.

"Please know me," he whispered into her ear. "Please know me and take me back. I'm sorry I left you. Please don't leave me alone in the dark."

He rested his cheek against her shoulder, tears freezing his eyelids shut.

"Come the spring," he whispered hoarsely, "we'll go on a picnic."

Walsh thought he could hear her sigh, though it may have been an errant breeze. Still, he smiled and let the cold take him.

LIFE

The Loneliest Man in the World
by Bobbie Metevier

Old Stanley Dodge never knew how they were going to behave until he got them strapped to the battered recliner. That last one had been a real corker, craning his rotting neck from side to side like some kind of pterodactyl. Stanley hadn't been able to get *that* corpse interested in the *I Love Lucy* DVDs to save his own life. He'd kept him around though, kept him right up until he broke into sixteen withered pieces.

Stanley was sentimental that way.

The neighbors complained—what few neighbors he had left, that is. After the outbreak, seven years ago, the survivors who hadn't fled had moved to the upper floors. Most corpses couldn't do the stairs. Their legs would snap away from rot somewhere around the third landing.

He had a girl strapped to the Lazy Boy now—her dead eyes staring straight ahead and her mouth snapping at flies.

"You have one of those awful things in there, don't you, Stanley?" It was Muriel Steinbeck from apartment 8G banging on his door again. She never could mind her business. This had been true before the plague, and not much had changed.

Stanley pretended to be asleep.

When she'd gone, he heard Little Hector firing his pistol from the rooftop. Years of practice had made Hector a sharpshooter, but it made for slim pickings where Stanley's DVD buddies were concerned.

Stanley moved about his cluttered apartment, steering clear of the corpse. He opened the window off the fire escape and hollered up to Little Hector, "Put that pistol away before you shoot somebody."

"Get back inside, Stanley," the voice drifted down. "You whack, and you need to keep yo' whack ass inside."

Stanley closed his window and sighed.

Little Hector had been waiting patiently, Stanley knew, for the People's Liberation Army to come "bust some caps" like they'd done in Union City. Actually—according to rumor—the PLA had swept Union City several times over the years. Stanley suspected that it would still be awhile before they made their way to his neighborhood. The inner-city projects were always last priority. This had been true before the outbreak, and probably always would be.

At least the powers-that-be had restored electricity. It took them five years to do so, but at least there was that. There weren't any television stations, but Stanley had looted the video store downstairs. He'd taken all the classics on DVD and a player to match.

It was good. The outbreak was good. Stanley hadn't had a real companion in years. Now, whenever the mood hit him, he plucked himself a buddy. He named them too—not that he was good with names.

If memory served, there had been a Stink, a Stink Two, a Baby Stink, a Firefighter Stink and a Stink Low. Stink Low had not been as stinky as the others. Once he found a young girl wearing a bent tiara and expensive shoes. She'd been known as Princess Stink.

Tonight though—tonight he wanted to find himself a real buddy, a corpse that might actually *enjoy Lawrence of Arabia* for a change.

And why not?

His refrigerator was stocked with root beer, and he had four unopened bags of cashews. Why shouldn't a man have a guest if he wanted one?

Now, it was only a matter of bribing Little Hector to help him take the girl—known affectionately as Sister Stink—down the landing to be set free.

They'd had a good ride, Stanley and Sister Stink. Just last night they'd watched *Breakfast at Tiffany's* together. Sure, she'd groaned through most of it, but had gone strangely quiet at the mention of champagne.

In the film, George Peppard said, *"I don't think I've ever drunk champagne before breakfast before. With breakfast on a few occasions, but never before before."*

That was all it took. She stared at the screen, filmy and colorless eyes blazing. Maybe she'd been a drinker in life, and maybe that's all it took. You had to grab a Stink and give him or her a glimpse into what they'd been before.

Stanley opened his window and hollered for Hector. "I've got a proposition for you, Hector. Come down here."

"A propawhat?" Stanley watched Hector's legs dangle over the side of the building. A moment later the fourteen-year-old was on Stanley's fire escape.

"I want you to help me get her out of here. Then I want you to help me bring up another."

"Whatchu gonna give me, you crazy shit?"

Stanley considered this. While there weren't any businesses open yet, Stanley knew they'd be opening soon. He'd seen the fliers. He knew about *The New Deal*—not quite as clever as President Roosevelt's had been, but it would go a long way toward restarting the economy. *Fifty thousand dollars to restart your business,* The New Deal promised, *loans to be repaid after five years.* Would money be a good trade off for Little Hector's services? Stanley didn't think so—not yet.

"I'll let you watch *Scarface* again." Stanley sighed in disgust. The idea of that trash playing on the very machine that had hosted

Philadelphia Story turned his stomach.

"Say hello to my little friend," Little Hector said, raising his pistol to the ceiling.

Little Hector hoisted her legs. His refusal to stand at the head of the corpse didn't surprise Stanley. While Little Hector liked to play gangsta, he was soft at heart and lost without his pistol—nothing like John Wayne in *True Grit* or George C. Scott in *Patton*.

"Her skin is comin' off under my nails," Little Hector whined.

"Just keep hoistin'."

They made their way down the fire escape quickly, not wanting to incur the wrath of Muriel Steinbeck from 8G. All the while the corpse's mouth snapped at the air, trapping the occasional fly. Stanley knew how to keep his hands away from the corpse's mouth. He carried her by the wrists, out and away from her decaying torso.

"Fuckin' stinks," Hector complained. "Fuckin' whack, man. Fuckin' whack. This *not* how I roll, *esse*."

"Almost there."

When they reached the lowest level, they released the corpse, dangling it over the side until its feet touched solid ground. Together they watched as Sister Stink lurched down the street, disappearing around a corner.

The plan now was for Stanley to select his new corpse and go back for Hector's help. The dead were slow walkers. If Stanley found his prize on Second Avenue, chances were it would still be on Second Avenue hours later.

"Go on up and watch your movie," Stanley said. "Meet me back here in three hours. I got huntin' to do."

Stanley Dodge stood on the street corner glancing at the burned-out Chicken Shack Diner, at the dilapidated Tina's House of Tacos and at all the *living* people. There wasn't a corpse in sight thanks to Little Hector and his pistol.

Stanley only sighed. It was always the same thing, the streets teeming with *life*. He longed for the good old days when there were Stinks swarming around every corner, just waiting to moan and writhe their way through *Citizen Kane*.

According to the fliers there were still plenty of Stinks to be had too—eighty/twenty split in favor of the Stenchies—but damn if Stanley could find them lately.

He had cashews for Christ's sake and a case of root beer to boot! He'd looted far into Grey's Bend to get these provisions too. He remembered that day, nothing but Stinks swarming farmland, but he could hardly pluck a Stink from Grey's Bend. The walk had taken him the day and until they lifted the ban on driving, dragging a Stink back from Grey's Bend was just too much trouble. They simply wouldn't fit in his Radio Flyer.

For now, he kept his eyes peeled.

What might a corpse look like who had enjoyed the classics in life? Stanley imagined a man in a tailored suit, a man of style.

He scoured the lower eastside and found only a child corpse coming out of an abandoned house. Later, he saw an armless cheerleader staggering toward Fifth and Beach Streets.

Reluctantly, Stanley turned toward home. When he arrived, Little Hector was sprawled in front of the television, a root beer in hand, deeply engrossed in the bloodbath known as *Scarface*.

Stanley collapsed on the sofa, his legs aching.

"Yo', seriously, Stanley, you need to clean up this shit-hole. You got dishes to the ceiling, and the whole place reeks."

"Duly noted," Stanley mumbled.

"That abandoned police locker has only a couple dozen boxes of ammo left," Hector said. "I'm gonna have to learn to use a slingshot."

"I'm sure you will," Stanley mumbled.

"This the last scene, *esse*. I'll watch one of your old school flicks if you want."

"You might like *Wizard of Oz*. It has some fine moments."

"Whatever." Little Hector rose to his knees and removed *Scarface* even before the credits had finished. He had never done that before. Stanley took heart.

"You'll love this movie, Hector. This was made back when MGM was really churning them out. I saw this one for the first time in Chicago, sat right up in the balcony." Stanley searched the overflowing coffee table, found the *Wizard of Oz* and passed it down to Little Hector. He almost beamed, seeing the boy insert the disc.

They watched in near silence. Stanley mouthed the dialog from memory, while Little Hector shifted restlessly on the floor, beat-boxed under his breath and stared at his own grubby knees.

When the outbreak first occurred, when most of the population still had power, the newscasters had invaded Stanley's television set. Even Turner Classic Movies had been interrupted, constant broadcasts from around the country.

First they thought the virus was in the water. Then they suspected the air . . .

Stanley fired off a letter to his cable company immediately.

When the Rialto Movie Theater lost power along with the rest of downtown, and he discovered that there would no longer be Saturday matinees, Stanley held on for awhile. Then eighteen months later, he found himself perched on the fire escape, ready to take a header into the alley.

It had been Hector who stopped him—not Hector in the flesh, but the boy's voice drifting up from apartment 7D. "I polished off daddy's pistol, and now I'm gonna bust some caps."

"Hector, get back here!" The boy's mother screamed.

Hector would have been nine-years-old then.

Regardless of his tender age, Stanley heard nothing but gunfire; afterward he smelled nothing but the charred aroma of spent ammo. Stanley stepped out of his apartment and stared over the railing. Little Hector glanced up at him from the second floor landing—corpses finally at rest were strewn across the first floor landing.

"You still alive, movie-fuck?"

Stanley nodded.

Hector stood idle, spit-shining the still smoking gun. "You wanna know something, Stanley?"

Stanley shook his head.

"It'll be a long time before they lift the ban on driving. You wanna know why?"

Stanley shrugged. He didn't really drive much.

"Cause if we was to drive into Union City or any of the fuckin' suburbs, we'd find out that those bastards are getting things that we aren't. We gonna be the last to get everything down here in the proj-ects. You wait and see if we ain't."

So Stanley had waited, his brief encounters with the precocious and violent boy sustaining him over many years.

When Hector fell asleep, Stanley leaned over him and quietly turned off the DVD, silencing Judy Garland in mid-song. There were noises in the hall, voices. Stanley pressed his ear to the door.

"Amazing, such innovation." A man.

"No, just a scarecrow."

Stanley thought the second voice belonged to Hector's mother. He opened the door and peeked into the corridor. A man with a clipboard and tie stood on the stairs. Hector's mother—his long suffering moth-er—stood with him. Stanley knew they were referring to the "scarecrow" on the roof, but it wasn't really a scarecrow—a corpse collared and staked to the top of the building. Nothing was better for keeping crows out of the rooftop gardens.

Stanley cleared his throat, and the man turned to him. "Please, sir, join us. I have plenty of unarmed guards posted on the landing."

Hector's mother grinned and stared at her feet.

Security hadn't really been an issue since Hector had learned to sharp shoot.

The man started toward Stanley. "Don't be afraid," he said, raising his hand gently as if he were approaching a frightened child. "I'm with the People's Rebuilding Project. We're gonna have these businesses restocked and reopened in no time. You're going to live well again." He gripped Stanley's arm and gave it a reassuring squeeze.

"Tell me," the man said, "how you managed such a high survival rate here? In Union City and Grey's Bend . . . in most places the rate was less than two percent."

Stanley shrugged and stared at the man's still-gripping hand.

"Here you have a twenty percent—"

"Who the fuck are you?" Hector, hair askew, shoved Stanley to the side, barreled into the hallway and faced the man.

"I've come to liberate you," the man said. "I've come to offer you school and . . . and cleaned up streets, jobs and rebuilding."

"I don't need school," Hector hissed. "My moms teaches me at the kitchen table. And you can't liberate us. Who the fuck are you after all these years?"

Hector drew the pistol from his belt, stepped back and held it on the man.

"Hector!" His mother gripped her own hair and swayed on the stairs.

"You know why you fuckin' suburban fucks have so many walking dead?"

The man, his eyes like saucers, shook his head.

"It's 'cause you *ran* from them. You got yourselves good and tired, holding up in packs, drifting into fucking malls. Yeah, I seen that movie, too." Hector cocked his pistol. "They fell on you good, didn't they?"

The man began to cry.

"Do yourself a favor and get the fuck out. You know what this plague means to me? It means my moms don't have to work two jobs to keep food on the table. It means Mr. Leary ain't been bugging her for the rent."

The man moved backward. The shadows of the unarmed guards broke away, casting sunlight across the landing.

"Keep moving," Hector said.

The man continued to back away. After a few minutes he was out of sight.

A tear spilled from Hector's mother's eye, but she didn't say anything, only turned and shuffled downstairs, back to her own apartment.

Stanley did the same, retreating to his own apartment and leaving little Hector to calm himself on the landing.

Stanley Dodge set about doing the dishes and cleaning up his dwelling. When the coffee table shone bright, Stanley stepped back and admired his work.

For the first time in his life, he took pride in his small apartment and in his neighborhood.

Later, watching *The Man Who Would Be King*, fighting to hear the dialog over Hector's rooftop shooting, he took heart. He wondered if the burnt out wasteland of the world would ever allow such majesties again, things like kings, queens . . . heroes.

Stanley picked up the DVD *Scarface* from the coffee table, turning it around and around in his hands. The People's Rebuilding Project would likely return, he knew. They'd probably fall hard on the inner-city after Hector's outburst, demanding they conform.

Stanley stared at the DVD, Pacino's face tough and ready.

Gunfire echoed across the alley.

"Say hello to my little friend," Stanley whispered.

Genuflect

by William D. Carl

"The body of Christ," Father Jim said, placing the piece of hard bread where the creature's tongue had once been located. The muscle had rotted from its head long ago. The zombie chewed with its yellow teeth before awkwardly genuflecting and shuffling to the back of the church. It was immediately replaced with another, this one dead for some years, judging by the gray pallor of its skin and the distinct absence of lips. Father Jim repeated his blessing as the monster daintily took the proffered host from his fingers with its decayed, shattered teeth. It knelt on one exposed knee-cap before limping to the back of Saint Michael's Cathedral.

The queue of the living dead awaiting Communion was another twenty creatures. Father Jim was glad Mass was almost completed. It wasn't as if he was in any danger from the zombies; the iron bars running down the length of the alter from floor to ceiling shielded him from their disease, allowing just enough space for him to fit the Communion wafer and his fingers through the gap between the slats, but not enough for them to reach him. Besides, the dead were more docile within the walls of God's home, as if they were children on their best behavior. In over sixty years, they'd never once attacked him through the prison wall.

No, Father Jim was merely exhausted. At eighty-four years of age, he found himself barely able to finish Mass, even when skipping the homily (though he had to admit, the dead were patient listeners). His arthritis was acting up, and the Deliverers hadn't brought him his medication for several weeks. Just standing in the heavy robes for forty-five minutes on Sundays had become a recurrent form of torture. His gnarled fingers shook so much, he was terrified of dropping one of the pieces of old bread, the substitute for the wafers he could no longer procure.

When he had been young, it had all been different. Sixty years ago, when the plague had struck, he had thanked God for his father, a stalwart iron worker who had separated the nave from the chancel with a long row of iron bars that traced the line of the transepts. As St. Michael's was an inner city church, the windows were already protected with bars and chickenwire. Even the basement was encased in iron; Father Jim, his parents, and Jane, the young Irish housekeeper/cook lived there. Ensconced within the womb of the prison-like church, they had remained safe for years, living off food from the soup-kitchen stores.

A few Sundays after most of the world had been devoured by the dead, Father Jim had heard something in the nave of the church. He had bustled into the chancel and was shocked at the line of zombies awaiting Communion. Patiently, the things had waited in the aisle of St. Michael's, emitting soft moans as if in terrible pain. Father Jim had stepped up to the barrier, and the first zombie in line carefully genuflected, then raised its face to heaven and opened its mouth. Curious, the priest had placed a Communion wafer on the thing's tongue, and it had crossed itself and walked out of the church. Then, the entire procession of walking dead had taken a single step forward.

"Before it stopped broadcasting, the radio said they're returning to places they remember, to places they loved," Father Jim's mother had said. "What if they so loved their God that they're coming back to partake of His supper?"

Jim's father had chuckled and shaken his head. "More like hom-
ing pigeons, probably. There's no brain there. Nothing human left.
Just crazy animal instinct."

"And if instinct leads them back to St. Michael's?" his mother had
countered. "Maybe there's still a soul in their rotting bodies. It would
explain why they want Communion so badly. They're feeding their
souls."

"It is a sort of cannibalism, isn't it?" Jim had suggested. "During
transubstantiation, the bread actually becomes Christ's body. They are
eating flesh. You think they can sense that it's the body and blood of
Christ? That they're just hungry for any sort of flesh, even if it's rep-
resentational?"

Jane had cleared the table while shaking a long finger at the priest.
"That's blasphemous, that is. You shouldn't ought to talk that way,
Father Jim."

"Why do you think they come back to the church, Jane? Why do
so many of them turn up here every Sunday at the exact time we used
to say Mass?"

She had pondered this for a moment before she'd answered.
"Because they're hungry for God. I believe your Mother is right.
They're lost souls, and they're lookin' for a way into heaven. The good
Lord knows, they've found their Hell right here."

None of them had argued with her. Jane was a stubborn woman,
and their isolation in the sacristy and basement allowed her to grow
even more obtuse. She'd go days without speaking, frustrated with the
close quarters. Over time, the group had grown argumentative
amongst themselves. A few years later, they'd turned quiet and
morose, becoming all too familiar with the manner in which their
world had altered. They eventually settled into a daily routine that was
as dull as it was necessary for their sanity.

The church was allowed to fall into disrepair, although they
cleaned the sacristy and the area around the altar every day and polished the tabernacle. Eventually, Jane would head downstairs to pre-

pare dinner from the leftovers in the church basement where the soup kitchen used to be. After dinner, Jim would read one of the books from the church library, usually aloud so everyone could appreciate it. Sometimes, they'd listen to the radio now that some survivors had started broadcasting again.

Father Jim's mother had succumbed to a flu virus, and his father died a few days later. The priest had been heart-broken, but he'd opened the back door enough to leave their corpses in the alley behind the church. He hadn't been surprised when he'd discovered them in line for Communion the next Sunday, heads lowered, feet scraping along the filthy carpet. He had placed the blessed bread on their tongues, had tried to ignore their identities, and he had continued with the rite of Holy Communion until all the creatures were sated. Then, he'd returned to Jane in the basement and wept over what was left of them. He saw them off and on for years, until their rotting bodies could no longer remain ambulatory. They just didn't show up one Sunday, and Jim was comfortable with the loss.

One day, Father Jim and Jane had heard a knocking on the wall of the basement. In minutes, the bricks had spilled into the room, and a group of what appeared to be mud-covered miners emerged from the hole. They were filthy, but they appeared cheerful. They were human, untainted with the virus.

"We're building a tunnel system," one had said over a sad little meal Jane had prepared. Their stores were running low, and the thirty-five year old housekeeper had been forced to become creative when cooking. "That way, we can all get help to each other. There's still a lot of us left. We're all just separated from each other. This way, we can deliver food or medicine or such to anyone who needs it without all of you being exposed to danger."

Thus, the Deliverers were born—a group of radicals who burrowed their way from place to place, bringing supplies to the church. Father Jim had been tempted to follow the group several times to see where the tunnels led, but Jane had been horrified at this concept.

"What about all of them out there, them things?" she'd asked, arms flying about in consternation. "They need you, they do. They need someone to give them the Host every week."

"You could do it as well as I can, Jane," he'd said. "You know the Mass inside and out."

She'd been flabbergasted. "I'm no priest."

"No, but in these times, I think the church would suffer even a woman if she were willing to give out Holy Communion."

"Ain't much of a church left, sad to say. Just us." Her eyes had filled with tears of loneliness and neglect. "Just us."

He'd had to admit they hadn't heard a peep from the Vatican in years. They couldn't even be certain it was still in existence. As far as they knew, St. Michael's was the only church left in Brooklyn, maybe in the world. The Deliverers didn't know of any others, but they were more of a local entity, channeling beneath the boroughs of New York. Sometimes, over one of the ever-sparser radio programs, someone would give a hellfire and brimstone sermon, but the radio mostly played static now. People seemed to have hunkered down, isolated themselves into small factions, like segregated neighborhoods. They were growing older, less adventurous, less interested in others. The human race turned in upon themselves.

And the dead kept coming to St. Michael's, searching for something, genuflecting at the apse and opening their decaying lips for the Sacrament.

In the sacristy, Father Jim folded his vestment, kissing the hem. The arthritis in his joints ached, and he winced as he stretched to put the robe on a hook. Peeking back into the church, he saw two of the undead shambling aimlessly in the maze of overturned pews. One of them, a young woman who couldn't have been dead more than a few days, moaned softly, and the sound echoed throughout the church. For a moment, he thought he recognized her, but her head and face were covered in bloody wounds.

Moving behind him, Jane said, "They look terrible lost."

"The ones who still show up," Father Jim agreed. "Aren't as many as there used to be, but they're always searching, always hungry."

"I'm hungry, too," Jane said, clutching at the priest's hand with her own. The skin felt thin, like paper, against his wrinkled fingertips. She continued, "I've got some canned spaghetti I'll heat up for us. Sal should be comin' today, so there'll probably be a treat for tonight."

Sal, the newest member of the Deliverers, had been bringing the two old people in the church food for several weeks now. Father Jim liked her—brash and sassy, with a mouth full of curse words and a head full of green hair. She was probably twenty-five years old, but it was hard to tell beneath the caked dirt from the tunnels and the odd clothing combinations she wore. She seemed like a baby to Jim, but since he'd passed the age of eighty a few years back, anyone would seem young.

If there's anyone young left out there, he thought, crossing himself and following Jane into the basement. His knees creaked as he descended, setting off a pang in his back. *Getting awfully old, aren't you?* he mused. *Old and useless.*

He sat at a long table. The others had been put in storage long ago, folded into themselves as though prostrated to some unseeable god. Jane fumbled about in the kitchen, eventually emerging with two steaming bowls of canned pasta.

"The propane's gettin' a bit low," she said. "Might want to tell Sal about that."

But when the Deliverer rapped the secret knock on the locked basement door, it was a young man with long red hair and a black trenchcoat. He gave them their supplies for the week—*Thank God my pain medicine is here,* Jim thought—and the young man accepted Jane's invitation to join them in some reheated SpaghettiOs. His name was Chuck.

"What happened to Sal?" Jane asked.

"Don't rightly know, ma'am," Chuck answered in a Southern twang. It had been so long since Jim had heard any accent other than Jane's Irish brogue and Sal's Boston Southie, that he had to take a moment to ascertain it was English the boy was speaking. "She went out on a run to the Bronx for a family in the prison, and she never came back. Guess the zombies got her. I went to the prison to check on her, but even the family was gone. Blood all over the place. Must've been something terrible happened in there."

"Lord have mercy on their poor souls," Father Jim, said, kissing his rosary. "Seems like our number's dwindling by the week. The number of humans left alive, I mean."

"More like by the day," Chuck said. "Between you and me and the fence post. . . "

"Watch your assignations, boy," Jane teased with a grin. She could still be charming, even at the age of eighty-five. "I'm skinny, but don't you be callin' me a post."

Chuck returned her grin and continued. "We still go out on delivery runs, but there's only about twenty of us left in the New York area, and I probably shouldn't say this, but supplies are getting low. All the stores have pretty much been emptied out over the years, and there's no way anybody's doing any farming 'round these parts. The old people are, beg your pardon, ma'am, dying out. And the young people. . . well, having babies don't seem like much of an option any more. We just struggle along while the undead fall apart and rot in the streets. There's a lot less of them, too. Still, they catch one of the living every once in a while, change 'em over into zombies. You still see young ones now and then."

"There was a young woman in church today," Father Jim said. "She was probably a pretty thing before they got her, no more than twenty or so. She looked very. . . lost."

"Didn't have green hair, did she? Could be Sal."

"No, I don't think it was her. I'd have recognized the girl if it was. Some other lost soul." Jim wondered for a moment. The girl's head had been severely traumatized. Could he have recognized Sal in such a state?

"I'm gonna miss that emerald head of hers," Chuck said with a long sigh.

"As will we all," Jane said, crossing herself.

"They still come, huh?" Chuck asked. "The dead people? To the church? I heard about them coming here. Ain't heard anyone mention it anywhere else, though. Just Saint Michael's. Like you're special here."

"Something draws them still," Father Tim said, nodding. "They're searching for some meaning to their existence, I believe. The body of our Lord nourishes them in a way human flesh can not. It's strange, but I think I'm saving them all somehow."

"Saving souls, Padre?" Chuck shook his head, a sad grin on his face. "Ain't no souls left to save in those things."

"Can you be sure?"

"Something with a soul ain't gonna eat his brother. I don't know my Bible real well, but I remember 'Thou shalt not kill.'"

"I won't abandon them," Father Jim said. "If they're searching for God, for forgiveness, even if it's just their way of seeking comfort, I will not abandon them."

"And if they ain't nothing but empty shells on autopilot?"

"Well, then, I may be wasting my time. I may be spinning my wheels here, but they may know more than we do. What if—and this is all conjecture—what if they have insight into the afterlife that we lack? What if they can see God, or sense Him?"

"A direct line to the Almighty?"

"Perhaps. Or they could be atoning for sins. They've seen the face of God, and they know what they do is wrong in His eyes, so they attend church, take the Holy Sacrament."

"Tell you the truth, Padre," Chuck said, standing from the table and stretching. "I look at those things, and I don't see any connection with anything holy. I see blank stares and open mouths. I think they're freakin' turnips."

"I can only hope you're wrong," Father Jim said, shaking the young man's hand. "Will you return next week?"

"If the zombies don't get me first," he answered, stepping into the tunnel. He turned on his mining hat with the light on the front to illuminate his journey back to what remained of the downtown Nordstrom's where the Deliverers were based. "Pray for me, Padre."

"I shall," Jim said, and he closed the door, switching shut the seven dead bolts. "I'll pray for us all."

"Seemed like a nice young man," Jane said. "From the looks of his ruby locks, he has a bit o' the Irish in his blood."

"You're a sentimental old thing, Jane."

"Aye, that I am. But, who you callin' old?"

Life continued, day by day, minute by minute. Jane continued to cook, and Father Jim said Mass once a day and passed out Communion to the shambling dead every Sunday. He often saw the girl with the crushed skull, and he wept when he discerned the green hair beneath the caked bloodstains. She took Communion from his hands without acknowledging him. She didn't even look him in the eye.

Jane and Jim talked about the past during supper, and he would check the generator every evening, adding gasoline as necessary. Eventually, two weeks passed, and there was another knock on the tunnel's door. Chuck ambled into the room, a bit thinner than the last time he'd visited. Jane set about preparing a decent dinner.

"We need to fatten you up a bit," she said. "You're gettin' terrible skinny."

"Too much running around," he said. "Lost a couple more Deliverers last week, and I'm picking up the slack. Those zombies out there are getting desperate, attacking with more force than before. Guess there ain't as much food."

"I'm afraid we found Sal," Jim said. "She's been attending Mass every Sunday. I didn't recognize her at first. Too much . . . well, too much damage to her face."

"Noticed the green hair, did you, Padre?"

"Yes. Yes, I did. God rest her soul."

Chuck laughed cynically. "Soul? You still on about that? Padre, you are the eternal optimist."

"No, I believe that was Jesus Christ."

"Whatever."

"Don't tell me you're not a believer?" Jane asked, crossing herself. "You've got to have some faith, Chuck."

"Not much left to have faith in. Another twenty years, won't be nobody left but the dead walking the streets. The books and art will rot away to dust. The last zombies will eventually fall apart. The sun and the rain'll eat away anything left over, and all of humanity's great accomplishments will disappear forever. Hell, I doubt it takes twenty years."

"Is it really that bad out there, son?" Jim asked. Jane touched his shoulder. "So bad you've lost all hope?"

When Chuck raised his haunted gaze to look Father Jim in the eye, his answer was written large across his face. He sighed, ran a hand through his long hair.

"Not much time left for us," he said. "We're probably all just as dead as those poor bastards out there who haven't realized it yet. Just a matter of time."

Father Jim set down his silverware, and he said, "I'd like to see the tunnels, Chuck."

"What?"

"I said, I'd like you to show me the tunnels. I'd like to see something good that man created, even if it's the last good thing. The idea of the tunnels was superb, connecting people, but we should've taken it a step further, come out of hiding. We should've used the tunnels to start communities all over again. We could still do it."

"I don't know," Chuck hedged. "You're not very fast. Sometimes, you need to run."

"You must see the possibilities. We make some central place a common area for everyone to meet. Stuck all alone like we are, we're dying out. If we could just find each other again . . . I don't know. It sounds far-fetched."

"It sure as hell does," Chuck said. "But it makes wicked sense."

"The Deliverers will have to take charge, get everyone to venture out of their hermitages. I'm going to start it right now. You lead me through the tunnels, show me what's out there. If we could find a suitable place . . . "

"You may have something there, Padre," Chuck said, with a less than hopeful grin.

"Of course, he does," Jane said. "Father Jim's always right. You take a note of that!"

"You really want to see the tunnels? We can go now. Probably as safe as any time. And I've got my pistol just in case."

"It's a crazy fool idea," Jane scolded them. "And don't be thinkin' you're gettin' me out there in those dirty mine shafts. I'll be stayin' right here gettin' your coffee ready for when you return."

"Ready, Padre?" Chuck asked, wiping his mouth and standing.

"As ready as I'll ever be," Father Jim said, and he cursed himself for the waver in his voice.

Chuck unlocked the door in the basement wall and opened it. Handing Father Jim a large flashlight, he turned on his miner's hat. A beam of light glanced off the tunnel's dirt walls. In the darkness, white roots emerged from the mud like grubs, probably from the bushes surrounding Saint Michael's.

"You'll be fine," Chuck said, waving the priest forward. "Just stay close to me."

Father Jim was terrified. He wondered what he was doing, eighty-four years old and scampering through precarious underground passages with some young fool. He was too old to be traipsing about in the dark.

I'm too old for almost everything, he thought. *Probably too old for this Earth. But, if I can do something to bring people back together, make some contribution, no matter how futile . . . God will smile upon me.*

He followed Chuck into the gaping tunnel, turning to tell Jane to lock the door behind them and to keep it locked unless she heard the secret knock.

"Be sure and come back," she said.

"Don't worry about me."

"That's all I ever do. My poor head's full of situations that could happen. And, you know . . . you know I . . . I have always . . . "

"Yes," he said, kissing her on the forehead. "I know. I've always known."

"Then, off with ya'. Have your fun, and come back to me, boyo."

He grunted, turned into the darkness, and followed Chuck's bobbing light. They moved slowly, and Jim knew it was because Chuck didn't want to lose someone who probably couldn't keep up with his sprightly walk.

The dirt walls smelled of iron and soil and mold. The roots grew more adventurous as they moved through the winding tunnel, and Father Jim had to duck several times to avoid getting caught in their tendrils. The floor was worn smooth by years of Deliverers traversing the tunnels. Jim felt as if he was inside an ant farm.

They came upon a crossroads, and Chuck stopped, turning to the priest. The light atop his hat momentarily blinded the old man.

"You want to go to the supermarket, or the high school?" the young man asked.

Father Jim was out of breath. "The school, I think. Is there a gymnasium?"

"Sure is. You think that's where we should all meet?"

"Let's check it out first."

Chuck nodded, then turned, and Jim was enveloped in musty shadows. He stumbled after the red-headed giant, losing track of how far they'd traveled.

The walls all looked the same to him. Some had more roots dangling from the ceiling, and some were more ragged in the walls, but in the flashlight's beam, dirt was dirt. The only sounds were their muffled footfalls and the trickle of water every once in a while. They didn't see another person, living or dead, while they hurried to their destination.

Father Jim knew he'd be lost if he was to become separated from his guide. They'd turned several more times, passed several closed doors, before they stepped into a large brick room with high ceilings and several benches and tables. A cafeteria, but the furniture was all shoved against one wall. Blood stains marred the white tiled floor, brown with age, but disturbingly sizable.

"The door isn't locked?" Father Jim asked as Chuck shut it behind them.

"No. The family that used to live here died out a few years back. Nobody else has moved in. Thought about it once, myself. Big place, plenty of air to breathe. Only, it's kind of lonely here. Spooky. All the echoes and such. And it makes me think of all the kids, what happened to them."

"Let's find the gymnasium, why don't we?"

It was still daylight outside, and the setting sun projected streaks of gold and orange through the dirty, high windows. The dim light only accentuated the desolation of the place, the eerie stillness of the hallways. Their footsteps reverberated along the walls, and it sounded as if they were the last two people on Earth.

When they arrived at the gym, Father Jim clapped his hands and smiled. The basketball hoops were pulled back to the ceiling, and the bleachers on both sides of the room remained intact. The windows were set twenty five feet off the ground, and the doors to the streets were locked with solid-looking bolts and chains.

"This looks like a good place to have a town meeting," he said. "A very good place."

"Padre, I think you're right. It's perfect. Not even any blood stains, and you have no idea how lucky that is. Hardly anyplace was left unstained after the plague."

"You think you could arrange for people to meet here?"

"I can sure try," Chuck said. "Like I said, it's a good idea. I'll get the other Deliverers to tell everyone on their routes."

Father Jim beamed. "Then, take me back to St. Michael's. I'm tired. It's pretty hard keeping up with a whippersnapper like yourself."

"Sorry, Padre," Chuck said, worry creasing his brow. "I thought I was going slow enough . . . "

"A joke, son, a joke."

The trip back to the church was long and circuitous, and Father Jim was delighted when he saw the door open. Upon his entrance, Jane gave him a big hug and a kiss on his leathery cheek.

"Saints be praised, "she said. "It's good to have you back home safe and sound."

"I'm . . . very tired, Jane. Would you mind terribly if I lay down for the night?"

Jane glanced at Chuck, and the big man shrugged.

"Course not. You go right along."

"Chuck," Jim said. "You do what we talked about. You tell them to meet, to gather together and get to know one another. Tell them. . . it isn't over yet."

"I surely will."

Father Jim was asleep before his head hit the pillow.

More days went by, each melting into the other. Mass was said. The generator was inspected. Dinner was prepared. But at the table, Father Jim and Jane were more animated than they had been for years. Word had spread about a meeting on Sunday night at the high school. During a brief visit, Chuck had informed them that there was to be a gathering at the gymnasium on Sunday night, that an old music teacher had tuned a piano at the school and was going to play Beethoven's "Piano Sonata #14" for them. Chuck had attempted to explain the way people had responded, the way their eyes had gleamed at the thought of a concert.

"And it's all due to you, Padre," he said. "You started this whole shebang. Started something really good. Probably saved a bunch of people from despair."

"I just made a suggestion."

"Well, it was a damn fine one. We'll see you there, of course?"

"Will you come to guide us?"

Chuck bowed before entering the tunnels again. "It would be my pleasure. And my honor."

On Sunday morning, Jane glowed, bustling around the sacristy, helping Father Jim prepare for Mass. She hummed an Irish ballad under her breath as she snapped up his vestments.

"You're in a cheerful mood today, Jane."

"Well, it's gonna be nice to see some other people. Been a long time, Father. A long time, indeed. You don't suppose they'll have beer at the concert, do you? That'd be lovely."

"Perhaps," he answered with a chuckle. "If Chuck has anything to do with it."

"That's a fine upstanding Irish lad, that is," she said. Looking into the church, she gestured to a lone figure. "Your girlfriend's here," she said. "Poor little thing. Back for her blessed sacrament."

Sal milled at the back of the pews. She'd deteriorated some, and the blood on her smashed forehead had gone rust-colored. A patch of emerald green peeked through, like the spring after a rough winter.

Father Jim said Mass, and the zombies lined up on the other side of the bars, patiently waiting for Communion. The priest blessed the bread, then tore it into smaller pieces. After a few prayers, he stood on the opposite side of the barrier and began handing out the sacrament.

"The body of Christ," he said.

The creature took it between rotting lips. Jim could see the bread in the dead woman's mouth through a hole the size of a quarter in her cheek. The next zombie took its place in front of the altar, genuflecting and gracelessly crossing itself.

"The body of Christ."

Father Jim thought of the people who'd be meeting in the school that evening, shaking hands, holding long conversations, listening to music played live for the first time in decades. Perhaps, they could build upon the relationships.

"The body of Christ."

He prayed they could. He prayed for new friendships, perhaps even a romance or two.

Sal stepped to the front of the line. She went down on one knee, giving Jim a clear view of the destruction of her skull. When she rose, she opened her mouth. He took a piece of bread and held it through the bars. She daintily leaned forward, sniffed the air once, and bit through Father Jim's forefinger and thumb. He screamed, fell backwards until he landed hard on the floor. Sal chewed, and he could hear the sound of his finger bones crunching between her jaws. She crossed herself and moved back to the far side of the church, dropping to her knees and folding her hands in front of her face. She looked serene in the colored light from the stained glass windows.

Jane rushed from the sacristy and knelt beside Father Jim. He clutched his hand, but the blood was pumping from the wounds, staining his vestments.

"Oh Lord, look at what she's done to ya', Father. Oh Jesus, Mary, and Joseph!"

"Get me to the basement," he said between gritted teeth.

They left the moaning queue of zombies still waiting for Holy Communion.

After running water over the bites, Jane bandaged them, then sat across from Father Jim, watching him warily.

"You know I can't stay here," he said.

"But, you can't go out there."

"I'm infected. I'm . . . one of them, now."

"Jesus, Mary, and Joseph."

"You're going to have to be strong, Jane. You're going to have to take my place."

"Don't be daft. You'll be fine."

"I'll be dead in twelve hours. Maybe less. You know how this works."

After a moment, she nodded.

"Good," he said, and he could feel his windpipe freezing up. "I'm going to let myself out into the church. Once there, I'll finish handing out Communion."

The tears fell from Jane's eyes, dropping onto Father Jim's bandaged hand, staining the immaculate white wrap.

"But, you'll have to say Mass and give out the holy sacrament from now on. Every Sunday."

"But. . . "

"I won't hear anything else. I need to know you'll do this. . . that you'll provide for those poor souls out there looking for some kind of redemption. If you ever loved me, you'll do it. For me."

"Okay, I will, Jim. I will. I swear it."

"I'll come back," he said, and he winced as a bolt of pain sliced up his arm into his neck and head. He continued, "I'll be back next Sunday. Spirit willing. I'll need my fix next week, and I need to know you'll be here . . . to provide it. I need . . . to know."

"I'll be here. I swear it. Until I can't stand up anymore. I'll be here."

"All right, then," he said. With a grunt, he stood and ascended the stairs to the sacristy.

The zombies were still lined up, waiting, moaning softly. Father Jim stepped forward and removed a key from a chain around his neck. He unlocked the door, picked up the bread in his hands, and stepped into the church for the first time in over sixty years. He sighed, tasting the air, and he could swear it seemed different than the stifling atmosphere of the area behind the bars. Passing the key back to her, he caught her eye. He continued to watch Jane as he passed out the bread to the remaining monsters.

"I'll be back next Sunday," he said. "If there's a God, I will want to be near Him. If I still have a soul, I will be back. Like these other poor bastards, I'll be back."

"And I'll be waiting for you," she said, sobbing into her hands.

He brushed the breadcrumbs from his hands and lingered while the zombies dispersed. When the church was nearly empty, he walked down the aisle and opened the doors. Sunlight streamed in, blinding him.

Sal watched, stood, moved after him. When she got to his side, she took his ruined hand in hers, and they stepped outside into the light. The doors closed with a bang.

Jane didn't attend the concert that evening. She begged Chuck to let her know what happened, and he filled her in on its success later. She lost sleep, wondering about Father Jim. She recalled the way his skin smelled when she was close enough, the way his skin felt when she helped him change vestments.

He wasn't present at Mass the next Sunday, but she still performed it for the attending zombies. She also broke up the bread and served them Communion, wary of her fingers at the bars, and feeling like a sinner all the while. Eventually, over the weeks that followed, the sensation that she was doing something wrong dissipated. She could detect something from the creatures, some sense of well-being when they partook of the bread. Her new purpose overtook her years of Vatican rules.

The surviving people of Brooklyn continued to gather in the gymnasium. The Sunday concert was followed by amateur plays, poetry readings, movies, budding friendships, and a romance or two. It took Jane several months to bolster herself enough to attend a production of Much Ado about Nothing, but she found herself in tears by the show's happy ending. Grasping Chuck's big paw in her tiny hand, she felt as if she was watching the human race slowly reassemble itself. Sixty years of scar tissue would take a long time to heal, but the people of New York were nothing if not resilient. She would sometimes lead prayers at the end of the meetings.

She often recalled Father Jim's words. "If there's a God, I will want to be near Him. If I still have a soul, I will be back. Like these other poor bastards, I'll be back."

But, although she often gave Sal her weekly serving of Communion, she never saw Father Jim again.

What Comes After
by Kris Dikeman

Reade glanced up as the cruiser rolled past the outermost barricade, into the countryside proper. It was a perfect clear September day, a crisp taste of fall on the breeze, but the blue sky stretching above the car like an ocean only made him feel vulnerable and exposed. The National Guard had done a good job of clearing up, but the wrecks and burned-out cars scattered along the gravel shoulders on both sides of the road made him nervous. They provided ample cover for anyone—anything—waiting, like a wolf in a fairytale, to gobble up unlucky passersby.

In the road ahead, a deep raw gouge cut into the blacktop where the bulldozer had moved the battered wreck of the school bus off onto the shoulder. The bus was back upright; it was filthy with mud and soot, one side horribly crumpled. It sat on its deflated tires in a drift of debris: gravel, slivers of chrome, bits of plastic, papers, and broken glass, lots of broken glass. Crash dandruff, Sheriff Howell used to call it. All the little bits of crap that accumulated, as if by magic, whenever there was a wreck.

Reade turned his face away from the bus as the car passed by, tried not to look at the smashed windows and the emergency exit door torn almost off its hinges, streaks of clotted blood and gore spattered across the sooty yellow paint. He put his foot on the gas, willed the car to take him away from this place, this bad place —crime scene, call it what it is, it's a crime scene—and saw a child's sneaker, a black high top, close to the edge of the road. The dirty laces stirred and flapped idly as the cruiser shot past.

Goddamn those Guardsmen anyway, he thought, Why the hell couldn't they have picked that up?

He knew his anger was irrational. The soldiers had done their best—done things he didn't like to think about—but the heat of indignation helped push back the queasy feeling in his stomach. With the wreck getting smaller in the rearview mirror, Reade remembered how Sheriff Howell had sneered when the Guard had shown up.

"Weekend warriors, Georgie," Howell had said, hitching his belt buckle up over his gut and reaching for his spit cup. "Soft boys in suits, pretending to be soldiers."

But they had turned out to be more, even Howell had admitted later. How much more had been made clear the night the innermost security fence had given way. The dead, pale and gray in the glare of emergency lights, had poured through the breach by the dozens. Reade remembered the look of calm control on the face of the Guard Captain as he had fired off the flame-thrower, into the vanguard of the zombie mob. They had gone up like kindling, their burning bodies lighting up the night.

The Branson place was coming up on his left. The windows and doors were still tightly boarded up, and except for the overgrowth of weeds and high grass, the house looked in good shape. John Branson and his wife had moved into town one week before martial law had been declared. Reade had come out and helped John board up windows, drain pipes, and get the house ready to stand empty for a time. While they nailed sheets of plywood into the window frames Branson's wife Lorraine, her face ashen, had silently carried boxes of clothes out to their minivan. The previous day, a zombie had come up behind her son Jason as he was picking tomatoes. Jason had been plucked himself, there one second and gone the next.

"I saw them things on the news, Georgie," John Branson had said, pulling another ten-penny nail from the jar on the porch and setting it against the plywood. "But I threw that fat fool boss of yours off my land when he told us to come into town. And now my boy is a monster, and his mother's heart is broken."

A sudden movement in front of him jolted Reade from his reverie. Adrenaline surged through him as the cruiser slowed.

A dead raccoon moved across the road before him in a crabwise shuffle, the track of the tire that killed it clearly visible on its flattened midsection. The animal glared up, eyes shining, teeth bared, misshapen body tensed to spring. Reade veered as the car reached it, closed his eyes as it crunched under the left front wheel and told himself that it was not possible for him to hear the pop of its brain pan under the tire. He looked in the rearview mirror and saw the dark stain left on the road twitch and quiver, teeth spilling out as the ruined jaws snapped mechanically.

He had almost reached his destination. And just beyond it, the cemetery.

The house was almost completely hidden by a high chain link fence, like the perimeter fence that encircled the town. As he pulled up to the gate and put the cruiser in park, Reade saw that the electricity was off. He took an enormous key ring from his pocket and searched until he found a key with a little piece of white tape and the words "Buren Fence" in Howell's fussy printing. Reade checked the rearview mirror, then the sides, put his hand on the door handle and took a few quick deep breaths, like a swimmer preparing for a race.

There is no need for this nonsense, he thought. The guard had sanitized the graveyard; there hadn't been a sighting in days. But when he touched the door handle, he flashed back to Bob Kerrigan, the town's Mayor, being yanked out of his Ford pickup. "I'll just be a minute, Georgie," Bob had said, "I left something on the kitchen ta—" and then the stinking, putrescent arm had reached in and grabbed Bob by his hair and yanked him backward out of the truck, and he was gone. Reade had sat, frozen, and listened to the sound of screams getting fainter and slurping sounds getting louder. Who's gonna sign the paychecks now? he had thought. And then he'd seen the keys dangling in the Ford's ignition and next thing he was tearing down the road back to town, to the shocked and unbelieving townspeople, and the Sheriff's black fury.

"You were supposed to look after him." Howell had thundered. "I can't run this whole goddamned town by myself, you know." And Reade had stood, head down, miserable, overwhelmed and out of his depth.

Now he fought to keep his breathing under control until the panicky feeling receded. He climbed out of the car and unlocked the gate, keys jangling in his hand only a little. He suppressed the urge to glance behind him, slid back into the cruiser and pulled the car into the driveway. As he re-locked the gate he tried to keep his back straight and his hands steady. He turned slowly when he heard the front door open. Sheriff Howell's star was a ponderous weight on his chest, the gun awkward and heavy on his hip, and he wondered for a bleak moment if he looked as ridiculous as he felt.

Mrs. Buren stepped out on the porch. "Hello there, Georgie," she said. "I'm glad you're here."

"Hello, Mrs. Buren." Her dress was clean and freshly ironed, her hair set in a familiar tight bun. She looked like what she was—a retired small town schoolteacher—and Reade could feel something in his chest loosen a little. She had deep circles under her eyes, and in the unforgiving light of mid-morning he could see the lines and creases around her mouth had deepened considerably. But her eyes were focused and clear, none of that glazed, far-away look he had seen so much of lately.

She's made of sterner stuff than that, he thought, and felt an unexpected surge of affection for this woman who had once terrorized his childhood. She had been the strictest teacher he had ever known, with high, exacting standards. He had barely kept his head above water in her classes. Now she smiled at him, and he realized she had been assessing him, too, checking to see what kind of stuff he was made from, and that smile, so open and genuine, meant she had not found him wanting. He was surprised and a little amused to find that her approval—so hard to win in the past—still meant a great deal to him.

"Well now Georgie," she said, "come on into the house, why don't you? I've made tea."

He came up the steps, and as he reached her she slipped her arm under his, like a lady being escorted to a fancy dinner. She gave off a fragrance of lavender and spray starch. Reade felt disoriented. In the jumbled memory of his childhood, Mrs. Buren had seemed a towering presence; this faded, delicate old woman barely came up to his chin.

Mrs. Buren pointed him to an overstuffed wing chair. "Pardon me dear, while I put pot to kettle," she said, and went into the kitchen. The tea things were already set out on a small rolling table—crustless sandwiches, china cups, silver spoons. The room was immaculate. There were ceramic figurines on the mantle, a grandfather clock ticking calmly in the corner, an assortment of pictures in antique frames arranged on a lace doily across the piano. He settled into the chair more deeply, closed his eyes, thought how it was nice to sit in a room without boards on the windows or blood on the floor.

"It's a comfortable chair, isn't it?" asked Mrs. Buren as she stepped back into the room. Reade jumped up and took the silver tray with the steaming teapot from her, set it down next to the little trolley. She picked up a cup and poured him out some tea. "That was my husband's favorite chair. That young captain from the National Guard liked it too. He made himself right at home here." Mrs. Buren frowned. "He certainly enjoyed giving me orders. He forbade me to set foot out of this house until you arrived. There's no milk, but will you take sugar?"

"No thank you, Ma'am." Reade took the teacup and saucer and balanced them on his knee, mindful of the faded Oriental rug. "I imagine those fellows from the Guard just wanted to keep you safe, Mrs. Buren. They caught h—they got a lot of criticism for even letting you stay out here in the first place after martial law was declared."

Mrs. Buren gave a small, tight smile of satisfaction as she poured his tea. "Martial rule, Georgie, depends for its existence upon public necessity. Necessity creates it, justifies it and limits its endurance. The Captain and I had quite a few interesting discussions on the subject. In the end, he saw the sense of my staying here."

"Yes ma'am." Reade took a sip of tea to hide his smile. He remembered the guard Captain sitting with Sheriff Howell in his office, a map of the county spread out across the battered oak desk between them.

"You tell the old bag she has to move out," the captain had said. "Every time I mention to her that she's living next to a graveyard, that fuckin' dead people are digging their way out of the ground at the rate of about two per day, she gets this stuck-up look on her face and starts in arguing with me. 'The civil law cannot be displaced, young man . . . let us call things by their right name, it is not martial law, but martial rule.'"

The Sheriff had tipped Reade a sly wink as he commiserated with the Captain on the frustration of dealing with an old lady so well-versed in the intricacies of the law. But after the guardsman had left, Howell's laughter had rung through the office. "He's a fair shot with a flame-thrower, Georgie, but he's no match for that old biddy. I'd sooner face a roomful of the dead than cross her m'self." Howell had said, wiping tears from his eyes. And Reade had laughed too, though secretly he felt sorry for the Captain, who was clearly used to people jumping up when he yelled frog. Unfortunately for him, Mrs. Buren was also used to giving orders, and it would take more than the end of the world to change that.

Now she passed Reade a plate of sandwiches. "Once those young men learned to respect my privacy, and not help themselves to things they shouldn't, things went well enough. Some of them turned out to be quite useful. I was almost sorry to see them go."

Reade looked over one of the dainty sandwiches. The bread was the same Government Issue whole meal everyone in town had been eating for weeks, with the crusts neatly trimmed. The filling was a single leaf of lettuce and a thin slice of pink meat. He took a small bite and chewed carefully. Spam. "It's the Guard's leaving that's brought me out here, Mrs. Buren," he said, and took another sip of tea. It had a strong, smoky flavor.

She leaned back in her chair. "You want me to come into town," she said.

"I do." Reade set down his teacup and looked her in the eye, hoping he sounded more authoritative than he felt.

"I'm afraid you've wasted your time, Georgie." She looked at him more closely. "I should be calling you Sheriff Reade, shouldn't I? You are the Sheriff now. And with the Mayor gone as well, really you're all the town has by way of an authority figure. Poor Bobby Kerrigan. He was such a good student, and a fine Mayor. You were there when he was killed, weren't you?"

Reade struggled to keep his voice steady; getting angry now wouldn't accomplish anything. "You know I was, Mrs. Buren." But I'm not ten anymore, he thought. I won't let you get the upper hand on me all that easy. "And since I am the Sheriff now, I may as well say what I've come to. I need you to pack up some things and come into town. All of this is far from over. This house is completely isolated. The idea of you staying here alone is just crazy."

To his surprise, Mrs. Buren's face quickly went dark with anger. "That is an inflammatory and imprudent thing to say, Georgie. I thought I taught you better than to speak so carelessly."

Reade flushed. "I'm sorry, Mrs. Buren, of course I didn't mean . . . now that the Guard has left, I'm responsible . . . " He hated the way the tone of her voice shot him back across the years, turning him into a frightened, floundering child again.

To his relief Mrs. Buren smiled at him, her anger gone as quickly as it came. "Of course you are. You just spoke without thinking. I know you're doing your best, all on your own. The guardsmen certainly cleared out in a hurry. Drink your tea, dear, before it gets cold."

Reade took another sip. They were both silent for a moment, then Mrs. Buren stood up and pushed the tea trolley back. "This house has been in my family a long time. Now that things are getting back to normal, I don't see why . . . "

Reade stood up too. "Nothing is normal. Now that the National Guard have left it's even more important to be careful. I can't guarantee your safety, all alone out here. Everyone else has moved into town." He sat down heavily, feeling drained. He pointed to her chair, and Mrs. Buren sat down too.

"No one can predict what will happen," he said, "or what won't happen. Like the graveyard out here. Everyone thought it was going to be a real mess, no one could figure out why they hadn't— why you hadn't been—hurt right away. Plenty of other graveyards in town gave up their dead, all the churchyards, even the old potter's field. No one gave any thought to how stony hard the ground was out this way. So they rushed all those guardsmen here, and it turned out to be a kind of turkey shoot, with the dead coming up so slow, it was actually pretty easy. . ."

Mrs. Buren looked away. Red spots of color bloomed on her cheeks.

Reade cursed himself and started again. "That's a dumb way to describe it, and I'm sorry, I know some of the people in that graveyard belonged to your family." He hesitated. "At least your husband wasn't there."

"There were quite a few of my people out there," she said, a little hoarsely. "But I was spared that, at least."

Mrs. Buren's husband had died in the Korean War, his body never recovered. Reade hated that he knew that. He could point to any person still alive in the town and say where their dead relatives were buried, or at least where they should be buried, and he hated that too. He thought it an awful thing that he knew more about the dead of his town than the living.

"Mrs. Buren, not all the dead come out of graves we know about.

We put men on shifts to watch the cemeteries, but there are family graves and plots all over the place—on farms, old estates, unmarked graves. Not all of them registered with the county. And then there's the other ones, hidden bodies that nobody knew about . . . "

She looked up sharply, and for the first time he saw a trace of fear in her expression. Reade was encouraged; perhaps he could convince her.

"Hidden bodies?" she said, "What are you talking about?"

"Do you remember Jennifer Collins?"

"Remember?" she said, her eyes wide. "Oh, oh, no. . . "

"I know she was a favorite of yours."

She lowered her eyes to the floor. "A teacher should never have favorites, but I truly thought I could help that poor girl. Growing up without a father can have such an enormous impact on a child. And then last year, that man she was living with ran off, abandoned her and their little boy. It was like a curse, passed down the generations. She turned out to be no better than her mother. What a waste," she said, her anger flaring up again, and Reade wondered what she thought had been wasted—Jenny's life or her own time.

"She killed the boy's father."

"Oh Georgie, what an awful thing!"

"Everybody knows he slapped her around, and I guess he went too far, maybe she was scared for the baby. She killed him and hid his body in the privy out behind their mobile home. That must have been tough, shifting a big man like him, but she managed it." I shouldn't be telling her all this, he thought, but found he couldn't stop. All the awful things he had seen and done in the past months were building up in him, filling him up like poisoned water in a well. If he didn't speak, he'd drown. "One night he woke up. He got Jenny, and the little boy, and about a dozen other people down in the trailer park. They all set off on a rampage, and there was hell to pay. We lost a lot of people. You could still see the mark on his temple where she hit him . . . "

"She was punished." Mrs. Buren's voice was a whisper. "Her sin came back to her. It was no better than she deserved, I suppose. But the baby, that innocent child, he never even had a chance, he deserved that at least . . . " Mrs. Buren put her hand in front of her face, shooing his words away like flies, and Reade cursed his own selfish stupidity. In his mind he saw Jenny Collin's little boy, barely a toddler, his blue pajamas covered with blood and slime. The baby had launched himself at Reade, right across the shattered, stinking remains of his father. Sheriff Howell had pushed Reade aside and the baby had fastened itself onto Howell's leg, a feral animal in footie pajamas. Howell had actually given out a startled laugh until the child's tiny teeth had pierced his skin; then he had started to scream. Reade had tried to pull the boy off of Howell's leg, finally torn him off, a goodly chunk of Howell's shin still in his mouth, the round baby cheeks filthy with blood. His squirming body had been so horribly cold.

He got down on one knee in front of Mrs. Buren like a suitor and gently pulled her hands away from her face. "You have to listen to me," he said. "I can't let you stay out here by yourself. They sanitized that graveyard out there, but there could be unmarked graves, there could be bodies we don't know about, making their way up. That soil is stony, and that makes it hard going for them, but there's something in it, something that makes the older dead ones more . . . preserved than normal. We had one come out of the church graveyard that was over a hundred years old, and it did a lot of harm before we could stop it. It doesn't matter how long ago they died, if there's even a scrap of bone and muscle left, it hungers, and if the head is intact, it'll hunt."

Mrs. Buren pulled her hands out of Reade's, stood up again and walked to the window. "You don't have to tell me these things. My people certainly are out there. We heard them at night, scratching their way up. Out there in the moonlight, the bones clicking against the earth reminded me of castanets. My husband and I took a trip to Spain once. That was just after we were married. Really, I think that was the happiest time of my life." She stopped for a moment and looked down at the floor.

"Two weeks after the soldiers arrived, I woke early and walked out to the fence to take in a breath of morning air. And standing on the other side to greet me was my dear cousin, Annabelle. She was just 15 when she died. I was 12, not allowed to go her funeral. Influenza, they said. But now I know the truth. She was there at the fence to greet me. And so was her unborn baby."

"My Lord." Reade sank back in the chair, overwhelmed and nauseous. Had he really thought of this house as safe? Had he worried about frightening this woman? It was a miracle she was still sane.

"She stood there, with her arms wrapped around her stomach, cradling her poor little bastard, her tattered burial gown swaying in the breeze. They buried her in white, that's funny, don't you think? She tunneled out of that stony ground, and the baby burrowed out of her. It yowled at me from her torn belly, with its horrible little puckered-up face. It was hungry."

Mrs. Buren walked back across to the tea tray and picked up her cup. "I think she killed herself. Or perhaps she simply died from the mortification of it. Either way, it was her shame that killed her. But the truth comes out. It comes up. Secret things don't stay secret forever. Like that soldier that ran away. Sooner or later he'll be found."

One of the guardsmen had gone AWOL just before his unit had been reassigned, taken some food and his gun and left the house during the night. The Captain had come to see Reade about it the day they shipped out, as worried as he was angry and embarrassed. Reade had promised to keep an eye out, told the Captain he'd keep in touch. On the desk between them was Sheriff Howell's revolver and badge. And down the hall, the zombie that had once been Sheriff Howell had raged and shrieked, throwing itself against the cell bars.

"Do you want me to do it?" the Captain had asked, and Reade had said no, no thank you, he would manage.

Now Mrs. Buren gave a shrill laugh—an unpleasant, brittle sound. "You think your old teacher is going to go crazy out here, don't you? Oh Georgie Reade! That is funny!" But through her laughter, he saw that black anger bubbling up again.

"Lots of people have gone insane," Reade said. He thought of Lorraine Branson, with her pale face and empty eyes. The night they burned her son Jason's body, she had thrown herself on the pyre. Reade had caught a glimpse of her, cradling her zombie boy in her arms, just before the flames had roared up.

He ran a hand through his unwashed hair and slumped down in the chair, suddenly feeling very tired. "I haven't been sleeping so well lately," he said. His voice seemed to come from far off. "I can't catch the knack of sleeping more than an hour at a time anymore."

"You'll sleep now, dear. For a while, I think," Mrs. Buren said. Reade looked up at her, and it took a moment for him to realize he was on his knees again. There was one more brief moment of lucidity before he pitched forward onto the carpet, then darkness.

He woke up slowly, head pounding, a taste in his mouth like grit. Masses of dull silver duct-tape secured his wrists to the armrests of a heavy straight-backed wooden chair; his own legs were strapped solidly to the chair's. Dim light filtered in from rectangular windows set close to the ceiling; he was in the basement. The cinderblock wall he was facing had been recently whitewashed, the red earth floor was neatly swept. The air was thick with a rank stench that was terribly familiar, cut with a strong smell of disinfectant. The Oriental carpet was piled in an untidy heap next to the chair. That's how she got me down here, he thought. She wrapped me up in the rug and dragged me down the stairs.

To his right was a small table covered with a bloodstained tea towel. On the towel were a roll of duct tape and a copy of *Gray's Anatomy*, with a small boning knife, laid across the pages holding the book open at a color illustration of a dissected bicep.

"You're awake, Georgie. That's good. I was worried I let your head hit the steps one time too many." Mrs. Buren stepped in front of him. Her hair was disheveled, and there were smudges of earth and something dark on the front of her dress. Behind them, Reade could hear movement.

He cleared his throat and tried to speak. "Mrs. Buren," it came out as a harsh whisper, "whatever it is you've done, we can talk about it. Please, just cut me loose."

"I'm sorry," she said again, and her eyes were so far away. "But I can't leave this house. He needs me. And we need you."

"Did one of the soldiers hurt you? Did you do something to them? If they hurt you whatever you did was self-defense." He forced himself to try and think clearly, past the steady throbbing in his head. He could feel blood trickling through his hair. His gun was still strapped to his hip.

Mrs. Buren looked at him with pity. "You don't understand, Georgie. I've done so much wrong. I've sinned, and suffered for it, as sinners should. But now I've been given another chance." She reached out and tipped his chair back on one leg, spinning Reade in neat pirouette away from the wall to face the other occupants of the basement. The soldier was taped to his chair in the same manner as Reade. Large sections of flesh had been neatly stripped away from the meaty parts of his arms, thighs and chest, leaving precise rectangular holes. His heart peeked out of a dark mass of rotting viscera and coagulated blood. The arms and seat of his chair were black with blood. Reade knew that the dead didn't bleed that way; the soldier had still been alive when the flesh had been stripped off him. He had crossed over—that was clear from the grey, grainy texture of his skin and the feral way his teeth gripped the wad of duct tape securing his head and neck. But he posed no threat now. His head was gone from the bridge of his nose up, the skull scooped out clean.

Just behind the soldier was a mattress piled high with quilts and blankets. In the center, hands and feet trussed with more tape, lay a zombie child. Reade thought he might have been about five when he had died. His flesh had the hard, desiccated look of a body that had been underground for some time. Next to the mattress was a stinking pile of rags, bits of bone and chunks of dried flesh all smashed into pieces. Further back, close to the wall, Reade could see two gaping holes in the cellar floor, one large, one small, with hard stony earth piled around their edges.

Mrs. Buren nodded toward the pile of body parts. "She came here after my husband died. Horrible woman. She said the boy was my

John's, that John had been planning to leave me and marry her, that she would be a truer wife to him, because she had given him a son. She said she wanted money, or she'd tell. So I gave her some tea, just like the tea I gave you, only stronger, much stronger. And I gave the boy some lemonade. Then I brought them down here and buried them and waited for someone to come looking. But no one ever did."

Reade tried to speak and found he couldn't.

"We've lived here together, the three of us, all these years. They were my secret. And then the dead began to rise. I came down here every night. I waited, and I prayed. And one night, when those awful men were off in town, I heard a noise, no louder than a mouse scratching for food, but oh, it made my heart light. He was finally coming up, coming back to me."

She gestured with her chin at the stinking pile of flesh. "I didn't regret killing her, that slut, that whore. But the child, that was wrong. Bastard or not, he was all that was left of my dear husband. Killing him was a terrible mistake, one I've regretted bitterly. But when I heard them coming up I knew I'd been given a second chance. Those stupid boys had searched the cellar the day they came. "Securing the perimeter" they called it. One of them had helped himself to a jar of my best preserves, and I pretended to be angry about it. I made them put a lock on the cellar and took the key. They had a good laugh at the foolish old lady, but they kept out after that, just to keep me quiet. By day I watched those men destroy what was left of my kin, and at night I came down here and listened. And when the time was right, when I knew they were ready, I told him." She pointed to the remains of the soldier. "He was the greediest. I've always been good at spotting the weak ones, the greedy ones. I told him they were here, and I needed help destroying them, because they were a secret. I offered him money if he'd come down here when the others were out in my garden, swilling beer, smoking God knows what to celebrate their last night. And he came down. He took care of that." She jerked her thumb again at the pile. "And then I took care of him. He turned out to be very useful. He lasted much longer than I expected."

She smiled down at the boy, her face radiant with affection, and in a distant corner of his mind Reade thought he had never seen her look so happy. She stepped over to the soldier's corpse and tore a dangling strip of flesh from his shoulder, dropped it in front of the child. Its head came up immediately, and cellar dirt trickled from the empty eye sockets. It wriggled forward towards the flesh, sniffed it with its ruined and rotted nose, and moaned in disappointment.

"But now my little boy doesn't want him any more, do you dear?" The child moaned again, and she made a little shushing sound. Then she leaned forward and gently squeezed Reade's bicep, testing its firmness. Suddenly Reade remembered that moment on the porch, her sharp look of assessment, her sudden smile of approval.

"Mrs. Buren." Reade said, "don't do this." He struggled for breath, for the words that would reach this woman. "He's not a child anymore. He's a monster, for God's sake. Don't hurt me. Please Mrs. Buren. Please I don't want to die!"

She stepped past him to the table. "But you won't die, Georgie. At least not right away. I've learned a great deal about how much to take, and where. I'm sure you'll last much longer than the soldier. And I'll be here to help you dear."

She glanced at the anatomy book for a moment, just as Reade had seen her consult her lesson plans before beginning class. Then she gave a short nod, picked up the knife and stepped towards him. Reade moaned. The zombie boy mewled with excitement. Mrs. Buren smiled.

"If you're ready Georgie, I think we will begin."

The New Dumb
by Kyle S. Johnson

We are living in dangerously weird times now.
Smart people just shrug and admit they're dazed
and confused. The only ones left with any confidence
at all are the New Dumb. It is the beginning of the end
of our world as we knew it. Doom is the operative ethic. . .
Guaranteed Fear and Loathing. Abandon all hope.
Prepare for the Weirdness. Get familiar with Cannibalism.

—Hunter S. Thompson

I'm sitting in this mobile fortress, smack dab in the middle of three-dozen methane-gas reeking bovine. It's horrendous. The bus smells like dung pancakes, heaped high with pomegranates and afterbirth. These are great men. Nay, Great Americans! Never mind their incessant, loose-tongued jabbering or glib, fat-mouthed laughter at infantile fart jokes. Get it straight, these men are now Kings.

As for me, I have no fucking idea where we are exactly. It's all Colonial America, all New England to me. Dense, lightless suburbs, row upon row. Me, my unfortunate entourage, and what I estimate to be a quarter-million dead people stumbling around in the dark.

It's almost sun-up. We, the whole, are looking for Fenway Park. These men have an obligation. To reignite the competitive flame, to bring the Fall Classic back from the dead. To live their childhood dreams and comfort themselves in their darkest hours. I have a side mission. I'm looking for the headstone that reads Here Lies the American Dream.

The last year's travels have led me to the east coast, and through the wire I heard about these fine men and their great cause. I considered personal safety. I decided in the interest of the story. So my contact passed me through their chain of command, I checked out for whatever reason, and the date was set.

Late last evening, a blazing silver steed with a pantless equestrian on the roof picked me up at my fortified hotel. I've been on this bus for hours, and I've yet to see anything promising. These men are savages. Brutish, squealing things bellowing at one another and making a mess of everything. But they have a well stocked bar, and they permit me to smoke in their metal tube. So I'm thankful to that end.

On the road, I see a guy—dead guy, I should say—reading a newspaper at a bus stop. He looks up at me as we roll past. I wave to him. He goes back to his paper. Even the living dead are discourteous little piggies.

I don't remember if I've introduced the topic, but the chicken-men are clucking about the election that was/wasn't/might have been. Then I'm blurting above their clamor, all about my theory for how this started, and it feels like I have two tongues bumbling around for control in my mouth.

"Okay, so we had an election year. The incumbent party in the executive branch could feel its black gloved stranglehold on the status quo slipping. They had to keep the goddamn status quo. So they need a plan to get their next sired boy in office, or to just fuck the whole damn system up and keep them there for good.

"Now, blowing up a couple more buildings and pointing fingers at a Jihad might have been a bit too obvious. Could have even backfired. So they had to come up with something air tight, the best solution for business.

"It's a well known fact that this administration had its roots tangled up in voodoo and mysticism. Or Crowley Magick. Or Chemical Warfare. Garden variety mind control. Queer elixirs and potions. You name it—they had druids burning candles for it.

"So, one day in September, all these bastards and she-bastards too dumb to realize they have a good thing going for them, which would be death, well they get up and start eating people, as you all well know.

"Ho-ho, but that's not all. See, the eaten people? Yeah, the left-overs. They join up with those other folks who decided death was too boring. They read the membership cards, scratch what they have left of their chins, and call the 1-900-number to join the parade. So before you know it, the streets are goddamn overrun with these monkeys. They're eating the postman. They're gouging the street cop's eyes out. They're even disemboweling little kids when they get out of school.

"So now you, as a concerned parent, have to gather up little Jack and Jill and get to running to wherever it is you feel like you can be safe. No more time to worry about an election, right? How convenient, no?

"So the three-piece suits are clamoring across the television, business as usual, claiming their intel places blame in Syria . . . no, no wait . . . Korea . . . yeah, what the hell, both of 'em . . . no, wait . . . Iran . . . no, Canada. Why those bastards have had it in for us all along. Aw, fuck all, why not all of them? It's their fault, and you need to focus on being afraid of them, way the fuck out there, not the undead folks who make a habit out of turning your friends into cinnamon tooth-paste on your doorstep.

"They ask for the go ahead to extend our president's term until we get this all sorted out. Nobody agrees, but he's still somebody's president a year later. And he still does those PR stunts we love so much. Thumbs up in front of a pyre of burning bodies, hunting trips for quail and reanimated farmers in the woods of Texas, etcetera."

And I notice how no one seems to care. Among the faces on the bus, not a one of them shows outrage or any discernable emotion aside from stupid drunk fervor. I worry for a moment that perhaps the events of the past year have killed my ability to captivate, to spin a tale worth hearing. But these men are simply not worth the spirits they're drinking. They had stopped listening to me some time ago, and by now we're already at Fenway.

I've been to Boston before, before all this, but even now it's oddly calming. Even with the emptied streets and failed roadblocks, it remains an elevated place of elevated folks. They still walk around, caught up in their hustle and bustle, wearing suits and Sox caps.

Except now they're all dead.

Some of them have these twisted looks about them, like they're considering chasing us down and consuming us like game day hot dogs. But the corpses know better. They want to see this game played just as much as these dim-witted louts want to play it. The dead know well that they can't hear the crack of the bat and smell that lush grass—which is probably as dead as they are—if they jump the gun and spill the catcher all over the asphalt. So they'll wait. They'll wait for the final score to be determined and they'll ambush us on the way out.

People think these things are dumb, but I see through that thinly-veiled disguise. They're conniving. They're shrewd and meticulous hunters. When the last out has been scored, we are in serious trouble. The men are adequately filled with drink, so we head through the turnstiles. The walls are adorned in reverence of great men. Fisk. Williams. Rice. Yastrzemski. Even Spaceman. And they tower over these pretenders, with their rag tag appearances and uncomely presentation. But the hooligans are nonetheless motivated, not shamed. They're ass-scratchers unaware of the steamy piss they're about to rain upon a once reputable game.

The dead people are simply unmotivated looters. They're everywhere and almost completely ambivalent to our existence. An occasional firefighter or janitor will swipe at us lazily, but they're simply not fast enough. No, you see, these men among men have been training. Or so I've been told. When it was decided amongst a small army of internet dwellers that two years without a World Series was two years too many, they stopped everything and began practicing their suicide squeezes. Their effort shows in their graceful trundling and doughy builds, and I am all the more encouraged that this game will be some kind of sight.

Some of the zombies are picking at the remains of beer stations and vendor booths. One of the fly-ridden jerks is yanking hard on a tap of Sam Adams. I admire its good taste but object to all the good beer going to waste and I cry, "At least drink it, you goddamn jackanape!" It could care less.

A bunch of them are following our motley crew, and they all blend behind me into a hodgepodge of snarling, drooling fools. The living dead stand out only slightly. They're hurricane survivors, refugees of war, cancer patients dumped out on the streets. We have nothing to worry from them. They're not interested in the swirls of red meat under our hides. Not yet anyway. They're simply coming to watch the game, bask in the glory of the Great American Pastime.

And these sultans among the living, these testaments to the rebirth of a great race of dunderheaded mouth-breathers? Well, they're sure as hell going to have a go at it.

Once we reach the field, I take a seat in the dugout down the first baseline. I scratch my groin, because I'm an old sport and I have to do my best to blend in. One of the players is unpacking his duffel bag next to me.

"What the hell do you even call yourselves anyway?"

He jumps a bit when I speak, which won't serve him well in the batter's box. A man with the jitters is a man unable to hit.

"We're the Sox. We decided we'd be the Sox when we picked the teams."

"No you're not. I've watched them play, I've met the men. You, my friend, are not the Sox."

He goes back to his bag and pulls out a bottle of water. He looks back over at me, then looks away.

I point into the opposing dugout and ask, "Well then, what about those other barbarians? What are they calling themselves?"

He clears his throat. I've clearly unnerved him. "They also wanted to be the Sox."

"Well that's just fucking loony. Ridiculous. I won't go along with that I'm afraid. They look like a lot of gutless cowards anyhow. They're the Non-Braves. You're the Non-Sox. That's how this is reported."

The player knows better than to argue. He may not be the brightest, but he knows that I will draw a line when it comes to journalistic integrity.

I had heard a story through the wire that, in this very ballpark, Jason Varitek had gotten the bug first and walked into the clubhouse during a homestand. By the time anyone was aware of what was happening, he had already bitten Terry Francona, who had in turn infected about half of the front office. The catcher also got to pitchers Daisuke Matsuzaka and Justin Masterson, who spread the disease to most of the rotation and infield. According to reliable sources, Varitek was going after Jacobi Ellsbury when newly acquired Jason Bay felled him with a clean cut from a bat. Unfortunately, these maple bats had a somewhat suspect track record, and this particular one splintered and impaled oft-injured J.D. Drew.

Of all the depraved sights I've seen, that is one I'm sad I missed out on. I had a grand on the Angels last year, anyhow.

The teams have taken the field to stretch, flood their engines with that white-hot burning American red-blood. There are twenty or so tag-along spectators above the opposite dugout swilling their brew and singing "Take Me Out to the Ballgame," and I stand and yell, "It's not even the Seventh Inning Stretch yet! Cool your fucking jets, man!" One of them vomits a geyser of lovely magenta, clearly over-served. Fucking mongrels, there's much more game to be played today.

The players congregate on the mound and flip a coin to decide who bats first. After much chuckling and heaving of great rotundity, it is decided that the Non-Braves will get the first at bat. I have decided to sit in with the Non-Sox, frankly, because they seem to have slightly better character. The Non-Braves' short stop has a face that droops like a sad horse that's been overridden through L.A. traffic. I'll be thankful to be no closer to that nightmare of a man than forty or fifty yards.

While the first inning is underway, I'm alone in the dugout as the team plays defense. They only have one reserve player, a reliever/closer sitting well out of sight in the bullpen. I'm appreciative of that, as pitchers are a race only a peg above the living dead on the intelligence ladder. They're all prattling prima donnas, venomous beings reliant on only one appendage and utterly useless once it's been ridden to shit. The game would fare better without them.

The Non-Sox's current pitcher is some astounding potbelly, but his mastery of the concept of pitching is paramount among those still alive. A two pitch man, he wields a fastball that looks like it tops out around eighty-one and a curve that breaks—badly—about four inches off the plate. He's boasted frequently in the handful of hours I've suffered his company that he was the best in his state three years running in high school.

It's a wonder that this broke-down steed spent the next twenty plus years of his life wasting away in some computer box. But now he's alive again, that same kid he was in high school plus about forty or fifty pounds. In the time it takes for me to light a fresh cigarette and butt it out on the dugout floor, he's retired the side. Credit given where due, the bastard got the job done.

In the stands behind the living spectators, the living dead are filing in, stylishly late to the party. Some of them have giant foam hands or pennants, stolen from ransacked vendor tables. One of the half-brights is wearing a big red hand on his head and lolls down the stairs like a walking contraceptive. Rather than pursuing the meat trays sitting just above the dugout—who don't even notice the arrival of the rest of the crowd—they meander through the stands, checking their tickets, looking for their proper seats. They might be dumb sons of bitches, but they haven't forgotten the time honored tradition of moving down a row or two when there are empty seats to be filled.

The Non-Braves' pitcher is in the worst shape of anyone, and it's being noted among the waiting batsmen in the dugout. A runner is waiting on first, a slender Asian man who poked a lazy pitch into the gap, and the pitcher continuously tries to throw him out with the generous lead he's taking.

I stand up and shout, "Quit sandbagging for chrissakes and throw the goddamn ball!" The team laughs, which is good. I've earned their trust for now. I've been envisioning that these men intend to leave me during their daring escape. I can see it twittering in their hand-cranked brains. But I intend to confront danger head-on and follow the story so long as there is one.

The bottom of the first is rife with horrible defense. The Non-Braves are perpetual fantasy practitioners. It wouldn't surprise me if they never got a chance to play the game because their parents were too concerned about their faces meeting with errant line drives. At least the men I sit with seem to have a buried knack for the game. Their day in the sun was probably long ago when they played for teams named after local printing houses and debt solution companies. Teams coached by their fathers. That day has long since passed, yet it too has risen from the dead, though moldy and worm-eaten. They are living out their dream. The American Dream. Playing in the biggest game of their lives. Rutting idiots prancing around in worn t-shirts and jean shorts, men-children playing a grown up's game. But they're enjoying themselves, and they forget about the world outside, even as it leaks into the stands. They figure if the world's light is finally flickering out, the wick might as well ignite a stick of dynamite in the process. They want to go out with some damn style, and I can respect that.

But that doesn't make them any good at it, God help them. I've been to charity softball games, opening night for expansion franchises, any number of tee ball outings. And this is, without question, one of the poorest excuses for a baseball game I have ever witnessed. Watching the Non-Braves play defense is like watching the zombies trying to field grounders. Humanity has finally been trumped by the slower, duller version of itself.

During a day's long third inning, I get in the habit of talking to Bill, the Non-Sox's second baseman. He's an odd but friendly fellow, completely covered in tumors due to a disease called neurofibromatosis. He tells me that it's always rendered him socially awkward, but he says that this drastic change to the way things work has given him cause to relax his self-loathing. He's happy to feel like he isn't the scariest looking thing walking these days.

"I want you to win. You know that, Bubba?"

"You're supposed to be objective."

"No sense in objectivity anymore. Objectivity is the tool of the hopeful, and the hopeful are the ones who are dead or undead. But we, you and I, we the proud have to be subjective."

And Bill is as sharp as a little tack. "Well, does that mean we're pessimists?"

"No, no, that means we know the Truth."

But before he can grunt his way into his next question, I spy the coward next up to bat.

"Why's he shaking so much? Does he have the palsy?"

"No sir. That's Guy, he lost his wife and kids. Guess he's a little on edge still."

"Christ, practically over the edge from the look of it. He's on the verge of implosion, he's a goddamn walking cucumber. Why's he still in the game?"

"He played college ball for a few years. Guy can hit."

"Could hit, but he doesn't want to." Guy gets into the box, knocks the dirt off of his cleats, and drops into his stance. He's brushed back in succession by three high pitches, not thrown in a form of strategic intimidation, clearly just the tank on the mound running on fumes.

Guy pats his chest and rips into the first thing close to the plate, a rope to left for two bases that knocks in a run.

Bill, the dog with the hemp rope bone and the bad skin, "What's the truth?"

"The Truth? Hopelessness, nothing new."

This is not what baseball used to be. Sure, runs have scored, but only for the Non-Braves' sheer defensive incompetence. Very few of these men can hit worth a damn, and not a one of them can come close to taking the ball out of this fortress. The only cause to direct any attention toward the Great Green Beast in left field is when one of the dead spectators drunkenly flops over the edge and splashes like a wet ragdoll into the field of play.

Bored and needing drink, I cut across the field to get to a concession stand. The zoo animals don't like that too much and boo and hiss in my direction, so I yell, "Pipe the fuck down and I'll bring you a hot dog when I get back. I'll even put relish on it."

I know I should still be in the dugout covering the game, but I've lost my passion. I haven't seen a baseball game in close to two decades, but I have fond memories of the game. And I hate that this will be my last experience with it. Imagine seeing the girl you had a crush on in high school, but twenty years later, and her tits are sagging to her knees and she's got four kids from four different male suitors. Now give her a hand grenade on a bad day, and you have what this game is to the mythos of baseball.

In the concession area, the televisions are on and President Georgie Porgie Puddin' and Pie is staging a debate. But not just any debate. The Great Debate of President v. Country. He's talking in what may as well be Swahili, all about taking aggressive measures in an aggressive age. He tells the world that he has taken the liberty of modifying the Constitution and naming himself to a third term. Both the main candidates and their running mates are dead, and he just dares us to vote for Nader. He's not using any of the cue cards his daddy gave him for the science fair. He's all on his own now. He's a mad dog loosed from his chain, a fiery televangelist spewing garbled sermons of malapropism and hellfire.

I pour myself a popcorn bucket full of Sam and King George tells nobody in particular—or maybe just me specifically—that he's been cleared to eliminate everything. That the world has been totally overrun, save for our shining City on the Hill. We have endured, and as the world's only remaining superpower, because we are in the ICU and not toe-tagged on the slab, we have the moral responsibility to bring peace to the entire planet.

Peace, as it occurs to the commander-in-chief, is complete annihilation. He says that all other nations, great and small, will be vaporized. After the smoke has settled, the remaining constituency of the United States will be sent out to repopulate the world at large. We will leave the country in his able hands and it will become his own personal playground. From there, he, his family, and a select few friends—chosen by lottery—will have wild orgies and burn each other with cigarettes and inbreed their way back into prominence.

And even unchallenged, George drowns in his own flop-sweat. He brushes back his silver mane, well coiffed to the last. He looks me dead in the eye and asks me where I'd like to go. I tell him that I'd always heard Mexico was nice. Parts, anyway. Then he tells me that I'm not fit for his Brave New World. He tells me his New World is not a place for the bold, for the unashamed. He tells me that the meek inherit the Earth after all, and that he is proof positive.

He pulls a fat cigar from his breast pocket, strikes a match to light it, inhales, and coughs uncontrollably for a moment. I drink from my bucket and drool dark fine lager like a dying beast. He composes himself, and one of his slaves, a sheepish boy in a tuxedo, wheels out a panel with a glowing red button in the middle. He wipes the froth from the corners of his mouth and asks if I shouldn't be covering the game. He puts on a ten gallon hat and starts caressing the button like an engorged clitoris. His hand raises and pokes out his index finger like an instantaneous hard-on, whistles as it descends down, down, and he mimics an explosion noise as he jams the red knob in.

He yeehaws and yells, "There goes Libya!"

The same motion.

"Yahoo! There goes Turkey, you turkey!"

Again.

"Lebanon!"

Again.

"Goodnight, Mother Russia!"

I remember my sidearm strapped to my ankle. I un-holster it, aim into the face of a mad-scientist-cowboy, and the television explodes in a decadent display of sparks and shattered glass. There are two more TVs in sight nearby, and I can still hear him.

"Cuba, so long!"

BANG!

"Auf Wiedersehen, Germany!"

BANG!

But the demon-president's voice is echoing throughout the concession area. Too many TVs, not enough bullets. I may need to save them for later, so I can back my way out of here when the time is right.

I stagger back to the field with a half-full bucket of beer, and then I stop where the stairs descend. A whole mess of dead people have wandered onto the field of play with still more slithering out of the stands. Two of them belly-flop off the Giant Great Wall in left field, pause for a second to collect themselves, and drag their broken legs behind them toward the outfielders. In the reliever's cage, a small herd of corpses are gnawing on each team's setup man/closer/generally superfluous pitcher. I can hear them wailing the highest in the commotion, like shrill coyotes in the setting Nevada sun. They're batting them away—ineffectively—with their ball caps, as it's a well known fact that pitchers cannot tow the lumber. Save for Sabathia and Zambrano. Those burly bastards sure could hit. I guess you could count Ruth, too. Hell, Bob Gibson was a fighter. Even Nolan Ryan knew how to throw a decent hook. But these two sloths just flail for spectacle's sake as the living dead rip into their arms and necks.

The scene on the field isn't any better. The benches have cleared, ladies and gentlemen. Panic, chaos, even a slight hint of jubilation. I swear I think I can see Billy Martin and Mr. October duking it out in the dugout. The teams have been dissolved by way of battery acid. One crazy asshole is swinging the first base bag around over his head, clipping anything within reaching distance, wide-eyed and screaming like a sloppy Persian warrior. The mound of goop that was pitching for the Non-Braves is now merely a lot of goop on the mound. His intestines stretch out toward the base paths in a literal telestrator for a 1-4-3 double play. Can't say I am too sad to see that sorry bastard go. There is much amok being run, folks are wielding baseball bats like fine medieval swords, doing the seductive dance of war. I haven't the heart to tell them that there's a nuclear (or nuke-u-lar) winter on the horizon, so I just sit on the stair with my beer and my cigarette and observe.

The game of baseball is now officially dead. Not killed by station-to-station game play, the designated hitter, Don Denkinger, or performance enhancing rubbish. It has been slain by these fools in athletes' clothing. It has been put to bed for good by the slack-jawed corpses tearing those same fools apart. But unlike these particular corpses, as for the sport of baseball, this puppy isn't getting back up, Bubba.

I've seen atrocity. I've seen madness. I've seen Nixon and the worst of every blow-hard politico trying to shape-shift before the great consensus, only to turn into a snarling and vengeful thing.

This is justified. This is warranted. Any sane jury of their peers or our peers would not convict the undead. These men, now under siege, have defiled a beautiful gal, and her daddy Abner Doubleday isn't around to protect her honor. So the fans have turned against the players, as any good audience would, and they eat them alive. The only difference in this strange new time is that the mauling is much more literal.

The living spectators have decided to get a jump on their inevitable trade to a new team. They've read the dirt sheets, seen the writing on the wall, packed their bags, talked to the press, and cleaned out their lockers. Before the ghouls can get to them, they're screaming hysterical-like, sobbing like grieving widows, and singing "Take Me Out to the Ballgame." And they're tearing each other open with bare hands and gnawing on fatty flaps and red-marshmallow entrails. One woman has hollowed out the stomach of some lummox and dumped her bucket of popcorn into her newly made gut-bowl. She sobs uncontrollably as she reaches inside him and scoops out handfuls of stale popcorn and viscera and shoves it into her mouth.

The real zombies, real in the sense that they have a legitimate reason to be a pack of lumbering oafs, have managed to move down from their nosebleeds into the best seats in the house. But not just any seats, mind you. No, these come with a complimentary meal. On the house.

Now they are melded together in a sickening tangle of living and not quite, bloated distended limbs and gnarly faces biting and snapping wildly at one another. A great swirl of rotting humanity moaning and screaming that they couldn't care if they ever get back. Which is a good thing, because they probably won't. At least not in one piece.

The drone in right field, the human zucchini known as Guy, leaps over the short wall and into the stands, practically doing the Lindy through a crowd of zombie spectators all the way to the exit.

Emerging in a strangely calm demeanor from the battlefield, Bill the oatmeal-faced man takes his seat next to me and steals a cigarette from my shirt pocket.

"Things sure aren't looking that great right about now, doc."

The screaming has died away, there are no more soldiers standing to fight. What is left of the teams lays heaped on the brown grass in messy red piles and jigsaw-shaped pieces. Some of the water-head ball players try to get up from their deaths while they're still being eaten, proving to the bitter end—and subsequently to the even more bitter new beginning—to be the sort of insensitive pricks who would spoil an honest dinner for no damn reason.

But Bill keeps his composure and says, "Shit is bad, real bad."

"I've seen worse before, my friend."

"Yeah, well I suppose we ought to leave all the same. No sense being here anymore."

But there's something about staying here that I can't seem to shake. I feel as though I need to be here, to see this through. This would be an exciting death, on one of baseball's greatest fields, under the lights one last time.

"I can't do that, Bill. I'm an old soul, I'm afraid, and I say the captain goes down with his ship."

"But this isn't your ship. Never was. You are a stowaway here, and I say we run like the rats would. We might be filthy rats, but we get to live to tell the tale, so to hell with honor in this case."

Telling the tale. Bill, past his bumpy face and hideous Minnesota accent, makes a lot of good sense.

"Besides, I like you. I have a feeling we're going to need a guy like you when the going gets tougher. Because it ain't getting any better anytime soon."

There's something endearing about Bill. He's completely genuine. And he's a man with a story. And there's nothing more important—especially now—than someone with a good story.

"Fine then," I agree, "let's get a move on. I saw a nice red Beemer in the street we could make off with."

He starts, "Well why don't we just take the bus? It's better fortified, there's food and water—"

But I snap him out of his stupor and fill him in on the bad news. "This will be a journey of most dangerous and frightening proportions. There'll be something bad at every turn, and probably something even worse sniffing at our asses. So we may as well travel with some panache. Top speed on one of those monsters is something around one-forty, and we'll need that speed to get where we need to be."

"Where do we need to be?"

"Don't ask so many fucking questions, Bill. You won't end up any wiser that way. We won't know where we have to go until we get there."

"Whatever you say, sir."

And as we jump into the car I remind him that this red BMW is a choice automobile with great features, though mostly unnecessary ones. The car will serve us well.

On the road out of Boston, Bill turns the white noise away and replaces it with the Duke Ellington CD in the changer and I mumble-yell about how the ingrate who owned the car before we absconded with it had to have some semblance of good taste. Bill just closes his eyes and listens, which is good. He'll need the rest.

And we barrel down the freeway between the battered and abandoned cars. It is here that I find the monuments in the graveyard that I have been looking for all along. The Dream is dead, but in our New Era of Craziness, death is more often temporary than not. I can only hope that if someone decides to hold the Super Bowl this year, it will be infinitely more entertaining.

Cured Meat

by Christine Morgan

The den is cool, the sand dry beneath us. We stir. Slow and sluggish, bodies stiff, joints cracking, tendons creaking.

Sunshine as we emerge. Early warmth baking into us, easing away the night chill, the lethargy.

Those with good eyes and ears take sentry duty. Watching. Listening. Alert for anything that might mean danger . . . or prey.

We are all very hungry.

We are always very hungry.

But first, we must groom.

There are ragged edges, peeling flaps, dangling pieces. There are stringy ends of veins, tough gristle, splinters of bone. There are bug-kind that burrow and lay eggs in us, clumps to be scraped from damp crevices.

The damp is bad.

The damp makes us soft, spongy, loose. The damp makes us slimy and green. The damp makes us rot.

We groom.

Fingers and teeth. Pinching, plucking, nipping, gnawing, nibbling. Skin scraps, bits of flesh. We rub with sand to scour and dry. We dust-roll. We turn to follow the sun.

The small or weak or damaged do their part, attending the big and the strong and the whole. Even those too impaired to be useful are good for one final thing.

We are all, always, very hungry.

The meat of our own kind fills, but never satisfies. We are sun-dried, salt-crusted, smoked. Hard to chew.

The meat of bird-kind, bug-kind, beast-kind, fish-kind. . . that meat fills and *almost* satisfies. Almost.

Once, there was other-kind. Moist and warm. Supple and sweet. With dark-hot-rich pumping blood. With juicy organs cradled in layers of succulent fat.

Their meat . . . their meat filled *and* satisfied.

But they are long gone.

Their great den-places are burned and flooded, rusted and crumbled, barren and overgrown. Full of sharp things that snag and cut, heavy things that fall-crush-break, hidden things that explode in fiery thunder. Holes, pools, pits. Bad, dangerous places that can end us.

Sometimes, our kind still go there. Drawn by habit, by hunger, by hope. Searching for the other-kind, for the meat that fills and satisfies.

A few who go, return. Most who go, do not. None who go, find.

There are only rumors.

Always, rumors.

Passed from group to group. . . mind to mind. . . by noises and gestures, by the raw blunt impressions of crude thought and meaning.

Rumors of bright, dry strongholds where other-kind gather behind barricades. Plump and tender other-kind, and fast strong other-kind, and weapons that can skull-shatter from far distances.

Rumors of enormous many-denned structures, where water leaps and fabulous things glitter, and the other-kind are packed so numerous that we could eat and eat and eat until our guts burst. An endless feast.

Rumors.

So many rumors.

None true.

But some of our kind believe, and even go. Hoping. Hungry.

Always, always so very hungry.

We groom as the sun climbs. The burly one, sitting on a sand pile above the den's opening, has a freshly-split scalp. It hangs in a tattered fold over a shriveled ear. Dull bone shows through. Damaged ones cluster around the burly one, eager to please, currying favor.

The legless one tears away that patch of skin and tangled hair. Offers it back to the burly one, who ignores it. The tiny shrunken one darts in to snatch at the morsel, misses, scrambles up the legless one's torso to grab again. The half-faced one uses the squabble to sidle in and take over the grooming.

There was a recent battle. Another group. We stood tall with arms upraised to seem larger, we groaned and wailed to seem fearsome, and when they would not give way, we fought.

We won.

We drove them off. We brought down two, crushed their heads, ate their brains, ate their meat. A salt-crust and a smoked. Some of us were scratched, gouged, bitten. The burly one's scalp was split. But we won.

Our group is strong.

A sentry, the one with only a single eye but a single eye that is very good, gives an alarm. All grooming stops. We wait, ready.

Dirt and brush. Ridges of stone. Dunes and cracked-parched gullies. The wide-above sky, sun, no clouds, no sense of coming damp. Faraway shapes of bird-kind.

No challenge from rivals. No entreaty-call from a stranger wanting to join us, or a wandering one come with news and rumors.

The air is silent, hot and still. There is only the whir and hum and click of bug-kind. It makes us hungry. Even for that poor meat.

We wait.

Some of us—hopeful, foolish—cannot keep from searching for a sign of the other-kind. The sound-throb-vibration of their machines, their music-noise, their weapons, their voices.

Hopeful. Foolish.

There is a group, we know from more rumors, who fed on other-kind that came from the sky in huge shining hollow-shells of metal that flew like bird-kind. That group waits, basking on sun-heated strips of black stone, sheltering in the broken hulls of the shining things. Day by day they wave the sticks that once summoned the huge shining things down from the sky, certain that some day, more will come.

Very hopeful. Very foolish.

Very hungry.

Always, so very, very hungry.

The single-eyed one gives a threat-warning. Long dry growth rustles and ripples. Dust puffs and drifts. The low forms of beast-kind appear. Narrow, lean and rangy. Matted pelts. Muzzles and teeth. Flat yellow eyes.

They growl their hate of us. They hunker and piss wet-yellow in their fear.

The burly one heaves up from the sand. The biggest one and the tall quick one also shake off or push away their attendants, and rise to face the beast-kind.

So do I.

The marked one.

Dark whorls and intricate lines. Smoke-black and blood-red. Like shadows beneath my skin. Symbols. Images.

Some believe that the marks protect me, keep me safe.

There is a small-finger missing on one hand. A chunk is gone from my calf, the wound an irregular scoop where the flesh was bitten away in a greedy mouthful. An ear-rim is torn off. But that is all. I am hardly damaged.

The beast-kind piss and growl. They want to leap upon us and rip us to pieces. They want to flee from us as fast as their four legs will carry them. They would not eat our meat but shun it, kick dirt over it, squirt more of their yellow fear-piss onto the ground. If they did bite off and swallow some part of us, they would vomit it out and *then* kick dirt and squirt piss.

All of the beast-kind fear and hate us.

They know we are hungry. They know we want to gorge ourselves on their meat that fills but does not quite satisfy. They know we would seek out their vulnerable little ones, eat them helpless, blind and squeaking. That is why they fear us.

They know we are not the other-kind. That is why they hate us. If they found one of us alone or unwatchful, they would attack. Tearing with jaws and claws. Goring with horns. Kicking and trampling with hard hooves.

All of the beast-kind hate us . . . but these ones . . . these beast-kind who once shared dens with the other-kind, who remember them as we do, who search for them as we do . . . they hate us most of all.

We are not alone, and we are not unwatchful.

We are many, strong, and ready.

The burly one raises both arms, and groans at the beast-kind. Daring them. Inviting them to come and try, come and try, we will peel their hides and break their bones, pull out their guts, scoop their eyeballs from their sockets and pop them sweet and juicy in our teeth.

The biggest one mimics the burly one, though with only an arm and a half because one ends in a charred-over stump. The tall and quick one does the same, the movement making the ragged line of old holes that run from shoulder to hip stretch and gape like more mouths.

I also do the same.

Soon we are all standing tall—those of us who *can* stand—atop the dunes and hills around our den. Standing tall with arms raised, groaning and wailing.

We are too many for them, too strong, too ready. But they are too many for us, too fast, too agile. A fight would be costly for both sides, and we all know it.

The beast-kind shrink and slink and finally retreat into the long grass. Our arms come down. The sentries go back to their places. The grooming continues.

I sit with my leg bent, inspecting my calf. The hole is not deep, but sometimes damp collects there or the bug-kind burrow into it no matter how often I scour it out with sand. I present my back to the hollow one, who picks carefully so as not to damage the marks that cover it.

Only the hollow one has the patience and precision for this. Only I find the hollow one useful enough to keep.

The hollow one is sun-dried and frail, scant meat clinging to thin bones. Knuckles and elbows and knees and chin are exposed where stretched-taut skin has split or worn away. Below the ribs is a gaping cavity where no organs nestle. Strands of gristle and cords of muscle crisscross like thick webs, helping to hold the hollow one's upper and lower halves together.

At last the day's heat shines full upon us. The shadows are chased away. The grooming is finished. We can forage and hunt.

Some stay behind to guard our den and the ones who cannot move well. They will dig and clean. They keep watch. The rest of us follow the burly one.

Bug-kind, we eat as we find them. Into the mouth, crunch, a spurt of bitterness and the barest teasing taste of meat. Too squirmy to carry back to the den alive, and too small to bother carrying back dead.

There are bird-kind, and eggs hidden in nests beneath bushes or up in the branching forks of trees . . . eggs that are not exactly *meat*, but good just the same.

Fish-kind, we do not often find, because we stay far from the wet places.

Then there are beast-kind. From the small and quick to the large and lumbering. Lone hunters and huge herds. Long coiled ones with darting tongues. Slow-moving ones with soft meat inside bony plates. Furry bodies with skinny naked tails. Spiny-bristly-pokey ones.

We hunt. We forage. Alert. Crunching bug-kind and small bird-kind. Our territory is close to hunted-out, almost empty. Soon we will have to leave our den and move on, into the unfamiliar. New territory, new den, new rivals, new threats.

But . . . new meat.

For meat, we would do whatever we had to do.

So very hungry.

The sun is at its highest when the burly one leads us to where the ground is cut by a narrow straight flatness. An other-kind thing from the days long gone.

It is hard like stone, dark like stone. Where it is not covered in dune-drifts and sheets of sand, it holds the sun's warmth well into the night. But we rarely come here, because it is the edge.

The battle was here. The burly one rubs at the missing patch of scalp. It could have been the burly one's end right then, if the skull was broken.

Some bones have been buried in wind-blown sand, some taken away by scavengers. Others lie scattered on the hard sun-warmed flat-ness. Stripped of every speck of meat, cracked and sucked clean of marrow. We left skulls smashed like eggshells, the dense meaty brains scooped out and triumphantly devoured.

There is an other-kind place on the far side, with bright-sharp glints in the corners of square holes. Stout posts. Round rings made of some solid black stuff even harder to chew than the tough flesh of our own kind. Jumbles of rusted machine-parts. Long snarls of thorny wire.

We pause, alert for trouble. The wind blows gritty, swirling sand and sending bristles of dry bush bouncing past.

A long-eared beast-kind hops and sniffs, hops and sniffs. A few small bird-kind dart and flit. Nothing else moves.

Our rivals seem nowhere nearby.

The burly one beckons, commands. We follow. Onto the flatness and heat. The air ripples around us. Puddles of not-wet glimmer in the distance. The sun is hot and good.

We cross the flatness. Beyond our territory now, into theirs.

The tall quick one makes a lunge at the long-eared beast-kind. It goes rigid in terror. Then its nose twitches, its hindlegs spring. But the tall quick one has it. A single wrenching bite and the beast-kind's throat is gone. Its hindlegs kick-flail-jerk, go limp.

Meat.

Not much meat. Not enough meat. And we are all so very hungry.

Two mouthfuls each. Fresh warm meat and slippery guts. Tufts of fur pasted to our faces by sticky crusts of drying blood.

We move on.

Toward the crumbling structure made by the other-kind.

The biggest one objects.

The burly one commands again.

We all know that sometimes there is food to be found in such places. Strange food-relics left by the other-kind, encased in metal that is bulged and weakened and distorted, easy to break open. Sometimes the food within is even meat of sorts. . . the meat of fish-kind or bird-kind or beast-kind . . . never the meat of other-kind . . . and most of the time it is plant stuff, inedible . . . but sometimes there *is* food.

There are also dangers in such places, even ones as small as this. The other-kind may have also left points, hooks and cutting edges. Things that could damage us. And if there *was* food, surely our rivals had found and eaten it by now.

The burly one has been our leader since the end of the large hairy one, who chased a beast-kind along a steep slope and was swept down in a rockslide. Limbs broken, skull smashed, brain spread in sticky lumps over a boulder so that we had to lick up the smears.

The biggest one would like to be leader. To have the most attendants for grooming, the driest spot in the den, the choicest bits of meat.

The burly one has been a brave and strong leader. We have held our territories, won many battles, increased our numbers the only way we can, by overpowering weaker rivals and taking their best into our group while feasting on the remainders.

But we have taken risks and suffered losses. There have been hasty-dug dens that seeped with rain, causing damp-rot. There have been battles and hunts gone wrong. The foraging has become poor, the meat scarce.

We wait as they argue. They go back and forth, the burly one and the biggest one, until the noseless one interrupts with an alarm.

An urgent, hungry alarm.

Beast-kind. A herd of them on the move, stirring up a haze of dust. Hunched backs and swishing tails. Horns curving out from their low heads, some blunt and stubby, some long and sharp.

Meat.

So much meat!

The argument is forgotten.

We go.

The beast-kind plod, eating the dry brown grass. As we get closer we can feel the thud of their hooves vibrating through the ground. Bug-kind buzz around their eyes and ears.

They are huge and heavy, large and solid. A single one could fill us all.

Fill, but not satisfy.

They are nervous. They shift and snort.

We attack. Arms raised. Groaning and wailing.

Hooves pound the earth, flinging up clods of dirt, billows of dust, shredded grass. The beast-kind bellow. A churning mass of meat, horns and hides . . . and we are in the middle of it. Grabbing, grasping, reaching, clawing.

Then there is blood. Thick dark splatters of blood.

A horn catches my hip, tears my skin, knocks me spinning. I fall to the shuddering ground with beast-kind thundering around me. A hoof slams down beside my head. Just misses. It could have been the end for me. It could have been the end.

I grab for the leg attached to that hoof. The beast-kind stumbles, trips, drops with a shaking thud. I yank myself up and on. A broad dusty expanse of hide is in front of my face. Short coarse hairs atop skin. The heat of a live-thing, the beast-kind's side rising and falling, a frantic beating throb from inside where its organs are.

My jaws gape and I bite. That coarse hair, that tough hide, resisting my teeth and then giving way. Now there is more blood. Thick and dark in a gush this time, into my mouth, pouring down my chin.

The beast-kind heaves and lunges but I hold on. I bite deeper. Meat against my teeth now, meat in my mouth, meat sliding down my throat as I gulp it in hot chunks. Others are with me, leaping upon the beast-kind, tearing at it while it squalls and kicks.

We eat. Ripping and pulling. Blood everywhere, blood all over us, damp and wet, but there is *meat*, meat and a loose flood of guts when its belly comes open, and we eat and eat and eat.

Finally we are full. Not satisfied, never satisfied, but full. Two beast-kind are dead in the flattened grass and blood-muddy dirt. There is much meat left, more than we can carry, more than enough for the ones back at the den.

But the burly one is not with us.

Bug-kind buzz around us now. Landing to sample the blood. We are damp with it and now there are bug-kind and we badly need grooming.

But the burly one is not with us.

And the biggest one is damaged. Gored. Horn-gouged. A deep hole is punched into the chest, another to the groin.

We find the burly one. Dragged, impaled, then dropped or dislodged or shaken off. The horn-gouge must have gone in through an eye socket and out through the top of the head. Bone-slivers jut up from the scalp.

The single-eyed one crouches and pokes probing fingertips into the wound, then when there is no reaction, grasps the edges and pries the skull apart. It cracks and splits. The single-eyed one scoops out the punctured brain, digging under until the stem is severed, and holds it out in cupped hands.

There is a long moment of uncertainty.

Our leader is gone.

The biggest one is damaged.

It is the tall quick one or me now.

The long moment stretches longer.

Uncertainty. Indecision.

With sudden resolve, the single-eyed one peels the brain into segments and passes them around to everyone. We may be full, but we still eat.

Already, bird-kind circle overhead and more swarms of bug-kind have appeared. Soon more beast-kind will arrive to scavenge their share.

We take as much as we can carry. The best meat, dripping slabs of it. Rich organs—liver, kidneys, eyes, tongue. We load ourselves until we are bent double and staggering from the weight. The rest of the meat, we have to leave.

Out of the grasslands. Past the other-kind place. Across the long narrow flatness. Into our own territory. Back to our own den.

Eating. Grooming. Standing sentry.

The wobble-headed one stays near the biggest one. The legless one pulls arm over arm along the ground, meek and submissive, toward the tall quick one. The half-faced one attempts to lick the congealing blood from my torso, but the hollow one is there with a hard shove and a warning snap of the teeth, and the half-faced one cowers. The tiny shrunken one snatches up a whole liver that the noseless one dropped and scurries off with it, down through the den's entrance and into some side passage too small for the noseless one to pursue.

Neither the tall quick one nor I take the spot atop the sand pile, above the den. Not yet. It will be one of us, must be one of us, but we do not know which, and dare not make a move too soon.

We eat. We groom. The sentries keep watch. We dust-roll to dry and cake the blood, then pick it away. I inspect the horn-scratch on my hip. The smoked flesh is ripped and uneven. The bone is nicked. But I can still walk. I can still hunt and fight.

The hollow one needs only a single chunk of meat. It goes in the mouth, is chewed, is swallowed, goes down the throat, and drops into the gaping cavity to be fished out and eaten again. Over and over. Until that single chunk of meat has been reduced to pulp. The hollow one is never full, can never be full, but the act of eating is enough.

The sun descends toward clouds. The air begins to cool and there is a hint of dampness. We feel night's approach in the growing heaviness of our limbs, the stiffness-sluggishness-lethargy that creeps into our bodies.

We enter the den before the sun's warmth has ebbed from us, and settle into the sandy soil.

The next day brings rain. We stay below, where it is dry. We are cold and hungry, but we stay.

The day after that brings sunshine again, raising steam from the wet earth. Also raising many bug-kind from the wet earth, and we feed on them eagerly.

The tall quick one defers to me. So do the rest of the group. The biggest one does so grudgingly, but does. I am the new leader. I sit atop the sand pile. The hollow one grooms me and will not allow anyone else to help.

A sentry gives an alarm. Then there is a hail. It is a wandering one, seeking permission to come near. The rest wait for me to grant or deny that permission.

I grant it.

The wandering ones belong to no groups because no groups will have them, and they form none of their own. They go alone from territory to territory, visiting for as long as they are welcome, sharing what meat will be shared with them, and then they move on, bringing news and rumors from one group to the next as they go.

The damp cannot damage the wandering ones, cannot make them rot, because they do not rot. They are not smoked or salt-crusted or sun-dried like the rest of us, but they still do not rot. Beast-kind shy away from them and bug-kind do not infest them.

They are embalmed. A sour reek lingers around them. Liquid oozes from their skin, beading like dew. Their eyes are milky and sunken behind loose, drooping lids. Some have long straight cuts from collarbones to breastbone and down the torso, the edges held together by metal clamps or loops of thin dark cord. More strings, these often pale and hair-fine, dangle from the soft, torn flesh of their lips.

Their meat is vile.

This embalmed one is pallid and ashen and bloated and slick. Like the belly of a fish-kind that has bobbed to the surface of some deep wet pool. One eyelid is gummed shut and the lips are shredded.

But if there is news, even only rumors, I want to know.

There is chewed meat-pulp in the bottom of the cavity where the hollow one's guts used to be. I scoop some out in my fingers and offer it. The embalmed one eats, slurping and smacking with those shredded lips.

News. News that seems like rumor. A group, not far from here, found other-kind.

We do not believe. Not all of us. Not immediately.

True, insists the embalmed one. Not rumor. True.

Some of us *want* to believe.

The embalmed one claims to have been there, claims to have seen-smelled-heard. Not to have tasted, not to have eaten. No group would share something as rare and precious as other-kind meat.

Warm, breathing, bleeding, tender, juicy, succulent other-kind.

Meat the way meat should be. Meat that fills *and* satisfies.

If it was true . . .

If only it was true!

The embalmed one insists that it is. We could go there, find out for ourselves. Eat for ourselves. The embalmed one would show us, help us. If we would share.

Our territory is hunted-out. We must move on anyway. And the chance of other-kind meat . . .

The noseless one groans. Imploring. Hungry.

The rest of the group join in. Their hunger and desire push at me.

I decide. We will go.

So we go.

Those who can move well help or carry those who cannot. The hollow one stays by me, and the embalmed one walks with us. I have the metal-toothed one, whose eyes are very good, keep watch.

That night we shelter in a ravine, beneath a rock-shelf overhang. The next night we must huddle together in the open, exposed under a dark sky of fierce bright spots. There has been little meat, no time to hunt. But the beast-kind who might attack us smell the sourness of the embalmed one, and avoid us instead.

At last we are close. The plants are short and squat and spiny. Stones rise in pillars and arches and strange shapes. There are stinging bug-kind and swift bird-kind that run along the ground. We find a cave that is large and dry, roomy enough for us all.

I send the metal-toothed one ahead with the embalmed one, with orders to return and bring me news. Real news, not rumor.

They do not return that day.

They do not return the next day.

We are all restless. There are squabbles. The tiny shrunken one bites the legless one, gnaws off both hands, leaves the legless one too damaged to be useful. There are squabbles over that meat as well.

I must do something.

I summon the tall quick one and the single-eyed one. We will go. The rest will wait.

We leave the cave when the sun is high. Bird-kind circle in the distance and we move toward them, until we find the place.

The carnage-place that was once a den.

Parts everywhere. Rot everywhere. The ground stained with dried fluids. A rippling, humming cloud of bug-kind roils above it all.

We stop. We are puzzled.

This was their den. This was their territory. They are all gone . . . or destroyed. Some torn to pieces in battle, or a squabble that became a battle. Some twisted in strange agonized contortions. Old damage seems torn fresh and almost new.

So much meat and all of it ruined. Decaying under the hot sun, decaying in that roiling cloud. Salt-crusted meat, smoked meat, sundried meat . . . maybe even other-kind meat . . . all of it rotting. Seething and teeming with bug-kind.

There are tracks and signs leading away, and we follow. Uneasy.

We find the embalmed one. Bloated huge and gassy green. Skin seeping with slime. Loose. Liquid. Dissolving. Blood is dried across the cheeks and chin as if from recent eating. The skull is intact, the brain untouched. But the embalmed one is ended. Somehow, ended.

Then the tall quick one gives an alarm.

Movement.

Tottering, staggering movement.

Approaching us.

The mouth flaps. The lips and tongue gabble. There are glints of teeth. There are sounds and wild gestures, pleading, begging.

At first the shape and form seem oddly familiar to me, and I hesitate. I almost mistake it for one of our own. But it cannot be, because it is other-kind.

Other-kind!

It does not have wrappings over its skin as other-kind should, wrappings that might be fine and flimsy or sturdy and tough. It is not plump and pink, jiggling with rolls of fat. It is as naked as us, thin and dirty, scabbed and scarred.

But it is other-kind.

Other-kind!

We go.

We go with arms raised and outstretched. We go groaning and wailing.

And hungry.

It stops as if astonished. There is a sudden stink of fear. Then it turns, and runs in a stumbling, faltering terror.

The tall quick one brings it down. It screams. It thrashes and kicks. Then the single-eyed one and I are there. We grab. Flesh in my hand. Warm. Pulsing with life. The other-kind screams and screams and *shrieks*. Fingernails dig and gouge. Blood flows. The tall quick one tears off a dripping chunk of thigh. The single-eyed one claws at the belly.

I bite.

Meat!

Meat like nothing else!

Moist and delicious!

Gobbets of it bulging in my cheeks, sliding down my throat. A thick vein throbs between my teeth, throbs at a furious beat, then bursts as I clamp down. A gush of rich blood spurts from the corners of my mouth, streams over my chin and chest.

We eat. We feast. We gorge.

The screams and thrashing finally stop.

We keep eating.

I remember the rest of the group at the cave, waiting for us, but we keep eating.

The meat is very salty. But it fills. It *satisfies*.

We crack the skull against a stone to get at the delicious brain.

So very satisfying!

When the brain is eaten, I pull open the other-kind's slack mouth to reach in for the sweet spongy tongue.

Again, I hesitate.

The tall quick one is slamming a legbone against a rock to expose the marrow. The single-eyed one is rooting around in the guts, delighted to find that the other-kind's stomach sack is full of yet more chewed meat as if the other-kind had recently gorged itself on flesh.

They do not notice what I do.

There is metal.

Metal on its teeth.

Peculiar.

As if . . .

There is not much left to seem familiar now, but it seems as if . . . as if this could almost have been our own metal-toothed one . . . the one we still haven't found.

But that is not possible.

This was other-kind. Other-kind! We caught and bit and ate, feasted, gorged on the meat that filled and satisfied. It was *not* one of us.

The metal on the teeth . . .

Not possible.

The saltiness of the meat, when our own metal-toothed one was a salt-crust . . .

Impossible.

I grip the tongue and pull until it rips loose. I am still hungry, always hungry, but I do not eat it. I save it to take back to the hollow one.

We are full and satisfied, and badly in need of grooming. Some bug-kind have already found us.

We gather what is left of the meat. The scraps and morsels clinging to the bones, some organs, tough sinew, most of a hand.

There is a long scabbed clot-blood scratch along the back of that hand. Where our metal-toothed one had old damage . . .

Impossible. And unimportant.

The cave seems far away. We trudge. Our feet drag. I feel heavy, swollen, satisfied.

Satisfied . . . and as we trudge on . . . strange.

Hot. Hot in the pit of my stomach. Hot as if I swallowed the sun whole.

And itchy. The stump of my small-finger, my missing toes, the rim of my ear, the long gash on my hip where the beast-kind gored me . . . those spots most of all, but other spots too, prickle with an intensifying, maddening itch.

The single-eyed one moans. The tall quick one rubs fitfully at old damage, the holes that cross the torso in a long ragged line. Those spots seem raw-angry-new somehow.

It takes a long time until we near the cave.

We all feel strange.

We ache. We tingle. We itch.

Something inside my chest clenches in a sudden painful squeeze-thump. I suck in breath with a gasp, let it out with a grunt. The sensation passes. Then it squeeze-thumps again. And again.

The cave is not far now.

My mouth is parched. My lips are cracked and dry. I am thirsty, so thirsty.

The sunlight is a harsh white glare, squinting my eyes, making them water. It burns on my skin, where the marks show in vivid color and design. The patterns they make . . . the patterns seem . . . more familiar somehow now . . . as if they have meanings. Meanings I can almost understand.

There is dampness on me. Under my arms, on my forehead, trickling along my spine. Damp even under the baking sunshine, cooler when a breeze gusts. More dampness, thicker and wetter dampness, is in the holes on my sore hip and calf. It seems like . . . blood. I feel it welling up, oozing down. I limp.

The noseless one stands sentry on a high flat boulder. Turned in our direction, alert.

Close now. Very close. The cave is just ahead.

But something is happening to us. Something horrible and strange.

I feel my bowels rumble. I feel pressure in my bladder. My breathing is shallow, raspy. I cough. It hurts.

My mind is . . . murky. Alone. Barely aware of anyone else. As if they are no longer there.

The tall quick one falters. Blood runs from the old damage-holes. Then all at once the flow turns into a flood. The tall quick one takes two more steps, stumbles, falls flat, does not move. A dark puddle spreads on the sand.

The single-eyed one cries out for help. But the cry becomes a gurgle as the single-eyed one bends and vomits up a lumpy pinkish stew. The single eye stares up at me, stark and afraid. The socket where there is no second eye has begun to dribble thick fluids.

The noseless one must have given a call that I missed, because the group is coming.

All of them.

The biggest one, the wobble-headed one, the half-faced one, the tiny shrunken one. Even the hollow one. All the ones we had left behind, the ones too damaged to be helpful in the hunt.

They are coming.

The embalmed one was right. That group did find other-kind, and eat them.

They are coming for us.

Arms raised. Groaning and wailing.

The meat. It contaiminated. Infected. Changed. Made old damage new again. Made the undamaged . . .

> They come for us.
>
> They are hungry.
>
> It *was* our metal-toothed one that we found, and ate.
>
> All, always, very hungry.
>
> And we have returned . . . with meat.

Dead Man's Land

by David Wellington

The dead man couldn't get away, no matter how hard he struggled. Barbed wire wreathed the outer perimeter of the WalMart parking lot, long droopy coils of it that bounced every time he tried to convulse his way to freedom. The blotchy skin of his neck tore open and a little dried blood sifted out. He pulled again, his arm held motionless by the wire, then stopped, confused, lacking the brainpower to unsnag himself, lacking the energy to panic.

The girl—Winona—threw a rock that bounced off his skull but didn't crack the bone. She had blonde hair pulled back in a braid curled and oiled until it looked like metal and eyes the color of old glass bottles. We stood on the loading dock of the superstore a hundred yards from the dead man. My hair and clothes still smelled like the cookfires burning inside. I couldn't wait to get out there, onto the road again. My cargo had already thrown one tantrum that morning, demanding she be allowed to stay. Too bad for her.

"Is this enough?" her father asked. He wore a bright orange vest and a baseball hat crowned with a ring of bird skulls. He was an Assistant Manager for WalMart and a man of some importance. He held out to me an orange plastic pill bottle. The label had been worn off long ago and the contents were a mixed assortment of colorful capsules and tablets, some of them crumbled near to dust, all of them decades past their expiration date. I nodded to the manager and grabbed the girl's hand. "Now you're mine," I told her, "and you'll behave, or else." Her father pursed his lips but I don't make my living coddling the civilized folk of the stores. I pointed at the dead man in the wire. "That's just what we call a slack. Too dumb and too far gone to hunt us, sure. You make too much racket throwing stones, though, and you'll attract his friends, and they *bite."*

She merely stared at me, those green eyes wide and vacant. A look she'd practiced, sure. She didn't care, wasn't going to care unless I gave her a reason. I pulled her along behind me as I stormed down the ramp to the parking lot. In my other arm I cradled my spring-lance, the one thing in the world I couldn't afford to lose.

"If any harm comes to her—" the manager shouted at my back.

I finished the thought for him. "Then you won't see me again."

It wasn't what he wanted to hear. Screw him.

There was no gate or door in the barbed wire for us to pass through. Instead a couple of boys who were watching the captive slack dragged out a sheet of plywood and leaned it up against the barrier, making a ramp for us. The girl refused to climb the ramp. Maybe she thought she'd get splinters. "My name is Cher," I told her. "I'm what your dad calls a Roadie. You know what that means?"

"Half human being, half wild folk," Winona said, watching the boys instead of me. "You travel between the Stores. You cross Dead Man's Land, to conduct our trade. That makes you our servant. Do you know what I am? I'm the daughter of a Manager and you've been hired to protect me."

"I suppose that's so, on this side," I said. I picked her up by the back of her pants and threw her over the wire. Behind me on the loading dock I heard someone gasp and someone else yell. I ran over the ramp and kicked it back, cutting off the only way in, getting shut of the place. I grabbed her yellow hair and stared into those green, green eyes. I showed her my spring-lance, a coffee can on the end of a wooden pole. The can concealed a spring-loaded steel spike long enough to skewer most heads. "Now we're in my world, little girl. Now you're nothing but ghoulbait. Understand?"

Why was I so hard on her? She needed to behave, of course, or she could get us killed. But there was more, a special reason to hate her, and it could be summed up in two words: Full up.

That was what they told my grandfather when he went to the great stores along the New Jersey Turnpike with me in his arms, back when the highways were still crowded with the fleeing going north and going south. "Full up," they said at Barnes and Noble. Full up at CostCo and TJ Maxx. No room for us who waited too long.

So he took me into the wilds, which at that time were lush and green but no higher than your ankle. The mowed lawns, the abandoned houses of suburbia. We hid where we could and moved on every morning. We lived on canned food and we listened to the radio in the dark, listened to static when that was all there was, hoping to hear of shelter somewhere, real shelter.

Full up. They were all full up before we arrived. Not enough food to go around, not any more room, they told him. He died in the wild and I could have joined a tribe in Montclair, they would have taken me in, but instead I crushed his head with a rock before I'd even begun to weep. I would not be a wild woman, a friend to the dead. I would not be a savage.

I didn't go hungry for long. The Stores needed me and my kind. We meant communication and trade and that meant survival. They let me sleep on their floors. They paid what I asked. And every time I looked one in the eyes I saw those words again, and I hated them all over again. There was no room in my heart for this girl. I was full up, too.

We couldn't make the thirty miles to Home Depot in one day but I wanted us as far from the WalMart as possible before nightfall. The commotion our leaving made would draw too much attention. For days to come Winona's father would be watching ghouls circle his perimeter, looking for the source of all that noise. He would lock his big loading gates and pray for them to leave him in peace, for his fence to hold them back.

We didn't have that option. I pushed us hard. I led Winona through a drainage ditch behind the store, through reeds taller than me and water scummed with mosquito larvae. On the far side we had to cross an old asphalt access road, a broken field of smooth black fragments with bright green weeds sticking up in unnatural rectilinear patterns. It took us most of an hour to get to the far side and over the sway-backed fencing there. It would have taken me a quarter of that time, alone. They don't need proper shoes in the Stores and what she had were old passed-down sneakers so well-used the laces were crusted in place.

Beyond the road the woods began, the real dead man's land. I saw the signs of ghouls everywhere, on every scraped tree trunk, on every broken branch. I was looking for one thing, to convince myself I wasn't just being paranoid. When I finally found it I felt almost relieved.

In a clearing in the shadow of a creaking utility pylon where the high grass grew yellow and thin I saw a splash of red. I pushed through the sighing vegetation to get closer and bent to touch the ground. A broad swath of grass had been bent back, crushed by the weight of a human being. Blood soaked the ground and turned the long stalks red. I dug around amidst the roots for a moment and came up with a broken leg bone—too long and thin to be human. Probably white-tailed deer. The femur had been cracked open so the marrow could be sucked out.

I squatted and ran a few blades of the grass through my fingers, letting the dried blood powder away like rust. Winona stared at the discarded bone as if it might come back to life at any moment. She'd probably never seen a meat bone before that wasn't in the bottom of a stew pot.

"There's one nearby," I told her, whispering. The dead don't linger when they've eaten and there was nearly no chance of the ghoul still being within earshot. Still I don't make a habit of raising my voice out in the woods. "He ate recently so he'll be strong and fast."

"But so he's full, then, and he won't attack us," she said, her fingers brushing the fibrous surface of the femur. She wasn't scared. The little idiot.

"A living thing, an animal might not. But this is a dead man. If he can't find human he'll eat deer or rabbits or mice. If he can't find meat he'll chew the bark off of trees and stuff himself full of grass. He doesn't care if he eats so much he pops, he'll still want more, even if it just slides down his gullet and out the hole in his belly. The more he eats the hungrier he gets."

She shrugged and laid back in the grass, probably exhausted after her long hike. I could see it in her eyes. She didn't need to worry, she thought. I would protect her.

So I did just that: I yanked her up to her feet and got us moving again, despite her exhaustion.

You smell them first, long before you see them. It's a mixed blessing—scent is a fickle sense to have to rely on. The stink of decaying meat keeps you on your toes, but you can't tell what direction it's coming from. You could walk right into the ghoul and not know it. They don't make much noise. They never talk or cough or sneeze.

I had him in my nose for most of the afternoon, on and off. Once I thought I saw him but it was only slacks, a whole line of them on the crest of a hill. They walked in single file, the one in front missing most of the flesh from his head. Just red-shot eyes rolling in a blank skull. Their clothes, filthy and torn, still kept the colors of the old time. Some of those colors never fade. In red and blue and purple t-shirts and dresses they looked almost merry up there, silhouetted against the setting sun. They walked without looking to the side, without knowing where they headed. This is their world now and they're safe within it as long as they don't get too close to the Stores. I kept the girl down, hidden under a berry bush until they were gone, just to take care.

In the middle of an overgrown housing development I hauled Winona over the splintered remains of a picket fence and into a house that had only been partly burned down, most of its roof missing but the walls solid as when they were put up. The stink of the ghoul was everywhere—he couldn't be more than a quarter mile away, even if he was upwind. Inside I held the door closed by shoving furniture up against it. It was the best I could do short of boarding us in and that's never a good idea. I let the girl collapse on an old water-stained sofa and searched the place. Green saplings grew through the floorboards of the living room while old pictures, still bright and fresh, lined the stairway to the upstairs. Smiling people out in the sunshine, boats on clean water. The frames of the pictures were riddled with wormcast and some had rotted away altogether.

Night came down, early as it does in October. The girl refused to sleep on any of the house's beds they were so infested with bugs. Instead she wanted to stay up and talk. I sat in one corner of an upstairs room under a hole in the roof, the spring-lance across my knees and listened, too tired to shut her up properly.

"My children will be managers," she told me. "Great men, great warriors and they will finally rid the land of the monsters. That is the destiny of my line. The story was told often around our fires."

I shifted slightly. The carpet under me was damp. "Is that why you're going so far away? To have babies?"

She nodded readily and gave me a smile that could have sold toothpaste in the old time. "To be wed to the General Manager of Home Depot and to bear his heirs."

"The big man's tired of fucking his first cousins," I guessed. "Makes sense. They've got bad skin out that way 'cause it's too close to the old chemical plants. Me, I never gave much thought to a baby. Just one more corpse to walk the earth in the end."

"That's doom talk, and it's not allowed at WalMart," she scolded me. She played with a DVD case she'd found in the entertainment center, the card insert showing a man dressed like a bat. She opened and closed the plastic with a snap, over and over again—snap-snap,

snap-snap. A good sound of well-made pieces fitting together perfect-

snap-snap. A good sound of well-made pieces fitting together perfectly. Everything sounded like that in the old time. "It's not just about
babies, anyway. This will be a strategic alliance, uniting two Exits and
drawing borders for future conquests to come. I imagine you have no
use for politics—"

"Shush," I told her. I'd heard something downstairs. She kept prattling on for a minute till she saw that I meant it. The sound came
again. Wood screeching on wood. Furniture scraping on a hardwood
floor. The ghoul was testing my barricade.

They can smell you, just like you can smell them, and they don't
need to rest. You can't hide for long.

A chest of drawers squealed and crashed as it fell over. A chair
tumbled away from the door. I lifted the window sill as quietly as I
could and gestured for Winona to go on, out onto the roof. The sec-
ond-floor window let out onto a slope of rotten shingles that skidded
out from under her and she wouldn't let go of the sill.

I crawled over her and carefully slipped my way down to the gutter so I could look over the edge. The ghoul looked up at the same
time and we made eye contact. He had on the loose grey pants of a
wild man, stained now with deer blood. Most of his hair had fallen out
and something had eaten his lips, leaving ragged skin that failed to
cover his crooked teeth. His eyelids were gone too, giving him the look
of a bloody death's head.

I skittered back onto the roof. Below I heard him redouble his
efforts, slamming a bookshelf to the side. He would be through the
door soon. Winona started screaming. "Kill it! It's right there! Just
kill it!"

It was an eight foot drop to the ground. There were some scrag-
gly bushes down there to break my fall but I landed badly and lost a
fraction of a second jumping back up to my feet. By that time the
ghoul had turned to face me, slaver running out of the hole in his face.
I could see the blotchy sores on his gray skin. I could hear his teeth
grinding together in anticipation.

"Do your job!" Winona howled. Her fingers couldn't hold her on the slope of the roof and suddenly she was sliding, falling on the loose shingles. I had been one step ahead of her, bringing the spring-lance around to line up my shot I was a breath's span away from firing when she called me. I managed to ignore the distraction of her falling off the roof. The dead man didn't. He swung his head up and to the side, looking for the source of the noise.

The spring-lance connected with his head, but not in the right place. The coffee can slid back, triggering a latch, and the lethal spike clanged out of the sheath and into his flesh. His jawbone exploded inside his fragile skin, yellow teeth flying from his mouth to clatter on the ground. The blow knocked him backward and off his feet but it had failed to penetrate his brain.

I jumped back and looked up at the roof. Winona had fallen into the gutter, which had bent but not broken. I only caught half a glimpse of her—a pale shape hanging in the darkness. Meanwhile the ghoul was recovering from my attack. The spring-lance was useless until I could crank back the spring.

He stood up, clutching at the place where his jawbone had been. His eyes focused on me with horrible slowness.

"Winona!" I shouted. "You stay there and be quiet!"

The ghoul started in to charge me, his head down, his broken fingernails stretched out to grab and tear my clothes and my skin. I turned around and headed into the woods, running as fast as my legs could carry me.

The dead are slow. You can outrun them, for a while.

"Come on, girl! Winona! Show yourself!"

She wasn't there when I got back. Which was the bad news. I couldn't find any blood or torn clothes, either, meaning the ghoul didn't get her. That could be very bad news. It could mean she'd run off on her own. I doubted it.

It took me most of the night to outrun the ghoul. He was a tough character, real strong, but none of them are ever as fast as a living person. If you don't exhaust yourself with sprinting, if you don't trip on an old curb and break your leg, you can escape them. It's how I've stayed alive so long.

I lead him in a wide loop through the subdivision, up cracked streets and through backyards full of playsets rusted down to twisted scrap. I could hear him behind me, smell him too, but I kept my eyes on my feet. I could step on an abandoned toy or even an old lawnmower lost in the high grass and it would be over. I could trip over an exposed cable or pipe. I could run right into a tree and give myself a concussion.

You have to not panic, is all. I kept my heading and I kept moving. Well before dawn his stench was just a memory in my nose, a last whiff of corruption that lingered on me well past the time I'd lost him. I circled back, made a wide circuit around the row houses in case he caught smell of me again. Eventually I wound up right where I started, ready to resume my travels.

Except Winona was gone. I tore the house apart looking for her, turned over every decaying mattress, broke open every closet and scared a few mice for my trouble. I looked all around the yard, constantly aware that the ghoul was still nearby. I searched the nearby houses.

Three doors down I found the remains of a campfire on what had been somebody's front lawn, a time ago. I found some old cans, emptied and licked clean. I found flat places in the grass where wild folk had laid out in the night.

I felt the ashes of the fire and they were still warm. I still had a chance, then. At least as long as the General Manager of the Home Depot didn't mind receiving my cargo slightly used.

It's not hard to find the villages of the wild folk on a calm day, even though they move from time to time, even though they are little more than tent towns and colorless and small. You look for smoke, is all, and it's something my grandfather taught me. You get to a high place, say the top of an old commercial building or you climb on top of a bent old power pylon and you look across the land. If you don't squint too hard you'll see them, the columns of smoke. Thin grey pencil lines rising in the air.

I tracked them down through a low defile that ran parallel to an old state highway. I moved quietly but I didn't waste time. I could hear them before long but I trailed behind, keeping my distance. I waited for them to camp and then I waited for the sun to sink over the hills. Only then did I move in.

There were maybe seventy of them, a fair-sized encampment and far more than I could take on with just my two arms. There were children with them, some as young as five. The wild folk have their babies in the woods and raise them where they can. Very few survive to puberty. It's why they keep their women pregnant at all times, and why they're constantly looking for new breeding stock.

I saw them like pinkish ghosts in the falling light, their undyed clothing and their pale skin moving between the trees like inverted shadows. I saw their fires and their animal-hide tents stretched over battered old aluminum poles. I saw their pet slack.

Every band of wild folk has one. A dead man, usually an ancestor, who they keep and feed. Some are simple totems, rallying points for the tribe. Some are valued because they can do tricks. I watched this one work his single gimmick over and over. The wild folk would bring him scraps of paper, bits and ends they had found in the old houses. The slack had a plastic pen wired to his hand. A girl of maybe ten years would fill it with ink from time to time as the slack signed his name, over and over. Who could say what dim chunk of his rotting brain, what curl of grey matter was left to him, that let him do that. He looked quite happy to sign and sign away, his fleshless face turned upward in a pure and innocent smile, his tattered body jiggling with the joy of it.

Every time he finished a signature the wild folk would laugh and cheer. It was something of the old world, something they might remember doing themselves. It was a thing of power, every name an incantation. I don't suppose it matters why. It was a good trick, for a slack, and entertainment is what you make of it out on the road.

I gave them an hour of darkness—just long enough to have their dinner ready—and then I stepped out of the shadows and into the light. I made myself known with a loud, warbling screech and threw my lance down before me.

Every eye in the encampment turned my way. Every hand reached for a weapon. Yet my intentions could not be more clear. I had dealings with the wild folk before, many a time, whether or not I knew any of this band. Their lives are unlike the life of the Stores. They don't hold to so many rules. But they still have a few, and I knew them, and how to make them work for me.

"I want some dinner, and I want some information," I said. I held my arms outstretched the way a ghoul might. In this case I was showing them I was unarmed.

The leader of the band came to me then. He was nearly my age—ripe, for a wild man—and some kind of fungal infection lined his cheeks and forehead with angry ridges. Muscles crawled across his chest and shoulders like vines pulled taut. He wore drawstring pants and shoes of fine deer hide. The top of a human skull, sawed away just above the eye sockets, perched atop his unwashed hair.

"You come to join us, Roadie? You come to be a friend to the dead?" he asked. He didn't look happy but he didn't look like he wanted to kill me, either.

"Not hardly. I've come for dinner, like I said."

He nodded. He'd be willing to feed me, in exchange for my leaving them alone.

I went on. "And I've come to be told where the girl is. The girl with hair like gold and eyes like old glass bottles. I'll be taking her with me."

His eyes narrowed. He moved sideways, scuttling around me, looking me over. He wanted to know if I had any real weapons on me. Say a pistol, or even a zip gun. Say a knife in a hidden sheath. He glanced at the spring-lance at my feet but it was well out of my reach.

"Finder's, keepers," he said, finally, when he was sure I was defenseless. He had a hatchet in his own hand, a steel thing at least half made of rust. It wouldn't keep an edge any more but it would do just fine for bashing in my face. "She's weak, but she can birth some babies for us. We won't be giving her up." He looked me up and down again but this time it was my breasts and my crotch he sized up. "Maybe you want to make a trade? Maybe you want to come be our babymaker?"

"Not hardly," I said again.

His brothers, his cousins, his uncles came out of the tents then or stepped up from their campfires or ghosted in out of the woods. They had spears and knives in their hands. Some of them wore leather thongs around their throats, tight as chokers, with finger bones dangling from them. That marked them as killers, as those who had fought before. They came close, close enough to strike me, but not close enough that I could touch them. They knew this kind of entertainment all too well. There was no chance of me taking them. I was a tough thing, all muscle and sinew, and stronger by far than any wild folk, fed up better on Store food, trained by hard life on the road. Against their leader, maybe, or maybe even him and his best two champions. Maybe. But there were just too many of them.

"Roadies are too smart for this kind of aggro," the leader said. "Too smart to come in here and start something they can't finish." He was figuring out my game, and far too soon. "You playing at something, Roadie?"

I shrugged my shoulders elaborately. "You won't give her back, then. All right." I took my water bottle from my belt and showed it to him. He turned away and spat. He wouldn't drink my water. It might be poisoned.

I shrugged again. I had to draw this out a little longer. Slowly, as if to assure them of my good intentions, I unscrewed the cap from my water bottle. Slowly I lifted the bottle, as if to drink.

Then the wind changed and a familiar smell lit up my nose and I smiled. I turned over the bottle and rabbit's blood spilled out on the ground.

Behind me, looming out of the shadows, the ghoul appeared, his broken mouth black and wide as a cave as if he would swallow the wild folk whole. I'd been teasing and taunting and coaxing him along all day and finally he had caught up. He smelled the blood and the hunger in him must have spiked. He came shambling for me, for the leader, for anything warm.

In the confusion I grabbed up my lance and slipped past their leader. I dodged around a cookfire and tore open the flap of the first tent I found. Inside a huddle of children looked up at me, terrified.

I'd brought death down on them, maybe. I didn't waste time on guilt. The next three tents I found were empty. Behind me the leader and his extended family were whooping with fear and running every way, their weapons up, their hands raised. The ghoul would lunge at one of them, then another. They would dance away from him, yelping like dogs. He stumbled like a drunkard from one body to the next.

I tripped over the slack in the middle of the encampment. He looked up at me and raised his pen hand, perhaps wanting another piece of paper. Endless copies of his signature littered the ground about his feet. My skin rumpled, my stomach flipped at the nearness of him, this harmless dead man. Reflexively I raised the spring-lance. But no. If I took the girl and ran this band of wild folk might forget me, after a time of seeking revenge. If I did in their pet slack, however, they would chase me like furies. I pushed past him and headed for the next tent.

Winona stepped out of it before I even arrived. Her hair hung loose around her face, piled in careless hummocks like the yellow grass revealed by the melting snows of spring. Her eyes saw me and I saw in them a hurt that went beyond blame. A hurt that needed healing of a kind I could not offer. She was stark naked, her little body smeared with dirt and ash and paint. I knew what that meant.

They had tied her feet and hands together with leather cord. She could shuffle forward but not walk with any speed. I didn't have the time to free her so I grabbed her up over my shoulder and I ran into the darkness, leaving the camp in chaos behind.

We hid in a tree, our exhausted bodies draped over the branches, and spent the night not sleeping, but listening for any sound, and smelling, our noses twitched, even as we dozed.

The next day I brought her back toward the Turnpike. We passed through the overgrown asphalt of an old school parking lot, climbing over places where the pavement had cracked like the top of a loaf of bread. The brick building loomed over us in silent decay, its windows broken, its doors standing open to let us look in on empty rooms full of dirt and dead leaves.

"They kept a dead man among them," Winona said to me as we climbed an endless on-ramp to the Pike. "They kept him like a milking cow, like a treasure."

It was the first thing she'd said to me since I left her in the abandoned house. I considered what to say long and hard. "They are the friends of the dead. It's why you call them wild."

"This much I knew, yes. That when one of them dies, they are left uncleansed. No relative will strike the sacred blow."

Which is what they call it in the Stores. The Final Duty of Kinship. The Sacred Blow. Which amounts to taking a sledgehammer to the brains of your loved ones when they pass. It's a necessary thing. I did for my grandfather, didn't I? I'm no wild folk savage. Still, I never saw it like some holy thing, as Winona's people did. I saw it as a sadness, a sharp sadness on the world.

"They have avowed never to strike a dead thing. They make a pact with their ancestors, you see. They will not harm the dead, which is sin, and in exchange, the dead will let them survive."

"The dead know nothing of treaties and pacts," Winona said, a little of her old uppity pride glowing behind her eyes. I guess maybe she was going to be all right. "Such foolishness. Such evil."

Now a Roadie may never judge those she trades with. So I kept my peace.

The ghoul found us again the next evening, just as the sky started turning orange. Maybe he got a meal out of the wild folk. Maybe they outran him. It didn't matter. He had my smell in his dead nose and he couldn't not come for me. He was a thing of nature, as pure, if not as innocent, as the smile on the face of the paper-signing slack.

For days he tracked me. For days I tried to give him the slip. It was for naught. We were like two arrows launched in the air at the same target. At some point our paths would cross. Smart as I am, I decided I would choose when it might happen.

I smelled him and then I heard him. I readied myself for him. I put Winona in an old storm cellar and locked the door behind me. Then I walked out into the middle of a suburban street with my spring-lance loose in my hands. I spread my legs a little, kept my knees unlocked. I tried to sense where he was, what direction he might be coming from.

He surprised me, as they do. He came from behind and I barely had time to pivot on my left foot, my right foot high to kick out at him. I caught him in the stomach and knocked him backwards. It gave me a splinter of a moment to bring the lance around.

His hands came for me, his broken jaws, his whole body swimming through the air as time slowed to a near stand-still. My eyes focused on his head until every little detail stood out. The dark veins beneath his cheek. The ragged hole in the side of his head where my spring-lance had caught him before, like a second, rotten ear.

His fingers caught at my belt, wove themselves through the cord to anchor himself to me. The next blow would tear my flesh open and make me bleed.

At least it might have, if I'd been a trace slower. I pressed the end of the coffee can against his forehead. It was a centered strike, a perfect placement. His own momentum pressed his face against my spring-loaded weapon. The coffee can slid backward and released the hidden latch. The spike jumped forward, its glinting point emerging from the back of his skull and catching the moonlight.

He fell on me, all spark of animation fleeing, and I might have been pinned by a collapsing chimney. His body sputtered out its last spastic movement and then stopped.

I rolled out from under him and lay looking up at purple clouds that stretched in thick bands across the whole of the sky. I waited a while, to catch my breath, before I stood again.

Atop three flagpoles in the Home Depot's parking lot long mylar banners snapped in the air, welcoming us to our destination. At the loading dock a party of warriors in orange smocks waited to receive us. They wore circlets carved of rosewood on their temples and had gold and silver chains wrapping their forearms like vambraces. The General Manager himself stood silhouetted in the doorway, a fire behind him throwing long shadows down toward us. He was a grey-haired old man with a white scar running across the full length of his chest. He wore nothing but a pair of tight-fitting elastic shorts, black and satiny with gold piping. Beads and bones and jewels were woven in his long hair. He smiled to see Winona, and he gestured to her to come into his arms, to come to his bed, perhaps.

"He doesn't waste his time," I said. We were still out of earshot. I'd planned on giving the girl a final lecture in what a beastly little hardship she'd been. Instead I wondered if maybe I shouldn't turn around and get back on the road with her.

"It is a grand destiny, to make the heirs who will rid the world of the monsters," Winona announced. She looked a bit scared, but not of the bulge in the General Manager's shorts. Something else had her in its teeth.

She turned to look at me with those eyes the color of old glass bottles. "He'll know," she said. "He'll know I'm not intact." Her voice was very small.

I stared at her. I stared and stared. I didn't like her. I never would. But I knew what they would do to her if they found out she'd been had by the wild folk. It was none of her fault but that wouldn't enter their calculations. They would be Full Up, if they found out.

We were women, both of us. Women of the world now. I sighed and took my water bottle from my pack. It was gummy inside with rabbit's blood. I filled it a little way up with good water and swirled it around, then pushed it into the girl's hand.

I hissed instructions at her. "You ask him to undress in private, and maybe he'll let you. You make it sound like you're shy, like you're just a little girl. Some men like that. When he's gone, you spill this out on the sheets and lie in it." I stared right into her eyes, for the last time. "Do it right, do it secretive and he'll never know."

She held my gaze and she nodded and then she looked away. Step by step she walked away from me, and toward her destiny.

The people of Home Depot owed me dinner at the very least but I didn't bother taking it. I was back in Dead Man's Land before I knew it, and glad to be there.

AUTHOR BIOS

William Bolen pens tales of Fantasy and horror from his home on the Louisiana bayou. When he's not being tossed about by malevolent hurricanes or gnawed on by rabid alligators, he enjoys reading the works of Peter Straub, Cormac McCarthy, and Jack Ketchum. He welcomes emails at dragonwulf@aol.com.

Gustavo Bondoni is an Argentine writer with over thirty stories published in five countries, online and in print. During 2008 he was a winner in the National Space Society's "Return to Luna" Contest and also won the Marooned Award for Flash Fiction. His genre fiction has appeared in three *Hadley Rille Books' Anthologies, Darwin's Evolutions, Flashing Swords, Every Day Fiction* and others, while his literary fiction has appeared in *Delivered, Amarillo Bay, Carve Magazine,* the *Buenos Aires Literary Review* and *Literary Magic.* His work has also been published in Spanish translation. (http://bondo-ba.livejournal.com)

Gary A. Braunbeck is the author of the acclaimed Cedar Hill Cycle of novels and stories. To date, he has published over 200 short stories, as well as 10 novels and 10 short story collections. He has also co-edited 2 award-winning anthologies, *Masques 5* and *5 Strokes to Midnight.* His work has received 5 Bram Stoker Awards, an International Horror Guild Award, 3 Shocklines "Shocker" Awards, a Dark Scribe Magazine Black Quill Award, and a World Fantasy Award nomination. His latest novel in the Cedar Hill Cycle, *Far Dark Fields,* will be released in August 2009. (www.garybraunbeck.com)

Jennifer Brozek, the creator and co-editor for the *Grants Pass* anthology (Morrigan Books, July 2009), is a freelance author for several RPG companies including Margaret Weis Productions, Rogue Games and OtherWorld Creations. She is also a freelance technical writer. She has contributed to multiple RPG sourcebooks (*Dragonlance, Castlemourn, Cortex, Serenity*) and has co-authored three books. She is published in several anthologies and is the creator and editor of the webzine, *The Edge of Propinquity*. When she is not writing her heart out, she is a loving wife to her husband, Jeff, and an indulgent "mother" to their three cats. (www.jenniferbrozek.com)

William D. Carl lives in Cincinnati, where he works at a bookstore by day and battles ennui by night. He's had stories in such collections as *In Laymon's Terms, Robots Beyond, Damned Nation, The Many Faces of Van Helsing, The Beast Within,* and *Skin & Ink*. His first novel was *Bestial: Werewolf Apocalypse* from Permuted Press. He cries at old movies, never met a pizza he didn't like, and he believes in werewolves. (www.williamdcarl.com)

Peter Clines grew up in the Stephen King fallout zone of Maine, started writing science fiction and fantasy stories at the age of eight, and made his first writing sale at age seventeen to a local newspaper. His latest short fiction can be seen at *The Harrow* and in the *Cthulhu Unbound 2* anthology. *Ex-Heroes*, his first novel, will be released in late 2009 from Permuted Press. He currently lives and writes somewhere in southern California, and can often be found ranting on his cleverly-named blog, Writer on Writing. (http://thoth-amon.blogspot.com/)

Kris Dikeman lives and works in New York City. Her stories have appeared in the magazines *Strange Horizons* and *Lady Churchill's Rosebud Wristlet* and the anthology *The Many Faces of Van Helsing*. She is currently working on her first novel, a romp through Manhattan, with zombies. Visit her website at krisdikeman.com

Walt Jarvis grew up in Central Texas, attended college in Tennessee and was a combat photographer in the Vietnam war. He now lives in Los Angeles. On and off he has been part of corporate America, and has learned that you don't have to be dead to work for a company like Esperionex, but it probably helps.

Kyle S. Johnson resides in Ohio, where every day is your birthday. He enjoys reading, writing, movies, video games, scrounging for clues in the sewer, and absinthe. Ladies—he's single, and he loves to mingle. His preferred zombie defense tool is a machete—sharpened or dull, no preference. "The New Dumb" is his first published work, so he's not fancy enough for his own webpage yet. But feel free to say hello to him at myspace.com/iamthedukeofnewyork.

Jack Ketchum is the pseudonym for a former actor, singer, teacher, literary agent, lumber salesman, and soda jerk—a former flower child and baby boomer who figures that in 1956 Elvis, dinosaurs and horror probably saved his life. His short story "The Box" won a 1994 Bram Stoker Award from the HWA, his story "Gone" won again in 2000—and in 2003 he won Stokers for both best collection for *Peaceable Kingdom* and best long fiction for *Closing Time*. He has written eleven novels, four of which have been filmed for the big screen—*The Lost, The Girl Next Door, Red* and *Offspring*. His stories are collected in *The Exit At Toledo Blade Boulevard, Broken on the Wheel of Sex, Peaceable Kingdom, Closing Time and Other Stories* and *Sleep Disorder* (with Edward Lee). His novella *The Crossings* was cited by Stephen King in his speech at the 2003 National Book Awards. (www.jackketchum.net)

Consumed with a passion for writing, but busy keeping house and raising a family, **Carole Lanham** originally began publishing short stories between diaper-changes and baking cookies. Recently, she set aside the Desitin and her spatula to write full-time. At long last, her moist and chewy fresh-baked tales of terror can be told. She lives in the St. Louis area with her family and an enormous collection of aprons. (horrorhomemaker.com)

Dave Macpherson lives in Worcester, Ma with his wife Heather and son George. He has been published in *Every Day Fiction, 13 Human Souls,* among others.

Since 2007, **Bobbie Metevier** has published fiction and non-fiction in various markets. Her most recent sales/publishing credits include *Doorways Magazine, Withersin, Tales of Moreauvia, All Hallows* and *Writers' Digest*. Bobbie lives in Rochester Hills, Michigan with her husband, two daughters and a dog named wieners. (bobbiemetevier.blogspot.com)

Ralph Robert Moore's fiction has been published in a wide variety of genre and literary magazines in America, England, Ireland and Australia, and translated into Lithuanian. He's been anthologized in the nineteenth edition of *The Year's Best Fantasy and Horror*, in *Read By Dawn* (edited by Ramsey Campbell), and elsewhere. His story *The Machine of a Religious Man* was nominated as Best Story of the Year in the 2006 British Fantasy Society Awards. His novel *Father Figure*, published in 2003, is now available as a free PDF download on his website. (www.ralphrobertmoore.com)

Christine Morgan divides her writing time among many genres: fantasy, horror, childrens' stories, thrillers, roleplaying games, erotica, even the sordid world of fanfiction. She's a guest reviewer for the *Horror Fiction*

Review and has tackled editing 'zines and convention-anthologies. She works the overnight shift in a psych facility, which is hell on her sleep schedule but gives her a lot of time to pursue her various projects. She's had a lot of luck and fun writing about zombies, and her other interests include pirates, superheroes, British comedy and cheesy disaster movies. Her husband is a gamer and living-historian, and their surly-goth teenage daughter recently sold a zombie story of her own. They spend a lot of time online and at conventions, but otherwise don't get out much.

Mark Onspaugh is a native Californian who grew up on a steady diet of horror, science fiction and DC Comics. A proud member of the HWA., he writes screenplays, short stories and novels. He was also one of the writers of the cult movie favorite *Flight of the Living Dead.* He lives in Los Osos, CA with his wife, author/artist Dr. Tobey Crockett. (www.markonspaugh.com)

Kim Paffenroth is Associate Professor of Religious Studies at Iona College. He began his horror writing career with *Gospel of the Living Dead: George Romero's Visions of Hell on Earth* (Baylor, 2006), which won the 2006 Bram Stoker Award. Since then he has written *Dying to Live: A Novel of Life among the Undead* (Permuted, 2007); *Orpheus and the Pearl* (Magus Press, 2008); and *Dying to Live: Life Sentence* (Permuted, 2008). He also edited the zombie anthology *History Is Dead* (Permuted, 2007). He lives in upstate New York with his wife and two children.

David Pinnt works for the federal government and lives in a suburb of Denver, Colorado with his lovely wife and myriad children and animals. In his spare time (what there is of it) he tries to write high-end literary fiction; however the end result is always something much like the story you've just read. Go figure. His fiction is also appearing in *Arkham Tales* this year. (http://dcpinnt.livejournal.com/)

David Wellington is the author of seven novels. His zombie novels *Monster Island, Monster Nation* and *Monster Planet* (Thunder's Mouth Press) form a complete trilogy. He has also written a series of vampire novels including (so far) *Thirteen Bullets, Ninety-Nine Coffins, Vampire Zero* and *Twenty-Three Hours* (Three Rivers Press). As an undergraduate he attended Syracuse University; in 1996 he received an MFA in Creative Writing from Penn State; and in 2006 he received an MLS from the Pratt Institute. Mr. Wellington currently resides in New York City with his wife Elisabeth and their dog Mary. Mr. Wellington got his start in publishing in an interesting way. In 2004 he began serializing his horror fiction online, posting short chapters of a novel three times a week on a friend's blog. The book was written in "real-time"; that is, each chapter was conceived, outlined, researched, composed and edited within twenty-four hours of its initial posting. By word of mouth readers learned of the project and returned to watch the story evolve. Response to the project was so great that in 2004 Thunder's Mouth Press approached Mr. Wellington about publishing Monster Island as a print book. The novel has been featured in *Rue Morgue, Fangoria,* and the *New York Times*. For more information please visit www.davidwellington.net.

BESTIAL
WEREWOLF APOCALYPSE

BY WILLIAM D. CARL

Beneath the dim light of a full moon, the population of Cincinnati mutates into huge, snarling monsters that devour everyone they see, acting upon their most base and bestial desires. Planes fall from the sky. Highways are clogged with abandoned cars, and buildings explode and topple. The city burns.

Only four people are immune to the metamorphosis—a smooth-talking thief who maintains the code of the Old West, an African-American bank teller who has struggled her entire life to emerge unscathed from the ghetto, a wealthy middle-aged housewife who finds everything she once believed to be a lie, and a teen-aged runaway turning tricks for food.

Somehow, these survivors must discover what caused this apocalypse and stop it from spreading. In their way is not only a city of beasts at night, but, in the daylight hours, the same monsters returned to human form, many driven insane by atrocities committed against friends and families.

Now another night is fast approaching. And once again the moon will be full.

ISBN: 978-1934861042

EDEN
A ZOMBIE NOVEL BY TONY MONCHINSKI

Seemingly overnight the world transforms into a barren wasteland ravaged by plague and overrun by hordes of flesh-eating zombies. A small band of desperate men and women stand their ground in a fortified compound in what had been Queens, New York. They've named their sanctuary Eden.

Harris—the unusual honest man in this dead world—races against time to solve a murder while maintaining his own humanity. Because the danger posed by the dead and diseased mass clawing at Eden's walls pales in comparison to the deceit and treachery Harris faces within.

ISBN: 978-1934861172

MORE DETAILS, EXCERPTS, AND PURCHASE INFORMATION AT
www.permutedpress.com

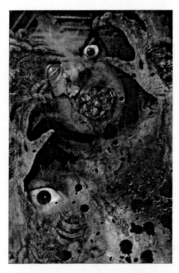

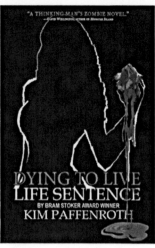

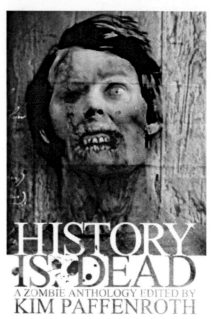
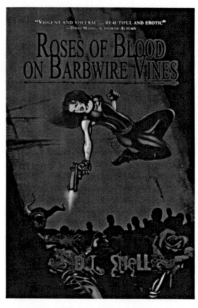

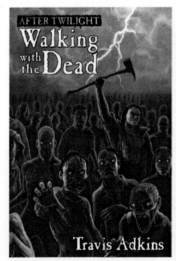

Zombies, Vampires and Texans! Oh, my!
The Novels of Rhiannon Frater

As The World Dies: The First Days
A Zombie Trilogy
Book One

Two very different women flee into the Texas
Hill Country on the first day of the zombie rising.
Together they struggle to rescue loved ones,
find other survivors, and avoid the hungry undead.

As The World Dies: Fighting to Survive
A Zombie Trilogy
Book Two

Katie and Jenni have found new lives with
the survivors of their makeshift fort, but
danger still lurks. Nothing is easy in the new
world where the dead walk and every day is
a struggle to keep safe.

Pretty When She Dies:
A Vampire Novel.

In East Texas, a young woman awakens buried
under the forest floor. After struggling out of
her grave, she not only faces her terrible new
existence but her sadistic creator, The
Summoner. Abandoning her old life, she
travels across Texas hoping to find answers to
her new nature and find a way to defeat the
most powerful Necromancer of all time.

All novels are available in both paperback and Kindle
eBook versions are available at smashwords.com.
For more information on the author, her upcoming appe
http://rhiannonfrater.blogspot.com/

Breinigsville, PA USA
29 October 2009
226720BV00001B/44/P